50 for 2

249

KW-051-406

30119 010203141 WA

London Borough of Sutton

STORE

**This book is to be returned on or before
the last date stamped below.**

01. OCT 86   01. MAY 87   02. FEB 88

08. OCT 86   14. MAY 87

5.11.86 US   17. ... 88

11. NOV   04. JUN 87 24. FEB 88

17. ...   27 JUN 1987

02. JAN 87   01. AUG 87   12. MAR 88
28. 1. 87 78   05. APR
Renewed   27 NOV 87   26th Apr. C.H.
11. 2. 87 N6 09. JAN 88

                                  13. MAY 88

REN.

THINK OF ENGLAND

by the same author

fiction

OBBLIGATO
THE EARLSDON WAY
THE LIMITS OF LOVE
A WILD SURMISE
THE GRADUATE WIFE
THE TROUBLE WITH ENGLAND
LINDMANN
DARLING
TWO FOR THE ROAD
ORCHESTRA AND BEGINNERS
LIKE MEN BETRAYED
WHO WERE YOU WITH LAST NIGHT?
APRIL, JUNE AND NOVEMBER
RICHARD'S THINGS
CALIFORNIA TIME
THE GLITTERING PRIZES
SLEEPS SIX and other stories
OXBRIDGE BLUES and other stories
HEAVEN AND EARTH

non-fiction

BOOKMARKS (edited by Frederic Raphael)
SOMERSET MAUGHAM AND HIS WORLD
BYRON
CRACKS IN THE ICE: VIEWS AND REVIEWS
THE POEMS OF CATULLUS (translated by
Frederic Raphael and Kenneth McLeish)
THE ORESTEIA OF AESCHYLUS (translated by
Frederic Raphael and Kenneth McLeish)

Frederic Raphael

THINK OF ENGLAND

JONATHAN CAPE
THIRTY-TWO BEDFORD SQUARE LONDON

First published 1986
Copyright © 1964, 1982, 1983, 1984, 1985, 1986 by Volatic Ltd

Jonathan Cape Ltd, 32 Bedford Square, London WC1B 3EL

British Library Cataloguing in Publication Data

Raphael, Frederic
Think of England.
I. Title
823'.914[F]   PR6068.A6

ISBN 0–224–02383–7

The stories in this collection have previously appeared as
follows: 'The Last Time' (*Fair Lady*); 'Work in Progress' and
'The People in Euclid' (*Fiction Magazine*); 'The Day Franco
Came' (*New World Writing*); 'A Kiss on the Cheek', 'Quixote
Shmixote', 'Seniority', 'Looking Back', 'Ave Atque Vale', 'A
Parting Guest', 'Portrait of a Lady', 'Standards', 'To Be A
Pilgrim', 'Union Jack Development', 'Bad Books' and 'The
Old Pro' (*Radio 3 Magazine*); 'A Long Story Short' (*Woman*).

WH
LONDON BOROUGH
OF SUTTON
PUBLIC LIBRARIES
F010203141
1 5 AUG 1986

Set by Inforum Ltd, Portsmouth
Printed in Great Britain by
The Alden Press, Oxford

FOR
NICK AND SARAH

CONTENTS

A KISS ON THE CHEEK

You probably know her better as Barbara Craven, but I always think of her, when I think of her, as Mrs Parsons. Today she calls herself Ms, of course, and has a creative writing professorship at San Diego, but today is a far cry from those yesterdays when I used to make the trip to Hampstead in order to attend the Siddonses' play-readings. Barbara was already separated, I have since realised, from Mr Parsons, but she was so young, to my young eyes, that it seemed inconceivable that she should already have abandoned a marriage which had given her two small children. She brought the second, creaking in a big basket, and parked it on the Siddonses' coat-covered bed, before taking her chintzed place in the drawing room. Sometimes she went to feed it during the coffee break. I would think about that unbuttoned blouse and the secretly offered breast as I waited for the Northern Line's last train.

I was still living with my parents in Putney, but I was happy to make the traverse of London to cadge some of the intellectual aura of N.W.3. Putney might once have been the residence of Sir Robert Walpole, but no one had ever lived there since. In 1950, the turreted red-brick houses, capping the hill with bilious green roofs, were manifest bastions of banality. What poet or painter was ever to be seen, hot for haddock, in Rudman's queue (Rude Man's was my father's preferred reading)? Deodar Road would one day be the Riverside Drive of S.W.15, full of darling girls with feminist fire, available for interview round the clock, but I confess that I never guessed it. I was urgent for distant horizons, setting off on the Underground, the windows still mottled by the webbing that once rendered them shatterproof in the Blitz, with the earnestness of a pilgrim for whom the oracle was but a distant shilling's-worth away. There might be a twenty-minute hiatus at Earls Court (time for an adult cough over a Gold Flake), and another at Tottenham Court Road, but these were the stations of no unendurable cross. How could time be of the essence when asphodel grew on Haverstock Hill? Helena Siddons was no demented Pythian, chomping the myrtle, but I could be forgiven for gracing her with prophetic powers when she told me that women were going to find me very attractive. (Oh, but when?) How could I not confuse her famous fruit cup — oh that *continental* tincture of Angostura! — with the true, the blushful Hippocrene? Had not poor little Johnny Keats cottaged in a neighbouring grove?

You could hardly accuse the Siddonses of running a *salon* — Helena was less *mondaine* than Madame Verdurin — but evenings at Verbena Walk were attended faithfully by the faithful. Giles scarcely disposed of (and certainly never displayed) a fortune sufficient to fund outings for any 'little band' of the kind to which *le petit Marcel* so patiently played second fiddle, before he blew the protracted whistle on them all, but it was a group with demanding ground rules. Infidelity brought instant anathema. A professor who had been on the Brains Trust, and whose Russian accent had proved invaluable, if disconcerting, in Chekhov, found that Helena's court had no machinery for hearing appeals. If he preferred to cuckold a colleague rather than play Vanya, that was his business, but it was nobody else's pleasure. Out!

The Siddonses and their circle had first come together during the war, in the Belsize Park Tube station. At first the bombs had kept them penned in purposeless proximity. They listened with increasingly unamused tolerance to the good folk who kept their spirits up, and the tone down, by reciting Nathaniel Gubbins and then, one loud night, Helena proposed that the happy few should read plays while waiting for the all-clear's monotonous relief. Soon the rattle of Sophoclean stichomythia and the boom of the bard enlightened their little corner of the south-bound platform with something of the heady allure of Fiesole when Boccaccio's naughty ingenuity made it a haven from plague-ridden Florence. By the time that I was admitted, as a probationer, to the company, it had repaired to the cosy drawing room of 5, Verbena Walk, but the brave memory of beleaguered days, and nights, gave founder-members heroic status and blessed the second Thursday of each month (except August) with the character of a ritual occasion.

Helena had presence. She did not clank like the Sitwell lady, but she did wear the enamel plaque of the poetess. On licence from the Muse, she also wrote wicked detective stories, but her flowing garments and her way of drawing back, with a light, light laugh, made her house seem somehow like a floral slope of Parnassus and herself a thing that belonged, at least in part, to the wild zephyrs. She and Giles had two daughters who were never in evidence at grown-up evenings. Reading – an impertinent inquirer was told once, and for all – did not happen to be their forte; they were happier where they were, wherever that might be. Helena had poise, but not even her dearest friend (who had appeared on 'What's My Line?', giving it some much needed bottom) could curse her with beauty. Giles had a profile that had been praised, in a student production, by James Agate, who had offered to show him David Garrick's nail scissors, if he liked, one evening, and his voice had almost been selected for training by a professional *maestro*. If lightly pressed, he would disgorge arias, accompanied by Felicity Prout, children's authoress of note. He had relinquished his operatic aspirations in order to '*prendre le relais*' (every man has two countries, does he not, his own and *la France*?) when his father had to retire from the small literary agency which he had founded.

Giles favoured a black overcoat with astrakhan collar and a Malacca cane with a silver boss that could curb a taxi at fifty paces. His ivory profile and matinée manner so closely resembled that of a famous actor-manager of the period that head waiters would often show him egregious preference. I never saw a man who could so quickly make a yo-yo out of a *sommelier*. He played the *grand seigneur* with ready relish, until that folded piece of paper appeared at the end of the meal, when he would defer, with infallible courtesy, to my father's expense-accountable seniority. (It was at a Dorchester dinner table that I first met the Siddonses.) My parents were never invited to join the play-reading repertory, but my Bohemian ambitions seemed to render me eligible. Of course, I could not expect very large parts, since Giles and Helena tended to have an option on the leads and those who had been in the Underground with them were next in line for lines, but I was mixing with intellectuals, wasn't I? We read Strindberg, not Feydeau; Shaw, not Priestley. After Professor Blank's lapse, Chekhov had been renounced, though Helena could not resist *A Month in the Country*. (*Dear* I.T.!) The frivolities of the Restoration were eschewed in favour of Jacobean double-dealing. The dark side of the moon, it was generally held in Verbena Walk, gave the most intriguing light.

How many readings did I actually attend that year before I went up to university? I can hardly have seen Barbara more than half a dozen times, yet those months seem full of her. I shall sound a lamentable hypocrite if I tell the truth, but what else can I tell? When Jocelyn Craven (I always called him Dr Craven, of course) began to pay Barbara rather obvious attention over the ground-bitter coffee and Huntley and Palmers, during the *entr'acte*, I thought him a shameless swine, never acknowledging that he was only doing what I wished to do myself. As I was already substantially committed to another girl (by substantially, I mean that we went to a lot of cinemas, but did not see a lot of films), my indignant jealousy was short on moral credibility, but there it was, and almost is, when I come to think about it. Barbara's white shirt, her simply pleated grey skirt, her silk legs and ebony, not too high-heeled shoes, the susurrant shake of her black hair and the humour in those unblinking eyes renewed their appeal with monthly punctuality. At first, I could not believe that Dr Craven had a chance. She treated him with watchful amusement, which I was quick to read for contempt. I did not then appreciate that when a woman watches a man very carefully (and he is not her husband) it is rarely because she dislikes him. Jocelyn Craven was cleverer than I knew, but not cleverer than Barbara knew, which was cleverer of her than of me. As far as I remember, he never mentioned that he wrote plays. Perhaps he had not started to do so. His fame, like his youth, was still ahead of him. She saw his future; I saw only his past.

One night, towards summer, Barbara came without her baby. Mother was in town. Dr Craven, I couldn't help observ-

ing, treated her with abrupt casualness: they were having a
brisk word as I arrived, and that was more or less all they said
to each other, except on cue, for the rest of the evening. When
we had agreed democratically with Helena and Giles' choice of
play for the following month, Barbara went for a glass of
water into their little cabin of a kitchen, Jocelyn went on his
way and suddenly she and I were leaving at the same time.
'Come on then,' she said, putting a silky arm through mine as
we stepped down on to the narrow pavement, that breast
against my Harris tweed ribs. 'I'll run you home.'

'I don't think you quite know what you're saying,' I said, as
we got into her little Morris. 'I live in Putney.' (There was, as
the screenwriters put it, a 'beat' between 'in' and 'Putney'.)

'Oh well,' she said, 'in for a penny, in for a pound. That's
what they say, isn't it?'

'Some of them may very well do that,' I said. I could be very
sophisticated when roused.

She smiled and kissed me on the cheek, as Jocelyn's
Wolseley breathed exhaust in at my window. I swear that I
was more afraid of what he might think than suspicious of
why she had thrown caution to the winds. Her kiss led me
into a ferment of desire; I put my hands lightly in my lap to
hide the evident evidence. I had been kissed by a married
woman, by someone who had actually done it, and often,
presumably. I sat beside Barbara, watching the smooth
articulation of her knees, as she changed gear or braked,
conscious of an efficiency which seemed positively erotic.
What did not? I watched her for some sign, some smile,
some wink, a gesture which would concede that Something
Had Happened. She drove me to Hyde Park Corner and,
when I said that I could easily get a bus from there, she did
not insist on honouring the whole of her rash offer. I sat in
the stationary car for a moment, wishing that I could take
the initiative, and wishing that she would. Perhaps I knew
that I had been used as a decoy, but I continued to believe
that I had not. I gave her a smile virile beyond my years and
went to wait for a 14, a 30 or a 74. On the way home, I faced
an appalling dilemma: was I obliged to declare my infidelity
before I took my regular girl to see *Up in Arms* on Saturday
night?

I had neither Barbara's telephone number nor the nerve to request it. She was a *mother*. I had to wait till the second Thursday of the following month (I was to read Octavian and murmur rhubarb where the menu called for it) before I saw her again. Things had happened in the meanwhile. She had had her first novel accepted, she had cut her lovely hair and she had gone to live with Dr Craven. They were engaged to be married. God, God, God. Now that she was impossibly inaccessible, I was tormented with fantastic lust and with Proustian consequences: I felt a combination of love and angry pity for the woman who had been so grossly misled by Jocelyn Craven's cynical overtures. I sulked, unaccountably so far as the rest of the group were concerned, throughout the reading of *Antony and Cleopatra*. When the question of the following month was raised, I mumbled that I might not be available. '*Might* not?' Helena said. The subjunctive smacked of opportunism: I sounded as if a hotter ticket was in the offing. 'I may have to go on holiday,' I said, making it seem, I hoped, as if darker motives were involved. 'On holiday?' Helena said. 'With *whom?*' She could be intimidatingly grammatical. Barbara, brutally happy, came to my rescue: 'Don't ask a young man a question like that,' she said, 'you'll embarrass him.' 'With my parents,' I said, proving that I had a pure heart, after all we had meant to each other, even if she did not. 'With your *parents?*' Helena said. '*Where* with your parents?' 'Possibly Deauville,' I said, loading that pretty place with doomy overtones in order to shame Barbara. She had turned away and was laughing with Jocelyn, the bitch, the beauty.

I never went to the Siddonses' play-readings again. It was not that I did not want to, not that I did not long to, it was simply that I could scream only by retreating into a sulky silence. It is not a nice characteristic, but there it is. I could not trust myself, as they say, since I could so clearly not trust her. When Barbara's novel was published, I was bitterly disappointed (the cliché has an accuracy I can't better) when I found that none of her *dramatis personae* bore the smallest resemblance to myself. I looked in vain for the scintillating boy who said precocious things. The novel had, no doubt, been at the publisher's long before our — or rather *her* — kiss in the little Morris, and I must have known it, but the reader of omens rarely has time for mundane chronology. Barbara soon became Mrs Craven, and soon after that the pregnant Mrs Craven, and I went up to Cambridge.

Life as it is lived has no 'Fast Forward' button, but when one looks back, everything seems to have happened at an accelerated pace. Jocelyn Craven wrote a radio play which became a stage play and then a musical: his fortune was made by the character of Dr Carmody, a modern Quixote with the figure of Sancho Panza, blundering, passionate and intrepid. I never saw the play and I have deliberately missed the T.V. series which has been repeated twice. I shall not be going to the ballet version when, as it must be, it is eventually staged. I hate the good and *human* Dr Carmody; I should imitate Horst Wessel rather than consult him. Barbara wrote more novels and became a regular reviewer, of a rather spiky nature. My own books avoided her barbs, or she avoided my books. I ran into her once or twice, as the Sixties poured publishers' parties from their brief cornucopia, and she told me, with something of her old apparently casual premeditation, that Helena Siddons had made me the murderer in her latest thriller. 'We're all in it,' Barbara said. She seemed interested in me, I was partial enough to think, and though she was now in her forties, she was handsome enough for a happily married man to sigh over what might have been, and still could be, perhaps. Her own novels spoke of jagged domestic earthquakes in a cold climate and, though she and Jocelyn were still together, the word 'still' gave the clue to what was likely to come.

The Sixties was, I need hardly say, the era of Film. I was fortunate enough to be quite successful in the movies at a time when it seemed the modal art-form of its day. Everyone was either making films or criticising them. Barbara became a film critic and her appointment to the classy post coincided with one of my own films coming out. It was an adaptation of a very long rustic tragedy, a classic novel, as they say, which scarcely provoked any of us to bold innovation, but which had its merits, even if Barbara did not care to see them. She was particularly severe on the script writer. I had, she told her readers, simply taken down the dialogue from the original, synopsised the events and supposed that I had performed a sufficient operation. So scornful was the review that a wiser man might have taken it for a joke, or a provocation. I was lacking in such resource: I was furious. Had I indeed done nothing but copy out the novel's dialogue and rammed it in the mouths of the actors, the film would have run for fifteen hours, not two and a half. I had been dexterous and she accused me of clumsiness; I had been ingenious and she accused me of the obvious. Love? I was cured.

I swear that it was not more than a fortnight later that I saw her at a first night. (For a short time, I was on lists.) I turned my back, or at least my side, but she came up to me: 'Freddie!' 'Hullo, Barbara.' 'Is something wrong?' 'Is something right?' 'You have the advantage of me,' she said. 'If I had,' I said, 'you'd be out of a job.' 'Do I follow you? But talking of jobs, I want to ask you a favour.' 'Ask,' I said. 'Well,' she said, 'you know dear Hymie Kenman, don't you? He's asked me to write a screenplay for him, from a perfectly dreadful novel, I must say.' 'Congratulations,' I said, 'those are the best ones to use, no risk of *mutilating a classic*.' (My emphasis.) 'And of course the money's marvellous – what you people *make*! – but there's just one problem: I don't know how to do it.' 'You just copy out the dialogue from the book and cobble together the incidents,' I said. 'It's not that simple,' she said. 'Oh surely!' I said. 'Can't Jocelyn clue you up?' 'Jocelyn and I aren't together any more,' she said, 'don't you read the papers?' 'Only when you write in them,' I said. 'What I wondered was, darling, if I do take the job, could you possibly spare a day to give me a sort of, well, seminar on what one has to do roughly?' Never has the delivery of a kiss on the cheek afforded me such pleasure. 'Darling,' I said, 'of *course*.' In the end, Hymie Kenman and she did not manage to make the deal, and our little seminar never took place, but what does Ms Craven now profess at U.C. at San Diego? The Theory and Technique of Screenwriting. I hear she's a whiz.

A LONG STORY SHORT

Wmust know. Emily Radford. I call her Em.'
hat's her name?' Ruth said.
'Oh look here, her name's Emily,' Gavin said, 'if you
must know. Emily Radford. I call her Em.'
'Hence the cryptic telephone message,' Ruth said. 'Got it! Emily Radford. Why does that name mean something to me?'

'She writes on wine in one of the glossies,' Gavin said. 'I expect you've taken her advice a few times.'

'So she has a nose too, does she, among other good things?'

'As a matter of fact, she's one of the youngest Masters of Wine in the business.'

'Master of Wine and Mistress Thine,' Ruth said. 'That's easy to remember, isn't it? And how young is youngest in the plonk game these days?'

'I believe Emily's about twenty-eight,' Gavin said.

'Oh, is there some doubt about it?'

'She's twenty-eight. I never wanted you to find out, you do know that, don't you?'

'Why not? It's a perfectly respectable age to start poaching other women's husbands, isn't it?'

'She's not interested in husbands, poached or any other way. And you know very well what I meant: hurting you was the last thing either of us wanted to do.'

'Yes, well, we're all very clear about what the first thing was, aren't we?'

'Look, Ruth, after sixteen years of marriage – '

'I wondered when we'd be getting a time check. And doesn't it fly though? You are a rotten bastard.'

'I certainly don't seem to be terribly good at it,' Gavin said. 'I am sorry.'

'I must admit you *look* sorry,' Ruth said, 'not to say

pathetic. Anyone would think you were the one who'd been given notice.'

'That's a silly thing to say.'

'Not as silly as getting your Miss Sniff to tell very inefficient lies.'

'She tells very inefficient truths as well,' Gavin said. 'She ain't never going to be Secretary of the Year. In fact, she's unlikely even to last the year. She was apple-green jealous, if you ask me, and couldn't wait to tip you the wink by mistake on purpose.'

'Well, come on, next question: how long's it been going on? I'll make an educated guess, shall I? At least six months, probably more like ten. Just about right for the loving lady to have got a wee bit careless about leaving panic messages about where to be when. Well?'

'If you must know, I met her on that wine-tasting thrash in the Médoc you didn't want to come to that time. It clashed with Alice's holidays and anyway you said you weren't all that bullish on claret.'

'At least I now know one thing you'll both have in common: brown teeth. And she was what you found to do between piss-ups, was she?'

'They weren't piss-ups. It was an educational tour. Piss-ups aren't tax deductible. As a matter of fact, she had such a crowd around her that we didn't exchange more than a couple of words until we were waiting at the airport on the way home. We had fog, you may remember. I called you.'

'So you did. You wanted me to notify the office, didn't you? And once you'd succeeded in making contact in the departure lounge, take-off for two followed without undue delay, did it?'

'We were stuck overnight,' Gavin said, 'and, well, it was just one of those things.'

'Not a trip to the moon on gossamer wings? I've heard a lot about them, but I never seem to be able to lay my hands on one. Who're my nearest stockists, do you know at all? Presumably Frank Livermore's been aware of it all along. I thought he was looking at me very strangely at the première on Wednesday.'

'Nobody has the foggiest idea. We've been extremely discreet. He was looking at you like that because he fancies you madly. Come on, darling, this isn't the end of the world.'

'It may not be the end of yours; it's very definitely the end of mine.'

'Nonsense. You're a beautiful woman. Good heavens, you're only — '

'Don't tell me my age, Gavin; I know it, I know it.'

'Her mid-thirties are the prime of a woman's life,' he said. 'I just wish — '

'You've had all your wishes,' she said. 'Have you told her all about us? Edited low-lights, no doubt: how I've smothered you with domesticity and forced you to become a successful furniture manufacturer instead of the dedicated cabinet-maker you really dreamed of being, how I — '

'I've told her nothing but good,' Gavin said. 'Emily and I've been completely honest about everything from the very beginning.'

'Yes, well, it's always towards the end that it gets more difficult, isn't it? What do you reckon's going to happen now?'

'I don't see why anything has to happen,' Gavin said. 'Emily has a life of her own, she doesn't — '

'Oh do ask her where I can get one of those. And when you get to the office in the morning, you can tell Miss Sniff to call and tell all those people I'm supposed to be cooking dinner for on Thursday that they can bring their sandwiches.'

'That's ridiculous. You know you love cooking. You're the best cook in London, for God's sake.'

'And as cooks go, I'm off,' Ruth said. 'Are you sure about Frank Livermore?'

'If you want to get your own back,' Gavin said, 'you can do better than Frank Livermore.'

'It's not my own back I want particularly,' Ruth said. 'It's the sixteen years that'd come in handy just now.'

Next morning, he got up early and squeezed frosted glasses of orange juice and put the Lapsang and the diet toast on the white wicker bed-tray. She accepted them politely, but she made no conversation; even though he left the paper for her, she did not look at it, or him. She said she was thinking. As soon as he reached the office, he told Miss Sniff to send flowers. He said nothing about cancelling the dinner party. Nor did he cancel his lunch with Emily Radford. She was wearing a red floral dress and a black straw hat and she looked wonderfully young, cool and sympathetic. They went to ¡Olé! a Mexican place with a patio which had been written up enthusiastically in several languages. The simple peasant food was extremely expensive and scorched their mouths.

'It was bound to happen sooner or later,' Emily said. 'The truth will out.'

'It does seem to have that unfortunate tendency,' Gavin said. 'What do you think she'll do?'

'You know her better than I do, Gav. Forgive you probably. I would. Much more to the point: what do you really want her to do?'

'There's Alice to think about, among other things.'

'My parents got divorced when I was fifteen,' Emily said, 'and look at me!'

'That presents no sort of a problem,' he said. 'I don't want her to divorce me any more than you do. You know what I'd really like, don't you?'

'Your cake and eat it too? Wouldn't everyone?'

'I'd like to have you all to myself for weeks and weeks – '

'And have your fill and then never see me again?'

'That's one thing that's absolutely out, not seeing you again. I love you, Emily.'

'That's really nice of you,' she said, 'and also very convenient, because I love you too. Have you got time to come up to scruffsville for a bit? My flat-mate'll be at work. We can always have a sandwich at least. If I eat any more of this, I shall have to dial 999.'

'I'll check my book,' Gavin said. 'Oh, what do you know? I've just cancelled my next appointment. I have two hours unexpectedly free.'

'That should be enough,' she said.

His flowers were in a bucket of water in the garage. His message was still in the little envelope stapled to the Cellophane. When he went into the kitchen, there was no sign of Ruth, or of dinner. The double oven was cold. The circular glass table on its melanite pedestal, a product of his own company, was devoid of plates or cutlery. She was not in the bedroom either. The bathroom door was locked.

'Ruth?'

'She isn't here. Would you care to leave a message?'

'Don't be silly, darling,' he said. 'Whatever are you doing in there?'

'Still thinking,' she said.

He bumped his knee nastily on her new vanity unit, but his yelp of pain turned no key in the bathroom door. Hurt, he went into the kitchen and ate a tepid omelette while reading the paper he had not seen at breakfast. She came downstairs as he was washing up. She wore no make-up, but there was a hint of humour in her eyes, which gave him hope, though he did not quite know of what. 'Well, hullo. Feeling better?'

'Much,' she said. 'I've decided to get a divorce.'

'That's not really what you want to do,' he said. 'You're trying to do what you think I want you to do.'

'Ha.'

'And I don't want you to, in the least.'

'Ho.'

'Are you trying to hurt me or are you trying to hurt yourself?'

'My mind's made up, Gavin.'

It was too. Of course, there were scenes and there were tears, hers and his, before the long business was concluded, but she never wavered. He claimed that he would never have been so vindictive. But what was vindictive in giving him what suited him best? He was now free to have a modern relationship with Emily and she, Ruth, would make the best of a bad job, or, as it turned out, of rather a good job. She had decided that if, as flattery promised, she was such a good cook, there was a future in turning professional. The idea had come to her in the bath, but she put it to prompt practical effect. Gavin had forgotten how, in the days before Alice was born, Ruth had been an astute and energetic partner in his then small business. By the time the divorce came through, she had rented premises (Frank Livermore staked her) and designed her kitchen. She recruited a small staff and began a gourmet take-away service. Soon her liveried motor-cyclists were buzzing all round those parts of London where people had the leisure to complain about the state of the economy over an impromptu dinner for eight. Gavin and Emily were nearly knocked over in Lowndes

Square by a rush consignment of Coquilles St Jacques au vinaigre de Xérès.

Gavin slightly resented the speed with which his ex-wife got over losing him. Emily avoided too immediate a show of exultation at having her lover to herself, but she did point out, after a few months of sexual and social commuting, how unnecessary it really was for them to maintain separate establishments. Her flat was romantic in its way, but it was pokesville, wasn't it? And her flat-mate, if tactful, was a drag. When they found a nice little mews house, everyone they knew assumed that they would be getting married. Gavin told Emily not to worry: he understood very well that marriage didn't interest a young woman in her position. 'I don't really have a position,' she said. 'I mean, tipping off the tippling public about a really rather ravishing and little known *cru bourgeois* isn't something a girl wants to devote her whole life to, is it?'

A month or two later they were married quietly and went to Venice for their honeymoon. Between churches, Emily ordered lots of glasses for the new house. A man of Gavin's status deserved the best and she was determined to have it. She revelled in the domesticity which she had never had as a child or been able to afford as an adult. She managed the house, and Gavin, expertly. The question of a baby was followed, quite naturally, by a baby; and the question of a brother or sister for Nigel was followed, no less naturally, if luckily, by Barnaby and Joanna. Emily proved as good a mother as she was a wife. The new house in Regent's Park Terrace was a splendid place to come home to, though it was odd how the interior bore such a resemblance to the one in which Gavin had lived with Ruth. Even the menus had a tasteful similarity to those which his first wife had provided. But then Emily had become an excellent cook, thanks in part to the Ruth Beaumont cookbook which was constantly on her Perspex kitchen lectern.

When Frank Livermore invited them to go on a tasting trip to the Burgundy country one Easter, Emily said she was sorry but she did not see how she could: Nigel would be on holiday and anyway, what could she do with the twins? She had long since given up her journalism and rarely drank wine. 'Heaven help us, darling,' she said, 'I do believe I've become a home body! Don't go and leave me, will you?'

'I love your home and I love your body,' Gavin said, 'and I certainly won't leave you.'

'But do go,' she said. 'You enjoy those things much more than I do. I'm not all that potty about burgundy, if the truth be known.'

'If you're sure you don't mind,' he said, 'I could use a break.'

Gavin's daughter Alice was now at university. He had seen Ruth from time to time, of course, but less frequently in recent years and never for longer than politeness required. Even now, after the surprise of seeing her at the first tasting, they had little opportunity for a *tête-à-tête*. Ruth had become very professional about wine. She had to be; her new restaurant was doing two hundred meals at lunch-time and scarcely less at night. The take-away service had become a sideline; she was into frozen food as well. Frank Livermore was advising her to go public in a couple of years. And had he heard that she was writing a monthly column in one of the glossies?

'You've fallen on your Ferragamo feet all right,' Gavin said, 'and I'm really glad. You're looking marvellous on it all, I must say.'

'You mean I'm using a lot of make-up.'

'I didn't know you were using any,' he said.

'You always were a sucker for strange women,' she said. 'You don't look so bad yourself.'

'A bit slow,' he said, 'but very welcome. I say, are you really planning to go to this shindig at the Hospice des Beaunes? The speeches'll be longer than the meal and we shall be surrounded with all those frightful dignitaries wearing faded velvet curtains. What do you say we slip away and dine somewhere together, just the two of us?'

'Are you making me an immoral proposal?'

'We'll have a table between us,' he said. 'How immoral is that?'

Ruth wore a new Missoni dress and she had found someone to do her hair the way that he had always liked it, pinned up just behind the ears, loose enough for threads of gold to glint against the whiteness of her neck. He learnt that Frank Livermore had never been anything to her but a reliable and

generous backer. There had been men, but there was no man.
She was jealous of her independence. They had, she realised,
done each other a really good turn, always assuming that he
was as happy as she was.

'I have the best wife in the world,' he said. 'After all, since
you've become a businesswoman, what competition does she
have?'

'And what about your mistress?' Ruth said.

'Mistress?' Gavin said. 'I wonder if this place has rooms.'

If it was as good for her as it was for him, it was very good
indeed. As a strangely familiar stranger, she seemed more
mysterious and more experienced and, in some way, more
exciting. They woke to the crispness of fresh rolls and the
ill-advised indulgence of home-made apricot jam.

'And are you still completely honest with her about everything?' Ruth said. 'Will you be telling your wife about this
woman you picked up?'

'Who picked me up,' Gavin said. 'Frankly, no. I don't
suppose I shall.'

'Very wise,' Ruth said. 'And shall you go on seeing her when
you get back to London?'

'I should certainly like to,' Gavin said. 'Not that I'm not very
happy the way I am, you understand, but what with the
children and the house, my wife . . . '

'I know how you must feel,' Ruth said. 'Of course, I ought to
teach you a lesson, but you're really much too attractive for me
to do that. And don't worry: I shan't leave embarrassing
messages on the telephone. The last thing I want is that you
should have to divorce what's-her-name.'

QUIXOTE SHMIXOTE

Jake Nathanson first spared me a few minutes of his time on a July afternoon more than twenty years ago. A mildewed diary confirms that I went straight to his office from a session with my accountant, whose name was Colin S. Lympett. Colin was a Southend commuter for whom 'dull' would be altogether too lively an epithet. Ditchwater sparkled by comparison. He confessed to me, over a cup of dusty coffee, that he was capable of literally boring himself to tears. His wildest dream was of falling asleep on a sandy beach and never waking up; he was an inverted Canute, pleading with some recalcitrant tide to come in and cover him up for ever. He was so tedious that H.M. Inspectors of Taxes took his word for what required thorough corroboration from more highly qualified men; anything was better than having him pop across for a bit of a chin-wag. Colin had been recommended to me by Aubrey Jellinek, who met him on a train, during a signals failure at Maryland Station, while on the way to visit his Dunroamin parents in their shingle-facing semi. Aubrey and I had been at Cambridge together a couple of years earlier, but he was already receiving royalty cheques from the Performing Rights Society and needed a financial adviser. Colin S. Lympett thus acquired his first client in show business. I was the second, I suppose. Aubrey had recruited me to write musical comedies with him and it was certain, he said, that I should soon need a subtle economic boffin (as well as a legal eagle) to manage my prosperous affairs. How do you do, Mr Lympett?

My partnership with Aubrey lasted a year and a bit, during which we attempted to make *Oklahoma* out of *The Mayor of Casterbridge*. The upbeat ending never really bonded with the

original material, and nothing very catchy seemed to rhyme
with Henchard. I left for Andalucia, without hard feelings or
the promised fortune, in order to write novels; I did not greatly
care if I never heard of a 'middle eight' again. Aubrey decamped to California, where he struck up a lucrative association with a lyricist with whom he is still minting old favourites.
A producer remarked that some people composed on paper,
and some people composed to the piano, but that Aubrey
composed to the radio. He must have listened to the right
stations, because he now has houses in Malibu, Puerto Vallar-
ta (he moved in the day before *The Night of the Iguana*), Èze
village (the breathtaking views!) and the Costa Smeralda (how
about those crystal-clear waters?). Colin S. Lympett did not
long remain Aubrey's answer to Pierpoint Morgan, but I had
no reason to seek flashier guidance. My income was in three
figures and unlikely to excite the avarice of the Inland
Revenue. As I left Colin's office, over the 'Dotted I' coffee bar,
a blonde with a beauty spot and a silky bosom of delectable
aquamarine blancmange was on her way up to check her
accounts. I was not, it seemed, Colin's sole remaining show biz
client.

My new novel, fat fruit of the Spanish sun, was in the hands
of the reviewers and I hoped, though I scarcely believed, that
its success would emancipate me from the vulgarities, and
temptations, of stage, screen and radio. In fact, since the
advance was already spent on family necessities, I badly
needed the job which it was in Jake Nathanson's gift, if not in
his nature, to offer me. He had told Robin, my agent at the
time, that he had never heard of me, which argued no singular
deafness, though it might have been more tactfully put. He
didn't, he went on, really fancy some up-market Oxbridge
dilettante for the screenplay he had in mind, but he could spare
me those few minutes of his time if I really wanted to make my
pitch. I could imagine more appreciative welcomes for a young
novelist whose first book had been hailed as 'amusing and
accomplished' (*Oxford Mail*) and whose second was said to be
'swingeing stuff' by the *Belfast News-Letter*, but that enemy of
promise, a pram, was in the rented hallway and a living had to
be made. Stay, Muse, while I make a brief *détour*!

Jake was not more than seven or eight years older than I, but we came of manifestly different generations. He had been a sergeant in the Tank Corps while I was still taking Radio Malt at my evacuated preparatory school. He was a published writer before he came down from Trinity, which he had reached, thanks to scholarship and energy, after an East End childhood. A Wittgensteinian from Brick Lane? Jake also was among the prophets! What public schoolboy, what covert Jew, what inhibited ambition could fail to wince at so quick a passage from barrow-boy to intellectual eminence? (In fact, Nathanson *père* owned several greengrocery shops and the family had lived in Stamford Hill ever since *boychik* was two days old.)

While still an undergraduate, Jake founded a magazine which enabled him to play the patronising angel to established names. Morgan Forster almost offered him a new piece of fiction about two pre-war Apostles who get given some irregular advice by a crone whom they mistake for the Pythian priestess and have a rather goat-footed evening in a rug factory afterwards. Jake's attack on Graham Greene's metaphysics, in the first issue of *Prospects*, was deemed outrageous, precocious and below the belt. In other words, people liked it a lot. Jake's black beret (without the Tank Corps badge, but with the holes from the pin still visible in it) and his 250 cc Norton made sure that he did not pass unremarked in demobbed Cambridge. There was usually a pretty passenger pillioned behind him, arms tightly enough around his corduroy waist to establish his virile credentials. Yet he was a dedicated student. Whewell's Court, where Wittgenstein held his exclusive seminars, knew his pious tread. When he had a shorter notice on Heidegger ('Being and Having Been') published in a philosophical journal, he seemed destined for academic preferment. As it was, his notoriety as a disputant survived the intervening years until I began to read philosophy myself. Russell had had to think for eighteen seconds before answering one of his points at the Moral Sciences Club.

Had *Prospects* not been let down by a defaulting Sartrean whose work in progress had not progressed sufficiently fast, Jake might never have abandoned the stringencies of logical analysis, but when there was a hole in the book suddenly, Barney Cohen was invented to fill it. In the event, like the fountain, he overflowed. As a Forties' hero, Barney went against the literary grain. *Angst?* He had enough trouble already. Dying falls? Who needed them when he was flat on his back? Sunset in the gardens of the West? So turn on the lights, somebody. Guilt? Turn the collar and sell it to the *goyim*. At a time when Sydney Stanley was an embarrassment which made my father straighten and re-straighten his Old Pauline tie before setting off for the suburban train, Jake Nathanson's creation was screwing *shiksas*, flogging clothing coupons and fixing foreign currency for the titled trade like as if Yossel was an amateur wet behind the ears.

Barney Cohen's aggression was shameless and almost alarming; there was anger in Jake's style, a deliberate quarrel-picking insolence which no amount of *schmaltz* could conceal. In spite or because of that, Barney caught the public imagination. In the nervous post-war world, he didn't give a damn; effing and blinding were as natural to him as um and er were to the rationed pin-stripers who were soon reading his randy adventures in their evening papers. Jake wrote his last philosophical essay on 'Sense-Data and Verification Again' and came down to London. In no time, he was doing pieces for just about every publication that could meet his meaty price. His Cambridge accent was shucked like his demob suit; he never bad-mouthed Wittgenstein, but Barney's loudest contempt was vented on pale-blue-oh-I-say-Rodericks and verse dramatists with Christian overtones. Jake's scoundrelly hero was turned into a musical (*Four by Two*) and a strip cartoon.

Unsurprisingly, Jake's accountant was in the Shaftesbury Avenue office when I arrived. The clutter of furniture seemed excessive, but Jake explained that he was taking most of it home; it had to pass through the office for tax reasons. I sensed the challenge in his brazenness; he was daring me to reveal middle-class scruples. He sat me down, had coffee brought in by Beverley, who looked as though she had not quite finished dressing, and rumpled his face into a sardonic smile. 'So you think you can write movies?'

I shall not rehearse the jejune phrases with which I sought at once to establish my haughty purposes in literature and to make it clear that I was up for grabs. He offered me a cigar, which I refused, and asked me to pass the oversized box of matches next to the third telephone. When he opened it, I could see that it was crammed with five-pound notes. 'Other box,' he said, helping himself *en passant* to enough fivers for six months' rent on the cottage I was living in. He still had difficulty shutting the lid. 'Think you can write comedy? Because I want somebody can write knockabout. Nothing subtle. I'll give you a for instance. Picture starts on the Rock of Gibraltar. Bloke feeding the apes, O.K.? The Barbary apes. Throws one a banana. Bugger throws back the peel, and our bloke goes arse over tip, knocks down this Arabic princess. She slaps his face and the stupid *schnook* falls helplessly in love. You married?'

'Yes,' I said, 'actually I − '

'Because if you want to be in the movies for the nooky, it's no use being a writer. You never get near the ammunition. O.K., so he's this modern Don Quixote, he thinks she's an Arabic princess, whereas in reality she's a nice Jewish girl from Dalston modelling *schmuttahs* on some cruise liner anchored in the bay. This bloke, he's so ugly she won't give him the time of day, but there's more to him than meets the eye. Has to be, you're right there. I've got Peter for the part; I've got a commitment from him and that's why I can't afford to piss about with somebody can't give me the crap I want. University boys're the kind of trouble I don't need. I want a hundred and twenty pages, tops, and it's got to be a knicker-wetter. Can you do it or can't you? Be honest, because if you're not going to be honest you've gotta be talented, and that puts a strain on people. If you want nooky, don't do it the roundabout way is my advice, my son. Look at that.'

He pointed out of the window. On the far side of Shaftes-bury Avenue a prostitute in a summer frock, white with rising suns on it, was touting for custom. She was a beauty. The promptness with which she attracted her next sheepish client was no surprise. Knowing the British, one would not have been amazed to see a queue begin to form. 'Better ways of getting hold of that than typing for it,' Jake said, 'but of course you're a married man and it wouldn't cross your mind. Mind's got nothing to do with it, right? So listen, you've written a novel, Robin tells me. What's it about? Don't tell me, I'll tell you. Sensitive Jewboy in a public school where he's not

appreciated and doesn't like compulsory chapel. Am I right?
First love. First marriage. Second love. Second thoughts. Am I
warm? Am I hot?'

'You're tepid,' I said. 'Tepid and loud.'

'*Loud?*'

'Just a little,' I said.

'You don't want the job, what did you come up here for?'

'You knew Wittgenstein,' I said. 'I didn't. He died before I
managed to meet him.'

'You want to see my copy of *The Blue Book*, is that it? Get
out of here!'

'Does Miss Anscombe know about this?' I said.

'Be worth a bomb one day, if only I had one. Know the
trouble with philosophy? No residuals. I'm going to get Frank
and Denis to do this one, not some pissy public school
Platonist.'

'They won't touch it,' I said.

'You're right: I asked them.'

'Do it yourself,' I said, 'why don't you?'

'Haven't got enough effing time, or I would. I'm doing two
for Columbia and one for Paramount and I've got Zanuck for
dinner.'

We talked about Freud and Wittgenstein until the shadows
lengthened over the gorgeous tart and I had to phone my wife
and tell her that I should not be home till after the rush hour.
Jake had been crude and jeering, but he had also been amused
and amusing. His voice had lost its hectoring edge as we
entered serious ground and he ended by being quietly informative about the influence of the Kabala on secular Jewish
thinkers; my ignorance about Gershom Scholem made him
almost tender in his dismay. I may not have got the job that
evening, but I did leave with a useful reading list.

My new book came out and, if I say so myself, it was
something of a success. There was a whole-page review in the
Daily Beaver. A reprint was ordered. The telephone rang in the
cottage and it was Beverley (pause), Jake's secretary. Hullo,
Beverley! She had Jake for me. He had read the reviews; he was
halfway through the book. 'Looks like you've got lucky,' he
said, 'because I don't think you'll bring it off, sensitive bloody
middle-class Jewboy, but who else have I got? I haven't got

anybody else. Your luck, my bad management and when can I have it? Tomorrow may be too late. Do I want it good or do I want it on time? I want it on time.'

The deal was struck. Robin was disappointed by the proposed fee; I saw a new car, a new bed and time for a new novel in it. Riches, in other words. I hated the subject and I did not delude myself into thinking that knicker-wetters were easy to construct. I told myself to get stuck in and succeeded only in getting stuck. However, when in the bunker and there's money on the match, one can only hack and hack until one gets out of it. The pages accumulated slowly as the allotted weeks passed. Jake called now and again and betted me I wished I'd never heard of Quixote/Shmixote (provisional title). I lied about how well it was going and how much fun I was having. Finally, when I read the script for the last time before sending it to him, I did actually laugh a couple of times, maybe three. The Barbary ape sequence was not too funny, I didn't think, but that was his responsibility.

The telephone did not ring. Its silence clanged like Bow bells. I had, no doubt, deceived myself into thinking that Jake was not merely my producer but also my friend. Your producer is never your friend (item one/one in the Tractatus Showbusinesso-Philosophicus). After two weeks, I asked Robin to press for the payment due on delivery. 'This abortion he calls delivered?' Jake was reported to have said. I was disappointed, but I was not crushed: I wanted my money and, after a while, I got it. Maybe Jake had had difficulty getting the match-box open. Robin revealed that Jake and Peter had broken their indissoluble partnership a week before my script hit the mat.

A year or so later, I was back with Colin S. Lympett, going over my annual accounts. Thanks to Jake, my income had considerably increased. I would actually have some tax to pay (so is bad news parasitic on good, like doubt on certainty). I can still see Colin's musty face as he told me that it would save trouble — and tuppence for the extra stamp duty — if I made out my cheque to him personally for the sum of £250, which would include twenty-five for his own fees. He would pass on the balance to H.M.G. I hesitated, but I did it. How could so lustreless a character be up to anything as interesting as no good? Several months later, I received an impatient demand from the Revenue for the £225 I still owed them. I called Colin's number and found that his office was now occupied by Gillian Green (Gowns of Renown) Ltd. Colin S. Lympett, further inquiries disclosed, had deserted Southend for the South of France in the company of a chorus girl half his age. I could see that aquamarine blancmange in a flashback which told me everything, too late. Colin had come to life, with my (and other clients') money. I cursed and almost smiled and made out a new cheque for the unamused Inspector of Taxes, a/c payee only. Nothing, I suppose, elicits less sympathy than the misfortunes of the fortunate when it comes to final payments, so I will be brief in recounting my further credulities. The close reader will remember that Jake's accountant had been in his office when I called there. It now occurred to me that there were unlikely to be any flies on Nathanson and I called Beverley for the chap's name. He took me on as a client and I thought my troubles were over. Two years later, Jake was in front of the Special Commissioners because of some scheme that Norman had devised for him and peddled to me and I had to extricate myself from another pit before the pendulum struck home. Jake was in big trouble, it seemed, and I felt sorry for him. I was writing fancy movies by then and could afford to play the old pal. I took him to the White Elephant. He was rather more cheerful and impenitent than I expected. We had a few drinks, and he had a few more, and he began to tell me about the deals he was making and the plans he had. His company was maybe in *shtook*, but he still had his wits about him. 'For instance,' he said, 'I've got a lot of projects Norman never got round to doing the paper work on them, they belong to me personally, like for example this script I had written for me years ago by some *schnook*, Peter was going to do it, cost me pennies. *Pennies*. About this character, sort of a modern Don Quixote. Load of rubbish but guess what I did with it last week.'

'I can't,' I said. 'Tell me.'

'I made a treatment of it, new outline, sold it to Frankovitch this morning for a hundred and fifty grand. I can use the original script I bought from this hack, doll it up a little bit maybe, and who's going to know the difference?'

'Probably there won't be any,' I said.

'Had a few laughs in it,' he said. And then he looked at me. I swear that I was not wearing my most reproachful expression, but something in my eyes must have been as clear as the waters off the Costa Smeralda. I never thought I should live to see it, but Jake Nathanson blushed. He blushed like one of his father's lovely beetroots. He almost steamed. 'You know what,' he said, when he had paused longer than Bertie Russell faced with a logical dilemma, 'you know what, Freddie, I was talking to Mike about you. It's time we worked together again. Believe me, my son, I could produce you like you need to be produced.'

'Not out of a hat?'

'Save the tired dialogue for working hours. Israel. Have you thought seriously about Israel recently? Because there's a subject. I read your new book; very nice, very good-hearted, very sensitive.'

'Come to the flattery,' I said. 'This is my lunch, you know.'

'What do you say?'

'I say you paid for the script and you're welcome to do anything with it you feel like doing.'

'So let's talk about Wittgenstein already. What do you still want to know?'

SENIORITY

Peter Crowman's *Seniority* has attracted remarkably little attention. There is perhaps something perversely unobtrusive about the title. One might suppose that it concerned the prospects for promotion in the navy during the Napoleonic Wars rather than the power structure of a public school. It so happens that Crowman went to the same place I did, even though he had left before I arrived, which may be the reason why his story had such an impact on me.

It is largely assumed that the public schools have changed out of all recognition. Any further denunciation of them is held to be as pertinent to modern life as, say, an indignant treatment of flogging as a military punishment. Those things simply don't happen any more, whatever they are. The dark days of Flashman have gone for ever. Certainly it was said, by those who bothered to say anything, that Crowman's book was an obsolete squib, a gesture of suspect sentimentality rather than of accurate indignation. However, the obsessive drive of the narrative and the vivid plausibility of Marmaduke Denton combined, so far as I am concerned, to make the house bully into something more haunting than a curiosity in an obsolete bestiary. Crowman turns the bully into an emblematic figure too enduring for easy burial. Tradition maintains that the bully is not all that much of a menace: he is always alleged to be a coward who collapses before the determined courage of his victim or the dismissive contempt of his moral superiors. In the old jargon, he is an outsider; his brutality may give him a temporary ascendancy, but — like pride — he must have a fall. There is something a little convenient in this confidence that the bully is an aberration rather than a recurrent phenomenon. It is Peter Crowman's skill to have depicted

Marmaduke Denton as a creature of the very system from which soft mythologies have always disqualified him.

The most obvious bully in the literature is, of course, Flashman, whose revision by George MacDonald Fraser has been a triumphant vindication of T.S. Eliot's remark to the effect that bad writers borrow from others, whereas good ones steal. Fraser has promoted Flashman into something much more attractive, indeed irresistible, than his original author would have found appropriate, or even tolerable. Yet Flashman was always as much a cad as a bully: the lineaments of charm were already there. One felt, even in Hughes, that he was really too old, too sophisticated for a place in Tom Brown's schooldays or Dr Arnold's school. He belonged to the world of tarts and pugilists where the young Byron (who was certainly no bully) found himself so deliciously at home. Flashman's behaviour owes as much to boredom with puerile circumstances as it does to innate sadism. Marmaduke Denton, warming himself at the only really hot radiator in 'Long Room', his rationed trousers too brief for his elongating legs, face plump with cadged jam and extra slices of National Loaf, could never have hobnobbed with gallants. Intimidating as he may seem to poor little Colin Black, the new boy, he belongs to the *dramatis personae* of Greyfriars rather than of Almack's:

> 'What's your name, grunt?'
> 'Black,' Colin said.
> 'You look a bit black. Have you ever had a wash?'
> 'Frequently,' the new boy said.
> Something physical seemed to change in Marmaduke Denton's attitude, though he did not shift his position. The flesh gathered in his face and made shadows under his cheeks. So does the still hunter remain not quite unmoved at the sight of his prey. 'Do you know what festive means, Black?'
> 'It means having a good time, doesn't it?'
> 'I'm asking the questions,' Denton said, and his eyes shifted to the door, as if he expected endorsement or possibly reproach from some watching senior. 'If you think it means having a good time, you've got a lot to learn about this particular little establishment.'
> 'I expect I have got a lot,' Colin said.
> 'Wait a mo. Where do you think you're going? Did I say you could buzz?'

'I'm supposed to go and have my voice tested,' Colin said. 'I have to go up to chapel.'

'Are you a frequent church-goer, Black? You don't look as though you are,' Denton said. 'My nose – and your nose – tells me different.'

'For the choir,' Colin said. 'Mr Effingham told me to be there at four. It's getting on for that now.'

'Nice watch,' Denton said. 'Did mummy give you that?'

'She did actually.'

'Mind you look after it then. Festive means insolent. It means showing signs of impatience when addressed by your elders and betters. And if you're going to do what Mr Effingham tells you to do with all the slavering oiliness of which you give rather disgusting evidence, you're going to find yourself involved in some very decadent goings-on before your course is fully run. Do you follow my drift, Black?'

'I'm not sure that I do.'

'My name is Denton. Use it. Respectfully. And I'm quite sure you do. Follow me. You're a tidge oily, Black. Your maker probably had a tar-brush in his hand when he was putting the final touches to your fizz. Well?'

'I didn't say anything, Denton.'

'No more you did. And I heard you. Are you clever, Black-amoor?'

'That's not for me to say, is it, Denton?'

'It's been said that you're a Hash Pro. Is that true?'

'Is that a scholar?' Colin said.

'No, that's a little swot who agrees to take money in order to come to this ancient establishment. Is that what you are – a professional? One who takes tin for putting pen to paper?'

'I can't help being a scholar,' Colin said.

'It's the things one can't help, Master Black, which give one away. It's the things one can't do anything about that land one in it. It's the things that nobody can do anything to change that are the most unforgivable of all. For instance, women can't avoid being women. Do you follow me, Black?'

'I don't think I do, Denton.'

'Have you ever been kissed, Black?'

'Kissed?'

'Osculated. Has the term escaped your scholarly attentions? Have you a dictionary? Kissed. On the lips. By lips. Ruby rim to ruby rim. Well? Have you ever been or not?'

'Of course,' Colin said. 'By my mother.'

'And is that the full roster?'

36

'Give us a chance,' Colin said.

'Remember what festive means, won't you, Blackie? I'd advise it.'

Colin manages to get away, but he is late for his audition and Mr Effingham, the choir-master, lisps his irritation. When he asks Colin to match a note on the rehearsal piano, the boy's voice seems to break at that very moment: he emits a 'froggish croak' and the other candidates laugh so loudly that Mr Effingham dismisses him, as if his sudden adolescence were an impertinent prank. Already we can see that Marmaduke Denton was right: what we cannot avoid is often held against us. Indeed, during his brief and dismaying encounter with Marmaduke the new boy has been warned of many truths and, in a way, inoculated against their pain. Denton makes him feel that he has 'been at the school all his life'. When he goes into Arrowsmith's Remove, the sarcastic rhetoric of the colourful master seems to echo that of Denton, although we soon realise that in fact Denton has learnt his polysyllabic ways from the lame usher. Denton has done Colin some kind of prophylactic service in singling him out for early treatment. If the new boy fears the menace of the bully, he almost craves it as well: when Denton is temporarily in Sick Room, Colin actually asks the hag how he is. He hopes 'at the same time to hear that he is dead and that he will soon be back'. Peter Crowman has the nerve to make Marmaduke both devil and saviour.

On the realistic level, it comes as something of a shock to discover that Denton is actually only one year older than Colin. In spite of his officious style and his assumption of privileged access to the radiator, he has no formal 'seniority'. He is a member of Long Room, just as Colin and all the other junior boys are. He too is a member of the proletariat from whom the fags, of various denominations, are drawn. Because of his age, however, Denton has merely perfunctory duties: he has to remove old newspapers and put them out for salvage. Once a week, he takes the obsolete mags − *Picture Post*, *Illustrated* and *John Bull* − from 'Hall', where the house Bloods congregate, and dumps them in Long Room, where the grunts can have their first belated dekko. He is also supposed to empty house waggerpaggers, but we find that Colin is soon doing this for him.

Marmaduke performs his duties with a rather surprising docility. We come to realise that he relishes the opportunity they give him to go into Hall, where he can eavesdrop on what the monitors are saying and so acquire the latest info with which to intimidate or blackmail the less privileged. In spite of his 'meaty menace', or because of it, Denton appears quite popular with his betters. The previous quarter, Kingsley gave him twelve and he took it without a murmur, even though Kingsley had 'taken a run and everything'. Now the monitors, especially Foxall, often engage him in casual conversation. Occasionally he gets offered a piece of charred toast. In return, he offers griff about 'the tone' of Long Room. It is appropriate that he is a lance-jack in the J.T.C.: his style is that of a non-commissioned officer, neither one of the men nor one of the officers. At once lubricant and irritant, he gives and accepts favours from both sides, without belonging to either. He is not trusted, but he is indispensable.

The analogy with N.C.O.s is not quite satisfactory, since Marmaduke's vocabulary and posture are decidedly nobbish. He may have blotted his copybook with his 'loutishness', as the punishment book describes it, but he apes the authorities whom he also challenges. Indeed, he likes to give the impression that he is too grand to jostle for status. (Even Long Room has its petty monitors − called 'Top Table' − who are, so to speak, auditioning for higher position in the house seniority. They alone, according to the strict letter of the law, are entitled to put their bums on the radiators, but none of them cares to 'budge' Marmaduke.) He likes to encourage the rumour that he will come into a title one day. His funny first name has led to his being given the obvious nickname 'Orange' and his reaction to it is typical: he will drub anyone who uses it, or whom he hears using it, but he also puts it about that he is descended from the 'House of Orange'. It is tempting to think that he has been turned into a bully, in some degree, by the sweet name his mother gave him at the font. His violent loathing for her (and, as a consequence, for all women) seems to stem from the humiliation of his endearingly precious name.

Denton's capacity for getting away with it, for the most

part, is due above all to his excellence at games. Although he never turns up for practice games and has a lamentable degree of 'House Spirit', he cannot be left out of the side. Equally, although he never seems to do any work, he manages to get quite decent marks. Colin finds that, despite his contempt for scholars, Denton is actually an exhibitioner: it is the lowest form of 'Hash Pro', but one which escapes the obloquy of the full-blown 'professional'. He holds his place in the 'A' set by a judicious amalgam of cheating and intelligence. If it amuses him to make Colin Black do his Latin verses for him, it also entertains him to correct the odd false quantity in the elegiacs which he has thus extracted from his 'slave'. His laziness is dangerous with alertness, just as his malice is armed with an intuition that is a counterfeit form of affection, shrewd with accurate attentions:

'Are you looking for me, young Black?' Denton has come into the bogs on his rubber soles, policeman and pickpocket economised in the same flesh.

'Not exactly, Denton.'

'Are you wondering what to do with yourself this sullen afternoon?'

'I've got to go to Godge,' Colin said.

'And what shall you do in that Surrey metropolis – look at the women's underwear in Silver's window?'

'I don't suppose so, Denton.'

'Do we never gaze at brassières and dream of what they may one day contain?'

'Not really, Denton.'

'Or knickers. Do we never wonder what nether regions will one day – or one night – be within those pink elastications?'

'Actually, I'm going to see if I can get some blackcurrant purée,' Colin said.

'Did I say you could leave?'

'Sorry, Denton, I didn't realise – '

'Realise, Blackie, realise! You know you don't really want to go, don't you? You ache to know what I require of you next, what vile demand I'm going to make on you. How are your marks, young Black, this quarter?'

'Not too bad, Denton.'

'We do like to be top, don't we, Blackamoor? We do like to shine. Well?'

'I do my best,' Colin said.

'I've had a thought. Yes, I have. Suppose — suppose *I* do your next set of Latin verses. Just for a change. Fair's fair. How would you like that?'

'It's very decent of you, Denton.'

'Then why are you shaking? Is it only because you're afraid you'll yellow your pants? I think I'll do your next set for you and you can hand them in without making any changes whatsoever and then you can show me how we've done afterwards. I shall, of course, be able to see if you've . . . *improved* them at all and I shall, of course, take a dim view of that.'

'I don't mind doing them for myself,' Colin said.

'Then you won't mind doing mine as well, will you? After all, I offered to do yours, didn't I? Tell me something, Blackamoor, what do you mind doing particularly? Anything? *Anything?*'

Peter Crowman here catches perfectly that mixture of social and sexual threat by which Marmaduke keeps his hold on Colin. The new boy, however bright, has a desperate need to conform with the ethos of a community to which his brains have given him access but where he seems not wholly to belong, since — apart from other reasons — it is part of a society where brains are suspect. Those other reasons are hinted at, if never fully articulated, in Denton's reference to Black's nose and, however improbably, to his negro streak. All distinction, it may be inferred, renders its possessor vulnerable, marginal, liable to ostracism. ('Taking exception' is a pretty piece of schoolboy slang.) Colin is a candidate for 'seniority', for a swift rise along the *cursus honorum*, but he is hardly less likely to prove a scapegoat on whom his fellows can visit their own inadequacies and fears. By becoming Marmaduke's creature, which he seems to do with a certain helpless complaisance, Colin acquires the cruel protection of the other boy. In a sense, he also becomes Denton's protector, even if the *dénouement*, with its neat irony, reveals him giving the very evidence which leads to the bully's downfall, although he imagines that the fact that the offence took place in the hols will lead to his acquittal. I shall not, of course, go further into the details of that ambiguous last chapter: to do so would spoil the pleasure of those who have yet to read Crowman's minor masterpiece.

What impression do we finally get of the character of the bully? He is like a copper's nark who has failed to enter the recognised force, but does its nastiest work. The discovery that Marmaduke actually lives not in some splendid Brideshead but in the suburban 'cottage' (to which, for almost inexplicable reasons, he invites Colin) may seem like a snobbish act of vengeance on the part of the author. The assumption is, of course, that Crowman and Black are virtually identical and that the novelist is, as novelists will, taking his time over getting his own back. However, it is, I now suspect, no miscalculation on Crowman's part that we begin to feel pity for Marmaduke rather than to exult over his banal background. His affectations of royalty are seen now to be part of an imaginative pattern, a longing to trump the court cards in the official pack. There is something almost heroic in Marmaduke's imposture: he may hate his mother for saddling him with an absurd Christian name, but he has somehow sought to honour her ambitions by bettering his betters. The tears which Colin sheds when he sees the bully carrying his trunk to the taxi are not those of the crocodile but, it must be admitted, more like those of the abandoned lover. We should not forget the last words of the novel:

> I'm free, he thought, and then he wondered why he did not feel more exhilaration. 'I'm free,' he said to himself, aloud, and could not think what could possibly be worth doing to celebrate his liberation. 'Free!' and his voice broke on the word. He was no longer a schoolboy, no longer young.

Soon after reading *Seniority*, I went with my wife to a restaurant for lunch. We were looking forward to a *tête-à-tête*, but a single man was sitting at the adjacent table and, with irritating flattery, he recognised me. Solitude made him garrulous and he said that he had been to the same school as myself. I looked at his half-spectacles as he surveyed the menu and guessed that he might have known Peter Crowman.

'Oh yes,' he said, 'I knew Crowman all right.'

'I suppose he had a hell of a time,' I said.

'Peter Crowman?' he said.

'I suppose he was terribly bullied,' I said. 'Have you not read his novel about his schooldays?'

Our neighbour laid aside the menu, as if his appetite had deserted him. '*He* had a hell of a time? When he walked through the house, we used to cringe against the wall. I've never known anyone else whose mere physical presence — the mention of his name — made me buckle at the knees quite as much as Peter Crowman. My sergeant-major at Mons was a positive — well, *nanny* — by comparison. Mind you . . . ' He stopped speaking, but it was as if the stream of words had plunged suddenly into a tunnel: one knew that it was continuing, though there was no sign of it. His gold-rimmed eyes were busy seeing old scenes; his balding head was full of dead dialogue. He blinked and turned to us again. 'I'm very rude, I'm afraid,' he said. 'Allow me to introduce myself. My name is Kevin White.'

LOOKING BACK

When exactly was Len Parker's first play performed? Did it open a little before, or just after, *The Sport of my Mad Mother*? Was it in the same season as *One Way Pendulum* or did it succeed *Yes — and After* (surely the best title ever written by an author still in his teens)? Was it directed by Tony or Lindsay? Or by Anthony or Bill? Although I did occasionally pass through Sloane Square during that second quinquennium of the Fifties when something was falling like rain and it was typewriter keys, I am not its reliable historian. The New Drama promised a social revolution which, with the right quotations on its banner, would radiate from S.W.1. to liberate the whole country from class and Terence Rattigan, but, like brave Crillon, I found no place in its battling ranks.

The nearest I ever came to getting a desert boot in the door was when one of the presiding Royal Court junta declared, with tremulous force, that my anti-bomb bombshell would certainly be staged during the next 'season' at the Court. Meanwhile I should regard the place as my spiritual home: I was welcome at any time. I took him sufficiently at his word to wander into a rehearsal of a new masterwork. The founder was on his knees barking at a very tall, thin director who seemed not wholly happy with his yap. 'If you like it, George, I *suppose* I like it,' the director was saying, in a very O.U.D.S. voice, 'but isn't it a bit Belgravia?' The bespectacled pooch at his suede feet snarled that he liked it quite a bit, or he would not have done it that way. The tall, thin director drew patient breath through a narrow nose and removed his twill leg, at which the founder was sniffing wittily before trying another yap, sarcastic and pointedly Battersea. The

43

purpose of admitting stray scribes to the rehearsals of other people's plays was to familiarise trios with the day-to-day problems confronting actors and directors. Such hospitality would weld a sense of solidarity between the various theatrical talents which Shaftesbury Avenue had been so adept in — to use an expression of Jean-Paul Sartre's — 'serialising'. By fostering the impression that directors mutilated scripts, that authors were intransigent and idle, actors merely pretty faces (and other parts), Binkie and his minions had deterred the workers from seeing how much they had in common. When the dramatist was summoned on stage to discuss exactly what bark he had in mind — was it a Surbiton snarl or a Wanstead woof? — I concluded that the Pierian spring had yielded as much knowledge as a student could be expected to quaff on his first day.

I went home to our basement on the Embankment and waited to be summoned for the first conference about my own work. The play was, I daresay, somewhat jejune, but there was one scene in *Do Not Go Gentle* of which I remain furtively proud: the American ambassador comes into his office with a golf bag containing, instead of clubs, a selection of weaponry of varying calibres and when an underling asks how the morning went, BRAD replies, 'I shot seventy-eight.' On such evidence, it is not surprising that I expected to be a shoo-in for a prompt production, but my sponsor was not, in the event, of sufficient *poids*. In fact, on balance he seems scarcely to have weighed anything at all. The smallest breeze made him shake so violently that he had to wedge himself under the desk to avoid being blown into the street. An aspen leaf was as steady as a guardsman by comparison. George had no difficulty in blowing him, and my play, right off the lot.

And so, always an easy sulk, I drew the quick conclusion that the theatre was not for me, nor I for the theatre. It was a disappointment, since my first ambition was to be a playwright. Two books had particularly impressed me when, as a war-time child, marooned in a Putney flat during television-less holidays, I spent much of my time wondering what to read next, or again. We had a decent small library: a mixture of Dickens, the Reprint Society's austere war efforts, my father's philosophical stuff from Oxford, the flashier fruit of pre-war

44

years in New York and some oddities, like *The Spanish Arena*, issued by the Right Book Club. My parents had elected to subscribe to this last organisation because they took it that the 'Right' in its title was the opposite of 'Wrong', not of 'Left'. In fact, the handsomely produced volumes in their Harris-tweed bindings were intended as a counterblast to the orangey agitprop published by Victor Gollancz. Hence my somewhat puzzled pre-adolescent self came into contact with the unnervingly virulent right-wing rhetoric, often deranged with anti-Semitism, which had continued to thud through our suburban letter-box until my father's belatedly close reading of the text led to its curtailment. The rant of the Right had an effect upon me which was not unlike that of the illustrations in a fancy edition of Oscar Wilde, which included a chastely suggestive impression of 'The Harlots' House'. In other words, the blood was summoned up in that mixture of excitement and apprehension which the cruel and the forbidden provoke in the sensitive and excluded. I was alarmed by the strident conviction of the Fascist mentality, but just as my war-time drawings were often of German officers strutting in high-hatted elegance, so I was bewitched by the snarling menace of those who had known, and admired, the dictators whose fall would save my skin. My later desire to adhere to the Social Revolution and to march in step with those whose drill sergeants were calling 'Left, left, left' owed something to the shameful furtiveness with which I was drawn to the apostles of autocracy. If I hated and feared them, for what they would almost certainly do to me, should their boots be shod with authority, I confess that the bragging insolence of their style, the sarcasm of their denunciations, made me wish, oh so very slightly, that I might be eligible for their faction.

But I digress, since the two books in my parents' shelves which turned me towards the theatre owed nothing to the adjacent works of Alistair Reed or G. Ward Price or Arthur Machen. The first was *Victoria Regina* by Laurence Housman, whose brother was a scholar-poet unrepresented on the Reprint Society's list, and the second was Noel Coward's *Play Parade*. Since my first seven years had been spent in the States, I was exceptionally awed by the map-reddening machinery of the British monarchy. Housman offered a literary entrée to the palace where I could overhear the chat of my betters and learn how the grand conducted themselves. (There is no limit to the number of doors, and windows, to which the suburban outsider dreams of putting his ear, and his eyes.) I was particularly heartened by the Semitic ease with which Benjamin Disraeli charmed his way to the Queen's quiescent heart and, with a few flowery speeches and a quiver of primroses, reduced Ma'am to girlish twitters. When he produced India, as lesser magicians come up with a rabbit, and offered Vicky the enticement of being *Ind. Imp.* as well as *fid. def.*, I saw how a single man, with his wits about him, could trump the Right and silence the Left. Bismarck's *alte Jude* was my kind of Englishman; Housman, with his neat dialogue, his easy command of theatrical narrative and *mondaine* society, alerted me to the hope of fame through the light touch.

As for Coward, his works were tricked out in an *argenté* edition which sparkled like a miniature of the Great White Way where he had enjoyed so many sophisticated triumphs with his devastating repartee (a yellow clipping, stuck under the back flap, drew attention to both). As adolescence added its bewilderments to my only childhood, I discovered through Amanda and Elyot what it was that grown-ups got up, and down, to when they were together on a Paris sofa: they talked in extremely clipped tones and had frightfully silly quarrels and — on a cry of Sollocks — terribly, terribly passionate reconciliations only to be interrupted by adenoidal maids and perfectly damnable telephone calls. I could hardly wait. Meanwhile, I was again struck by the one thing Housman and Coward had in common: they entered the hall of fame on payment of a remarkably exiguous entrance fee. Novels, I noticed, contained many more pages than plays and their authors were, on the whole, required to fill the space from margin to margin. A dramatist could have someone say 'Open this door' or 'Ecstatic' and move immediately to the next double-spaced line. I had a long way to go before I could hope to appear between hard covers, but I could already recognise a short cut when I saw one.

The second important virtue of the drama was that it was not a solitary vice: others were soon implicated in it and their larky participation (as petty experience in school plays had already proved) gilded the gingerbread of authorship. Occasionally, during those Putney holidays, I was able to persuade a pretty neighbour to come and read the Master with me while our parents played sixpenny bridge at their place. We rattled through the *risqué* dialogue with briskly innocent knowingness, desiring each other madly, darling, without ever so much as a kiss on the cheek. Later, it is true, we did proceed to certain scandalous experiments in the tennis club loo, but since the smoke turned us wickedly green and did no good whatever to my overhead, we soon desisted. Were life a novel by Howard Spring, I should in due course have written a hit play and turned Dorothy into a West End star. In fact, she turned into one without my agency and was notably successful in her representation of the Queen Empress, a part which she had never played in our occasional rep. I have written a good deal of dialogue since those days, but little of it has been spoken across the footlights. My first love has been pretty well without issue and I am obliged to pretend not to be sorry.

As it happened, my first novel was published just as the play was proving to be very much the thing. No one in a purple suit was reviewing fiction, but Ken was in the stalls and the *Observer* every week. Here was a triumph of the will indeed: determined to be the new Agate, Tynan needed grist for his ego and his demanding enthusiasm summoned the new drama into existence that he might have the pleasure of being its eloquently stammering barker. Virgin playwrights came mothily to his flame. He was a caustic Dr Frankenstein to whom nothing talented was monstrous. Osborne was but the most scintillating of his promotions; his recension of *Private Lives* set in that hitherto undiscovered country known as The North, where no French windows looked on to bird-loud borders, gave the author of *Look Back in Anger* the crown of the dramatic republic whose advent it trumpeted. His rhetoric was barbed with intimidating venom. When he declared that the Royal Family was 'the gold filling in a mouth full of decay', it was not only dentists who quailed at the diagnosis; everyone was open-mouthed, as it were, for the next touch of the drill. The middle class came to be insulted and wasn't going home until it was. Osborne was not only a great talent, he was also a great liberator, little as he might relish the tribute today. Len Parker might have been successful without Osborne's example, but he would never have been so bold or so brassy so soon. His first play, *Where Are You Going?* (the answer was, of course, 'out'), did not excite K.T. to the dithyrambic flights he reserved for Osborne, but he did observe that Len's play was 'half pat on the back, half kick in the tripes' for that 'just below the middle-class belt between the lumpen-proletariat and the lumpy *booboisie*'. (Mencken served in the office of coach for those who would soon be exporting the red gospel of the Berliner Ensemble at a buck a word.)

Where Are You Going? was a considerable near-hit. Was it Tom or Alan or Ken or Albert who impersonated Parker's 'callow, sly, sensitive, coarse, inhibited, randy, foul-mouthed, silver-tongued scholarship lad, Pat Sully'? Here, someone said, one Sunday when I was writing my *tristia* on the undiscovered Costa del Sol, was a 'new voice not too inhibited by glottal stoppages, effing and blinding its way out of the provincial wilderness and hell-bent on running after the band-wagon fast enough to kick its passengers where it hurts, before pinching their cushioned places'. Some of Ken's colleagues had to work a little too hard to mix a metaphor to match his. Another of them, positively psoriatic with emulation, weighed in with 'the sticks have come to town and they're in no mood to apologise for cudgelling us smug metropolitans black and blue'. Oxford wits were markedly prone to effusive welcomes for those fortunate enough not to have had their advantages.

Len's suburbia lay between Manchester and Liverpool. Its air was sour with an unbreathable mixture of non-conformist cant and creeping Jesuitry. Sully's R.C. youth was a sorry season of burgeoning skin complaints and morose lust. As for the adults whose oppressive hypocrisy drove him to such frenzied fantasies, they were the 'kind of sunless souls you would expect to find trapped under the stones of booze, bitching and butties' (critics always think that alliteration clinches an argument).

Len wanted to call his next piece *Shit Off a Shovel*, but the moribund Lord Chamberlain summoned his waning powers to interdict it. *Swing Those Arms* (revised title) was alleged to be a 'devastating go in the ghoulies' at 'that parodic paradigm of the class system, the British armed forces', with its officer-

and-men dichotomy 'reinforced by regimental rhubarb and patriotic custard'. If the recent Suez episode had established that the sun could set on the British Empire, Len's supposedly scathing Muse was surely ambivalent about those khaki targets in which the raving reviewers were so sure he had planted such dead-centre bull's-eyes. I only saw the film, but it seemed to me that Len was more kissing than biting the hand that had fed him bromide and wads. The later work surely bears me out: *See You Round* (1961/2?) looked back, not in the least irascibly, as Pat Sully, now a poly lecturer, with a wife and mortgage, attended a reunion of his old Canal Zone unit. When Major 'Pickles' Branston drops dead among the sausage rolls, one of the ex-squaddies praises him faintly by saying that 'he wasn't a bad bloke at times'. Len Parker's *alter ego* lets him have it:

SULLY: Not a bad bloke, did you say, Smitty? Effing shit-bag you can be sometimes. Quite often, in fact, now I come to think about you, which I don't do more than I can help. Old Pickles could've had you on a charge time and again.

SMITTY: Charge? What charge is that then?

SULLY: Bashing bishops in the regiment's time.

SMITTY: Watch it, Sully. Just because −

SULLY: *Watch* it? It takes a stronger stomach than mine, old son, to do anything like that. Remember the time the Major put his arm up to the elbow in a jakes full of Pharaoh's revenge in order to save that poor bloody cat from a fate worse than the Last Judgment? And you talk about not a bad bloke! He was an effing prince.

ERIKSON: Shouldn't we call a doc, Sully, if the Major's really gone and swallowed his last?

SULLY: Not before we've poured the poor old bugger one for the lonely road, Jacko. Because this was your genuine article. More holes in him than nature's unsubtle economy ever budgeted. You don't get that bit of ribbon he wore over his left tit for filling in chitties for skiving squaddies like Smitty here. He went bare-kneed across that bloody desert when the rest of us were doing the two-times table and hadn't even started wondering what mucky Marlene had under her gym tunic she was damned if she'd let us have a look at. He went out like an officer and a jenkelman did Pickles and I'm going to pour a snort of the genuine Napoleon down that dry old gullet of his before you call for stretcher-bearers,

and his corpse to the ramparts they hurry. Squad, 'shun! Slo-ope
ipes! Major salute, present ipes!

(As SULLY *puts the bottle to the Major's blue lips, the sound of a
smart parade presenting arms synchronises with the clumsy tribute of the half-drunk company at the reunion. Scowling,* SMITTY
at last takes a menu, rolls it and blows the last post.)

Bruno Lazlo snapped up the film rights to that one, and
quite right too, and he then asked me to write the screenplay,
which was surely quite wrong: Len Parker was an experienced
technician and a much more agile adaptor of his own material
than I was likely to be. I suspect that Bruno asked me only
because we had had a certain success together and he was
superstitious about changing a winning team. He liked working with, and quarrelling with, people he had worked with,
and quarrelled with, before. I refused to be bribed or flattered;
whatever was 'missing like hell' in the stage version could best
be supplied by the original author. *See You Round* featured in
a recent round-up of Fifty Years of British Cinema (the
presenting arms scene was always effective), whereas the
only English post-war film whose female star won an Oscar
was ignored, so Bruno's faith in Len Parker was clearly
vindicated.

Len became a well-paid screenwriter as well as a rated
dramatist. The reproachful nostalgia with which he glared at
his early years was never purged from Pat Sully's character, or
from the characters who manifestly doubled for him in plays
like *Two Up, Two Down* and *How Long Are You Here?*, but
as Len became accustomed to fame and fortune, so too Pat
Sully's progress from polytechnic lecturer to text-book author
and affluent publisher led to new sexual and social horizons.
He remained married to the sweetheart who had shared his
dripping butties, but there were, *disons*, problems. Len himself, as Sainte-Beuve would assume, was no less faithful, and
probably no more, to Beryl than was Denise to Pat. The split
level Richmond house in *Desirable Residence*, and the *au pair*
who did reparable damage to Sully's self-esteem, mirrored
pretty exactly the Parkers' own detached house in S.W.
something.

The success of *See You Round* (Dirk played Major Pickles to
a very nicely) led to further collaborations between Bruno and

Len. Indeed Bruno praised Len's skill often enough for me to feel a twinge of vexation. If I was relieved no longer to be telephoned every day for ziss or zat, I was not amused when, absent-mindedly, Bruno called me 'Len'. I doubt if Bruno was sufficiently bothered consciously to play Len and me off against each other, but a certain muted rivalry developed, even though we never actually met in the magazine-littered waiting room in Bruton Street, or even on the threshold of the unreliable lift. I became involved in American movies, a leap which Len never chose to make: Beryl said he was loyal to his roots, others that he was parochial. If he refused to go whoring for dollars, he was not short of pounds. Yet, resolutely un-trendy (Douggie Hayward never designed him a safari jacket), he never so much as gave a glance at a Roller or even joined the White Elephant. He remained as tenaciously working class in accent and attitude as if his talent depended on it. Perhaps it did: he had money, but he could not afford to become smooth. Rough edges were essential for the sparks he liked to strike. Sully too still called magazines 'boooks' and when he counted it was from wan to ten, and on up. In *Inland Revenue* he was rolling in lucre, but his best speech was the wan in which he pissed on the effete neighbours who thought that the only way to treat their children's neuroses was to slap therapeutic ten-pound notes on them.

I never imagined that Pat Sully would approve of our buying a small house in the Lot-et-Garonne, but it did not make me hesitate very long over doing so. One spring day, we were sitting in a small restaurant in the middle of the French countryside, certain that no one could ever guess where we were and that if the telephone rang, it could not be for us, when a rather lugubrious, tallish person in N.H.S. glasses, his plate charged with the self-served *hors d'oeuvres* for which M. Popaul deserves to be renowned, came and stood over us and gave us a lop-sided toothy grin. 'Didn't you used to be Frederic Raphael at wan time?' he said.

'I'll take the Fifth,' I said.

'Len Parker,' he said. 'Bruno told me you'd bought a place down here.'

'There's no keeping anything from him, is there?'

'We're over there,' he said, indicating a big round table at the far end of the long room, 'why don't you come on over when you've finished your . . . ?'

We did not much want to be sociable, but what could we do? Len introduced us to Tone, his new director, and to Beryl, who was large and amiable. If she was not a bit 'rude', as Bruno had reported her, we could see where Pat Sully's earth-mother wife Denise had come from. The Parkers had been staying with a millionaire composer on Ibiza, working on a pirate musical (a musical about pirates, I mean, of course). They had, as Len's mimicry made clear, had a less than relaxed time. Their host was anxious about his furniture and picky over his diet; they had, as it were, walked on egg-shells without the compensation of enjoying the omelettes. Tone, who was to direct the new Pat Sully instalment, *Up and Coming*, had the beard and the undenied accent which promised that he was second-generation Court. He endeared himself to me at once by asking if I had ever done anything apart from writing production-line movies. His wife gave suck to their two-year-old at the table, which established their integrity.

I am not sure how or why I ended up by paying for all the coffee and Armagnac which Len's hospitality dispensed to the company, but I did so with the good grace of the sucker and, silly with unaccustomed midday liquor, I positively forced our local address on Beryl, if they were ever passing. I had, I confess, been gratified by the laughter with which they had all greeted my imitations of Bruno Lazlo. 'You should develop that character,' hairy Tone said, 'it could be quite amusing.' I really liked him, didn't I?

We were sufficiently genial in our memories of the Parkers to invite them, that winter, to the private view of our daughter's graduation show at Camberwell College of Art. R.S.V.P. was at the bottom of the card, but the Parkers neither came nor replied. Probably they were out of the country. The following summer, we were in our *gîte* in the Lot-et-Garonne when the telephone rang: 'Freddie, it's Len.' The tone was so assumingly amiable that I reacted with unpremeditated warmth. He said that they were not far away and could they pop by and see us?

They came to tea. They stayed to supper. My wife asked if they had booked anywhere for the night. Len said that they were just wandering homewards from Formentor and had no particular plans. They stayed the night. We really did have a nice evening. Len imitated their latest hosts to perfection: *he* was a homosexual Hungarian whose tantrums made Bruno's seem like an instance of Anglo-Saxon reticence and *she* was his designer-cum-*châtelaine* whom gin made very explicit about how, in a pinch, she could accommodate Yves sexually. Other jet-set guests were effortlessly conjured up as Len began to enjoy our *eau de vie*. As we were going to bed, Beryl said: 'How did your daughter's show turn out?'

'Very well indeed,' I said, wishing that she had not now disclosed that they had indeed received our invitation. I should have preferred to think that it had been lost in the post.

If we were very nice at breakfast, we were determined that they should not be there for lunch. Beryl made us a nice speech about putting up any of us who happened to be stranded in Richmond without a bed and they were off down the drive in the red Ford Granada estate. I suppose that I could have endured not receiving a postcard of thanks (modern manners are devoid of the hypocrisy which once demanded fulsome insincerities about generous welcomes and delicious meals), but I did find the last act of *Foreign Rights* an inch or two below the bourgeois belt. The expatriate screenwriter who rabbited on about his daughter's brilliance as a painter and his put-upon wife whose every attempt to speak is greeted with 'Just let me finish this' were not, I am quite certain, direct transcriptions, but the accuracy of certain details put the pointed boot in. (The set was a *gîte* in the Lot-et-Garonne, with Mexican bark-paintings on the walls, alongside that talented daughter's daubs.) I need hardly say that we did not receive invitations to the first night. We saw the piece only because Bruno, who had acquired the film rights, wanted me to be the screenwriter, 'for once'. Since *Full Fathom Five* was going into production in New York and he would be unavailable, Len was particularly keen that I should do the job of adapting *Foreign Rights* because, he had admitted to Bruno, it was partly thanks to me that he had managed to lick that worrisome last act. Having declined the honour, I did drop him a postcard acknowledging how much I appreciated the kind thought. Whom should I bump into on the way back from the pillar-box but Tone, the director, walking his new calfskin boots? 'When are you going to write that play?' he said. I said I was thinking about it. I am too.

THE DAY FRANCO CAME

D on Antonio – '
'Another time, woman.'
'Don Antonio – '
'Did you not hear me? Another time, I said. Later. Another time.'

'But when, Don Antonio? When? You always say – '

'Later in the day, woman. This morning I have more important things to do than listen to you. Much more important.'

'It's impossible ever to speak to you, Don Antonio,' said Carmela.

'Very well, it's impossible. You've worked in this house long enough to know why I never have time to waste.'

'But, Don Antonio – '

'Shall I tell you why I'm particularly busy this morning? Shall I? Tell me, what do you think this is?' Don Antonio waved a blue envelope so thick that it clicked as he flapped it. He held it an inch from his cook's withdrawn face. 'I'll tell you what it is. This is an official letter from the Military Governor. You know what that means? You think after getting a letter like this I have time to waste listening to your complaints about Paco's meat?'

'It's not that, Don Antonio.'

'Whatever it is, it must wait.'

Carmela passed her hands in front of her face, touching her nose, her chin. 'Don Antonio – '

'Not now.' The Mayor of Torreroja unsheathed his yellow Malacca cane from the umbrella stand against the wall of the vestibule. 'You have no idea of my responsibilities. I certainly don't expect to be bothered by people in my own household, at times like these – ' The blue letter clicked again. 'I'll tell you.

The Caudillo himself is coming to Torreroja. The Caudillo. The Head of State.'

'I know,' said Carmela.

'You *know*? How do you know? I didn't know myself until this morning.'

'I know,' said Carmela, 'that the Caudillo is the Head of State.'

'Now perhaps you understand why I have no time to waste on domestic nonsense. Do you realise by any chance that the entire responsibility for making this village respectable in time for the Caudillo's visit depends exclusively, *exclusively*, on me, on the Mayor, and on no one else? Do you?'

'Yes, yes.' Carmela tightened the string around the waist of her ballooning black dress. 'Yes, yes, yes, but — '

'I have no time for domestic trivialities.' Don Antonio tapped the ferrule of his cane on the tile floor of the hall and turned for the door. It was a double door, wide enough to admit a horse and cart. Within it, on the left-hand leaf, was incised a second door, of normal size, its bottom a foot above the level of the floor. As Don Antonio approached, the knocker on the outside was lifted and allowed to drop, gently. It was the knock of someone who was expected.

Don Antonio withdrew into the doorway of a side room; the Mayor could never open the front door for a visitor. In this room, all shuttered darkness, the creaking of a cane rocking chair alone indicated someone's presence. Doña Elisabeta, the Mayor's mother, sat invisible but for a wand of light which ruled her from the crown of her white head down to the buttons on her black boots, between which an ebony stick went to the floor. The pressure of her crossed hands on the silver head of the stick rocked her chair in the darkness. Don Antonio waved Carmela to the door. 'Come along, come along. Open it, open it.'

'Antonio, is that you? Antonio?'

'Yes, Mother, it's me. Only me.'

Doña Elisabeta could sit in the dark and imagine a house full of her children. 'Antonio, is that you?' she would call, as if it might have been Jaime, María, Pepe, José, Sandro or Pia, or as if it might have been the Colonel himself, Colonel Alfredo Francis Xavier Martin de Córdoba y Albeñiz, whose presence she sensed on the threshold of her room.

'I'm about to go out, Mother.'

'Go with God.'

'Yes, Mother.'

'Antonio,' said the old woman to herself. 'Yes.' He could hear the chinking accountancy of her rosary. 'Jaime, María, Pia, Sandro . . . '

Don Antonio frowned. The wounds of the victors should be forgotten. To grieve was to have lost. Still, had he himself not given Torreroja its Garden of Remembrance? Ah, but he did not sit in the dark calling the roll of the dead. 'The Caudillo is coming to Torreroja,' he called through the door.

'Praise be to God.'

'I am in charge of the arrangements.'

'Clearly,' said the old woman. 'Who else but a man whose father campaigned at his side?'

'Come along, woman, what are you doing?' said Don Antonio to Carmela as she scuffed past in her black slippers. The stirrup-sized iron key snapped back the bolt on the brown door. A mat of sunshine fell on the chessboard vestibule.

The visitor was a young man with a pale, freckled face, broad shoulders, some stomach and bandy legs. His eyes were narrow behind the shell-rimmed glasses. Stepping over the base of the door, he spread his eyelids to recover his vision. He had books under his arm and a white skull cap on his head.

'Good morning, Mr Stern.' Don Antonio was looking at his watch. 'My son is waiting for you.'

'I've been correcting his exercises,' Adam Stern said.

'He is a clever child, Mr Stern. But, of course, in a village like this — you can imagine what the schooling is like. He has had little chance to develop his intelligence. That is why I am so glad that you have come to live among us. You can enlarge his world, help him to make the most of his talents. He's progressing, I trust?'

'Oh, yes, indeed.'

'Once he really begins to grasp a subject, he will learn very quickly. He is an exceptional boy. Of course, his mother's death — ' Don Antonio frowned. Carmela was standing in the patio door. Don Antonio came closer to Adam Stern. 'It affected him very badly. A tragedy of that kind — it goes without saying. It was a great shock. Then living here, a village of this kind where the people are ignorant, superstitious – well, you must go to your work and I must go to mine.' Don Antonio clicked his blue envelope. 'Francisco is waiting upstairs. A clever child can always catch up if you keep him off the streets away from the rabble, isn't that so?' Don Antonio swung the door back and forth using the key as a handle. Sun-shafts sawed at the umbrella stand. 'Now if you can help him make up the ground he's lost, if you can get him to the university eventually, if you can – ' The Mayor broke off. 'Have you nothing to do, woman? No work to do?'

'I am waiting', said Carmela, 'to close the door for you, Don Antonio, when you go out.'

'Insolence,' the old woman hissed in her darkened room and pressed on the head of her ebony cane. The rocking chair squeaked.

'Find something to do. I can shut the door. Go away and find something to do.'

'Yes.'

'Go along, go along. Servants! No, the trouble with people in this village is they have no idea how civilised people live. How can Francisco have anything in common with them? Do you know I saw the children drinking urine in the street the other day? Drinking urine, can you believe it? They don't want to be civilised. How can I let Francisco out with children like that? A child as sensitive as he is? If people behaved as these people do where I come from, in Castillo that is, well – my mother would tell you. People down here have no conception of civilised behaviour.'

Carmela's broom brought her into view at the patio door.

'Well, I'm late now. I have a great many things to arrange.' The Mayor held up his blue envelope. 'Official duties.'

In the street, Adam Stern could hear the simmering of children's laughter.

'Even when schools are provided, you can't make them go. Now what are they up to? Thank heavens Francisco doesn't have to run about in the street like a wild animal.'

Don Antonio appeared high on the heel of his front door. His black brows were joined and the jut of his chest built a turret for his house from the top of which his sentinel eyes glared at the children in the Calle José Antonio. The fire was withdrawn from them; their laughter lapsed; they looked up in silence at the Mayor whose stick was over them.

There was a blurt of laughter. It came from a child who seemed unaware of Don Antonio, a girl taller than her playmates, who wore a ragged dress, sleeveless and too short. She had thin, bent legs and scabby knees, a narrow chest and a stalky neck barely strong enough to support her head. Her feet crabbed at pebbles in the road bed. She lifted a blank face to Don Antonio; broken teeth showed behind worried lips. The eyes were flat, black buttons in the white slice of her face. Clotted hair hung over her ears and was cropped unevenly at the back. The sleeveholes of her rusty cotton dress were so tight that Don Antonio could see stubs of hair in her armpits. Yet her chest was that of a child, without the barest swell of a breast or the prick of a nipple. She gobbled her laughter at Don Antonio and the humour of the other children began to bubble once more behind their nostrils.

The girl pointed. 'Umpump.'

Don Antonio lifted his chin, to be taller. In the midst of the children he could see the back of a spotted dog, pink skin under a white coat blotted with black. The children spread out to give him a view. Now he saw that the high back of the spotted dog was due to the bitch beneath him, a short-legged, shaggy vagabond who had been disowned by the barber, José Poblet, on the corner. She cowered now with an air of meek resentment, looking round at her hindquarters from time to time, as the stabbing of the dog grew in intensity, his forelegs bracketed about her as he glanced solicitously sideways at the Mayor.

'Umpump.'

Giggles went off like firecrackers among the children. The spotted dog stretched his neck along the back of the bitch and worked himself up. A tear drooled from the corner of one of the bitch's eyes. The Mayor swung his cane, scattered the children, made for the dogs.

'Get away, get away, you filthy beasts. Get away.'

The dog unlatched his forelegs, but the pink tassel of his penis still tied him to the bitch.

'Get away from here.'

The dogs fell back from Don Antonio as he swung at them with his cane.

'Umpump,' pointed out the girl, crouching like a mechanic. The other children ran all over the street, giggling and dancing and slapping at each other. Don Antonio stamped his foot at the dogs; they lurched round a corner, intimidated and snarling. The Mayor turned on the children: 'Be quiet! Get away from here! Do you want me to fetch Don Luis? My son isn't idle garbage like you. He's working at his lessons. He's learning something.' Don Antonio pointed to the window of the schoolroom. Did the skirt of a shadow move away from the window? The shutter hooded the glass, making a wedge of concealing black. No, more likely Francisco was sitting in his place at the table, scrubbed knees neat beneath his knicker-bockers, his socks — his English woollen socks — neat over elastic garters at the top of his shins, buckled shoes resting on the wooden slat which shackled the ankles of the desk. As for his face, that sensitive face so like his mother's in its olive serenity (so Don Antonio saw his son and remembered his wife), it would be turned attentively on the American professor. 'You should all be at school, learning something.'

'Too old,' said a boy at Don Antonio's waist.

'My son is almost fourteen, almost fourteen, but he's at school. That's where you should be. Now get out of this street. My son is trying to work.'

They trotted away. The girl, however, stayed in Don Antonio's path. He sidestepped her and strode along the lumpy road towards the Plaza. Almost there, he whipped round, cane raised at the children gathered once more at his front door. They scattered, fresh giggles. The girl was still in the same place. Don Antonio clapped his cane against the side of his shoe and pivoted on his high heel.

Don Antonio's office put him above the villagers; he was one not with them but with the régime. As Mayor appointed by Madrid, he was part of Madrid. When he taxed and bullied the Torrerojans, it was not for personal gain or satisfaction, it was to impose upon them a proper sense of humility and obedience. If the new café he was in the process of erecting was likely in the end to take custom from the Casino and from the smaller bars in the village, that was Torreroja's deserved bad luck: everyone knew what Torreroja had been. The more he enriched himself, the more powerful was Madrid in the life of the people, the more loyally did he represent the master whose imminent arrival was proclaimed in the blue envelope which he clasped, like an Order, against his chest.

Don Antonio had a number of appointments that morning; it was almost noon by the clock on the tower of the new church (the destruction of the old one was a flagrant instance of the crimes for which Torreroja had to atone) before he was able to start along the *carretera* to see how work was progressing on the café. He had first to pass the bar where the gypsies congregated.

'Going to see how his cock is growing,' said one of them as he went by.

The Mayor had decided to name his café The Cock. Its tall tower would, on completion, allow Don Antonio to advertise the presence of his Bar-Restaurant for several kilometres in either direction. As the tower grew, so did the volume of local comment. Don Antonio had already had Manolo sack one labourer for alluding to it as 'the Mayor's prick,' and now the gypsies, godless animals, had picked up the joke. They could say what they liked; he would teach them a lesson eventually. Their 'King', Don Ferdinando, had adroitly evaded tax on a desirable piece of land he owned adjacent to the Garden of Remembrance.

Manolo came stuttering up on his motor scooter. He stopped just past the Mayor, who swung himself on to the saddle behind his agent. Manolo released the brake and the Vespa jumped forward.

'How is it going?' shouted Don Antonio.

'Well, very well,' said Manolo, as usual.

'Franco is coming on the eighth.'

'Franco!' Manolo wrung his hand and looked back, looked forward again to swerve past a blinkered donkey as it advanced, into the *carretera*. 'Gypsy!'

'Can we be ready?'

'Ready?'

'To receive him at The Cock?'

'Today's the seventeenth!'

'We must be,' shouted Don Antonio. 'All we need is the

terrace, the bar and the downstairs lavatories, in case — '

'It might be done.'

'It must be done.'

Manolo jigged the scooter in under one of the plane trees at the front of the café site.

'You go on.' The Mayor dismounted. 'I must see Pepe.'

While Manolo went on his pointed, polished toes (no worker Manolo) up the steps to the terrace, Don Antonio returned to the entrance of the Garden of Remembrance. The Garden ran adjacent to the *carretera*; it was seventy-five metres long and thirty metres deep. A gravel path ran the length of it, formal with benches; where a second path bisected the other, behind a tiled kerb, a shallow pool was decked with goldfish. An earthenware mermaid, glazed green, stepped in the centre, the spout of a narrow water jet held between verdant breasts. The force of the jet could be regulated by a tap ensconced under the plaque which informed those who enjoyed the Garden that it had been planted in memory of Doña Pilar, Don Antonio's wife, who had died in 1951, aged thirty-six.

Pepe the gardener stood with one hand in the pocket of blue cotton trousers, a yellow cigarette in his lips and the ear-flaps of a leather cap popped together on the top of his head. His thumb was over the nozzle of a hose. As he moved his wrist, a fan of water spread casually over a cracked marigold bed.

'Good morning, Pepe.'

'Don Antonio.' Pepe squashed his cigarette against a horny thumbnail before putting it behind his ear.

'Gypsy children haven't been — ?'

'No, no.'

'I gave that Ramón a clip he won't forget.'

'You did.'

'None of the children in this village appreciate what a garden like this means. They're better off throwing orange peel at each other. Well now, Pepe, I've got some news for you. The Caudillo is coming to Torreroja.'

'I heard.'

'Oh? Well, I'll tell you something you haven't heard. He's going to come directly through here, through the Garden of

Remembrance. Along this very path. With his staff. What do you say to that?'

Pepe wrinkled his brows and switched the arc of water to another bed.

'After refreshments, the Head of State will pass along this very path, through the arches you will be putting up and so eventually to the cars which will be drawn up, down there, to receive him.'

Pepe's eyebrows jumped and descended.

'You can see how much depends on you, my friend. I want Torreroja to have the best decorations in the entire province. I have decided on solid wooden arches plaited with palm and cane, with laurel wreaths at appropriate places and a large silver slogan across the top of each: "Welcome to Our Saviour." '

'*Saviour?* To me — '

'He saved us from Communism,' said Don Antonio. 'In any case, I shall be speaking personally to Placido about the lettering. I happen to know where you and I would have been if the Reds had won. Up against a wall. Believe me, I know. One doesn't argue with a father, two sisters and four brothers. I want three arches. One, two and three, so. All right?'

'Very well.'

'And then there's the mosaic.'

'Mosaic?'

'To commemorate the visit. I have already ordered it from José Lerida. I have not been idle, I can promise you that. Yes, the mosaic's to go — come with me, man, come with me — here, directly in front of the fountain. José will show you what to do. You can count on its being one metre square. Exactly.'

On the terrace of The Cock, Don Luis, the local Captain of the Civil Guard, was fingering the bulbous brown mole which grew in the centre of his thin black moustache. A heavy man, bulging from the narrow café chair, he had exceptionally large ears with pendant lobes. He came from Bilbao.

'I am sorry to be late,' said the Mayor, looking round for his coffee, 'but you can't get them to do anything around here without having to push them, push them all the time.' He clapped his hands. 'Come along, come along.'

Don Luis rotated his lacquered hat on the table in front of him.

'If it weren't for people like you and me,' said Don Antonio, 'nothing would ever be done around here.' He took crested papers from his pocket. 'Well, we've got a few things to discuss, eh?' First of all, Don Antonio proposed that all shops be shut from lunch-time, so that no one might have the excuse of business to prevent them from paying their respects to the Head of State. Pressure was to be put on the owners of shops and cafés along the *carretera* to make them festive with flags and decorations. All kerbstones would be whitened and patriotic slogans stencilled in the roadway. All schoolchildren would have a holiday. To none of these proposals did Don Luis offer the smallest emendation. From time to time he tugged at an ear-lobe, nothing more. Don Antonio, however, argued each of his suggestions with a full range of reasons. There would be nothing of which the Captain had not heard. 'I assume', said Don Antonio, reaching the actual day itself, 'that there will be no question of a siesta for the police or the Guardia? No leave, no rest.'

The Captain rotated his hat.

'The Caudillo arrives at four forty-five. We shall need maximum security for the entire day up until that time. Otherwise who knows who might sneak into town, conceal himself and then, when the time comes, make some sort of disturbance? We shall have to keep our eyes open for anyone who looks as though he might — López, for instance.'

'López?'

'The carpenter. I'm told he's an anarchist. He reads books published abroad.'

Don Luis picked up his hat and inspected the red silk lining.

'He wishes to emigrate to Australia,' said Don Luis.

'Precisely. Well, you have thought of all this, of course; I raise the point so that you know where I stand.'

The Captain nodded and eased his trousers. He was ready to put his hat on, but Don Antonio was not finished yet. He had still to secure agreement to the notion that to complete the terrace where Torreroja was to entertain the Caudillo was a matter of public interest and should be subsidised by public funds. To this, cosseted by his favourite *seco*, Don Luis made no objection. He could scarcely see how the issue fell within his sphere. Nevertheless, Don Antonio argued his case forcefully and in full.

By the time the two men left The Cock, it was twenty minutes past two. Don Antonio marched through the roasting village. The clip of his Malacca cane announced him to the tenants of the houses along his road. The sunshine in the Calle José Antonio blazed up to the eaves of the houses. He had hoped it would be empty, but it was not: she was waiting for him again. Her feet crabbed pebbles from the burning bed of the roadway. She was not waiting, he told himself: she was simply still there. She ignored him until he was practically at his door, then she looked up and showed her broken teeth. The Mayor could see a tag of fresh blood on her chewed lower lip. He tapped on his front door with his cane.

The girl squatted in the road and lifted her skirt up to her waist. The Mayor banged for Carmela. The girl was squatting down right in front of his own house. Look at her! He couldn't help seeing the clump of hair in her groin. He thumped again with his cane. 'Come along.'

The door opened.

'Look at her. Look at her. You've got to do something about her. She can't stay around here all day. Look at her.'

'What?'

'She — ' The girl was standing a little way down the road. Her back was to the Mayor and she was crabbing stones with her feet. 'She was squatting down there a moment ago like an animal. She's too old to piss in the road. I know what she is, but she's too old. It's an insult to public morals. She's got to be trained. She can't go on pissing in the road and that's all there is to it.'

'Where did she?'

Don Antonio strode to where the girl had been. 'But I saw her,' he said. 'I saw her, right here, she — '

Carmela was inspecting the dry place.

'Yes?'

'She lifted her skirt, she squatted down — I saw her with my own eyes. Well, what else did she do it for if not — ? You've got to do something about her, send her away. She mustn't be allowed around here.'

65

'Where can I send her?'

'I don't know. She can't stay around here.'

'No.'

'You say no, but what happens? She sits outside my front door all day. What kind of an impression does it make when people come to see the Mayor and find an idiot? She can't come here. If you can't arrange something, you'll — Why not your sister?'

'She's working now. They can't fish. She has to go out to work. There's no one in the house.'

'She can still stay there.'

'She won't. She goes out.'

'Tie her up. I don't know — but something has to be done. It — ' Don Antonio pointed to the dry road, ' — it can't be permitted, that's all.' He barged through the front door of his house. 'It can't be allowed.'

'Antonio, is that you?'

'Yes, Mother, yes.'

Don Antonio slotted his cane in the umbrella stand and continued into the patio, where lunch was laid. His son was at one end of the blue wooden table, eating grapes from a fat bunch.

'Is something wrong, Father?'

'That girl, did she disturb you this morning?'

'Not really.' Francisco put both elbows on the table and attacked more grapes.

Don Antonio clapped his hands. 'Either she disturbed you or she did not disturb you. What were you doing this morning?' He had to wait until some pips were worked to the front of his son's mouth and ejected. 'You put too much in at the same time. If you eat too much, you'll get fat. If you get fat, you can't work. When is my lunch coming?'

'Now, immediately, Don Antonio.'

'Now. What were you doing this morning?'

'Oh, a lot of things. We talked about America.'

'What about America?'

'The life of the people. It's very different from here. For instance, the young people, people of my age — '

'Why were you discussing this? In what subject?'

'English.'

'You spoke in English of this, the life of the young people?'

'Yes, Father. She's been doing her mess in the street again, is that it?'

'Never mind. She should never come around here.' Carmela came in from the kitchen with a plate of *boquerones* fried in yellow batter. 'She has a bad effect on everyone.'

Francisco slid off his chair.

'Where are you going?'

'To work. The American set me some sums to do.'

'Excellent. You must learn to cope with figures. You go and work. No one will bother you, I'll make sure of that. Come here a moment.'

'Father?'

Don Antonio pulled out his handkerchief. There were scabs of grapeskin clinging to the phantom moustache above his son's mouth. 'Always keep your face clean. Your mother wouldn't like you not to be clean. Always keep yourself clean for her sake.'

'Yes, Father. Father — '

'Yes, my son.'

'Is it true that in America she wouldn't be as she is?'

'She? Who? Oh — what, you mean — ? Of course not. What's wrong with her comes from God. No one could do anything about her except Him.'

'She couldn't have been cured in America?'

'No. I told you. No.'

Carmela was standing in the kitchen door.

'Go along.'

Don Antonio pushed his plate from him. Carmela came away from the doorpost and removed the plate. She returned with some fried liver and a dish of shredded lettuce in the middle of which two tomatoes fell open in wet, red flowers.

'Don Antonio — '

'Already?'

'May I speak to you?'

'Now what is it?' demanded her employer, as though he had dealt with one request and was now faced with another. 'Well?'

'Don Antonio, you told me that when the new café was finished — '

'It's not finished. Please don't bother me until it is.'

'It will be by the time Franco comes, won't it?'

'Who told you about Franco?'

'I still owe money to the doctor. You said that when the café was completed I could work in the kitchen, as cook. Now they say a cook is coming from Malaga; they say — '

'You listen to too much gossip. Nothing is settled yet.'

'It's the money, Don Antonio. I still owe the doctor.'

'Do what your sister did when she owed Leon money. This liver is tough. It's leather. You and Paco — And overcooked.'

'You told me two o'clock. Don Antonio, you did say that I could earn more money when the café opened; you said — '

'Do you think I don't know what I said? You dare to stand there and tell me — serve food like this — you ruin my lunch and then you — ' Don Antonio pitched his plate on to the tiles. 'Get it out of here and that daughter of yours as well. Clear it up, stop sniffling and get out.' He pushed back his chair and went indoors.

'Is that you, Antonio?'

'Yes, Mother, yes.'

'She's insolent, that woman, insolent.'

'Yes, Mother.' Don Antonio went into his office.

The rocking chair squeaked and creaked, squeaked and creaked.

In the patio, Carmela was picking up slices of broken earthenware. The ends of Don Antonio's liver she placed carefully on the largest section.

Don Antonio did not sleep during the siesta hour. Sitting forward on his swivel chair, he listened to the silence of Torreroja and knew that in every instant of it he was drawing ahead of those who might have competed with him. The sun forced Torreroja to close its eyes, but the Mayor, mantled in the thick shadows of his study, kept his wide open. He lifted his head from his correspondence and listened. Somewhere he heard the rustle of whispering voices. He capped his Parker and left the room.

'What's she doing here?'

Carmela grabbed the side of her chair. 'Don Antonio — '

'How many people do I feed in this house?' He wrenched the plate from under the girl's hand. 'What's this? No wonder I had tough liver. *She* gets the tender pieces. An idiot gets the master portion!'

'It's what you threw on the floor.'

'I've told you before. I will not have my house used as a lunatic asylum. Now get her out of here, at once.'

The girl smiled and took the last of the liver and put it in her mouth.

'She's not to come here. She'll shit in the hall — there's no knowing what she'll do. My son lives here. If his mother knew that a girl like that was coming in and out of the house — '

'If you'd given me money for the doctor, Don Antonio, she would not be as she is.'

'Why didn't you go to him on your back?' whispered Don Antonio, for his mother's sake. 'Like your sister did? She managed. You could have got the drugs if you'd really wanted to.'

'He needed money himself, to buy them.'

'He's got plenty of money. All doctors are cheats. I've paid him enough in my time. Anyway, I gave you some money myself — '

'A hundred pesetas! I needed five thousand.'

'Five thousand! *I* need five hundred thousand, does that mean someone's going to give it to me? Five thousand pesetas for this?' He raised the girl by her shoulder and dragged her from the table with a piece of bread in her hand. 'I don't ever want to see her in this house again.'

'She has to eat.'

'She doesn't have to eat *here*.' Don Antonio stopped at the door to turn on Carmela. 'And you want to work at The Cock! How many people are you intending to give free meals to *then*, eh?' He yanked the girl through the house. She smiled at him. 'You go out of here and you don't come back.' She smiled.

'Father, what's happening?'

'Where have you been? I thought you were going to work.'

'I went for some chocolate, that's all.' Francisco stared at the girl as she slipped by him into the street. She grinned and made claws.

'Francisco, go upstairs and get down to that work of yours.'

Carmela was sobbing in the kitchen.

'Woman!' Don Antonio banged the front door so that the knocker rapped, like a ghost.

'Antonio, is that you?'

'Yes, Mother, yes.' He went into his study and banged that door too.

The rocking chair creaked and squeaked.

There was a knock on the study door.

'Now what?' Don Antonio swivelled his chair to the door.

'I'm going to my house.' Carmela had a basket over her arm and a scarf round her head. Her black dress was closed over her throat.

'You're leaving, yes?'

'I'm going to my house.'

'Then go.' Don Antonio swivelled back to bend over his work. 'Why don't you?' He picked up his pen. 'What are you waiting for?'

'My money.'

'Money? Haven't I been feeding your entire family?'

'My money, Don Antonio, and then I go to my house.'

'Go back in the kitchen and finish your work and stop bothering me and we'll say no more about it. It's forgotten.'

'My money, Don Antonio.'

'Do you ever think that I might have better things to worry about than you? Do you realise that this whole town depends on me?' Don Antonio leaned forward. 'Just who do you think you're going to work for if you leave here? Who's going to employ you?'

'Foreigners. They pay better; you work less.'

'Foreigners! You leave this house, you leave this village. You leave the province. You go to prison if necessary.' Don Antonio went to shut the door of the study. He held his wrists vertical. 'With handcuffs on, you understand? I know you're a thief. You're all thieves. I know. You work in this house or you don't work at all. Finish.'

'You promised me work in the café – '

'I want young girls in the café, sixteen, seventeen – '

'But to *cook*, Don Antonio.'

'What do you know about restaurant catering? Modern methods? Nothing. You fry a bit of fish – '

'I'm the best cook in Torreroja.'

'And you work here.'

'Don Antonio, the doctor – Don Antonio, I've cooked for twenty or thirty people in this house. I can cook for as many as you want. Any number.'

'I want the best restaurant on the coast. I'm not handing out a few pieces of fried fish.'

'I'm going to my house.'

He grabbed her. 'You have no house. Your sister rents a house, that's all. I can have you all turned out if necessary. They owe rent.'

'My brother-in-law can't fish.'

'Exactly. You can be turned out whenever I say so and you won't find a house between here and Madrid.'

'Very well.'

'You'll be in the street.'

'Very well.'

'You're mad. You're mad. All of you.' He shoved Carmela's shoulder. She let go of the neck of her dress and backed away. 'Mad.' He pushed her and she fell on to the low leather-covered *chaise-longue* under the shuttered window. The springs grated. 'I want you to understand for once and for all, no one goes out of this house.' Don Antonio leaned over her and gripped her shoulders. She tipped backwards and her bosom rode up in her dress. He pushed at her knees. The springs of the rusty *chaise-longue* grated and ground.

'I don't like people to threaten that they are leaving,' said Don Antonio at last.

'And you built her a garden,' said Carmela, pulling her dress out from under her hips and making the springs grate once more.

'What are you talking about?'

'Accident,' said Carmela. 'Ha!'

'Get on now. Here, take this. And I don't want any more nonsense.'

'I don't want your money.'

'Take it, when I tell you.'

'Garden of Remembrance!'

'Go on. And I don't want to hear any more about the doctor.'

'Ha!' She closed her black dress over her throat.

Don Antonio pulled Carmela back into the room and opened the neck of her dress and put his hand in on her warm breast. 'Now go on.'

Francisco was sitting on the third step of the stairs. Carmela passed him without a word and went into the kitchen. He was carving a piece of cane into a flute with his penknife. Carmela sat down at the kitchen table, hunched her shoulders over her plate and went on with her meal. She finished by wiping her bread round the plate and then drank a cup of water although there were glasses. She closed her black dress over her throat.

Don Antonio was in the washroom which opened off his study. He always used potassium permanganate.

The rocker creaked in the dark front room. The chink of the rosary paced a litany of names: 'Jaime, María, Pepe, Sandro, José . . . '

The day before the Caudillo was due in Torreroja, the Military Governor drove out from Malaga in his black Seat. Don Antonio and Don Luis met him at the Municipal Centre. They joined him in his car for a tour of the route, after which the car returned to The Cock.

'Such are our modest preparations, Your Excellency.'

'We shall now rehearse the actual arrival of the Caudillo,' said the Military Governor to his aide. 'For the purposes of the rehearsal, I shall impersonate the Head of State.'

'His Excellency wishes to rehearse your arrangements for the actual arrival of the Head of State. For this purpose, he himself will impersonate the Head of State.'

'What a good idea, Your Excellency!'

The Military Governor pursed his lips. His sun-glasses were quite opaque. He had already had a full rehearsal in Malaga and he had inspected all the little villages between that city and Torreroja.

Don Antonio and Don Luis waited on the terrace of The Cock. The Military Governor's Seat vanished round the corner past the red-brick castle which gave Torreroja its name and reappeared at speed. It drew up in front of The Cock, from which the two local officials came down to meet it. Don Luis sneezed at the Military Governor's dust. As they emerged from the car, the Military Governor whispered to his aide. 'The

Military Governor thinks you should not *descend* to the Caudillo,' the aide said to Don Antonio.

'Of course not, Your Excellency, of course not. If Your Excellency would care to — ' Don Antonio indicated the steps with his hand. 'I believe I am right in thinking that my father, the late Colonel Alfredo Francis Xavier Martin de Córdoba y Albeñiz, once had the honour of accompanying Your Excellency, who was then — '

The Military Governor was brief with his aide.

'His Excellency thinks you must be mistaken.'

'I understood', said Don Antonio, 'that His Excellency was impersonating the Head of State. It was to the Caudillo himself that my late father once — '

The Military Governor spoke to his aide.

'There is no need, His Excellency says, for you to repeat to him every word you intend for the Caudillo. He is concerned with security, not with elocution.'

'As His Excellency wishes,' said Don Antonio. 'Now, if you would care to step inside — '

All was complete. The coffee machine was in place. The bottles were ranged in rows. The stools were at the bar. The restaurant tables wore starched skirts and bore refulgent glasses. A special counter was being installed in the main reception room where delicacies expressly ordered from Malaga would be available for the distinguished guests. Don Antonio snapped his fingers for Manolo to join them. 'If there is anything Your Excellency thinks we should do further, my assistant — '

The Military Governor looked round. 'It seems suitable enough. The Caudillo doesn't like immodest display.'

'No, no, of course. We are only a modest village — '

The Military Governor spoke to his aide.

'His Excellency wishes to know if this café belongs to you.'

'Yes, Your Excellency, to myself and to some associates of mine. But of course on an occasion like this, it is nothing more nor less than Torreroja's. In fact, so far as my own personal pocket is concerned — '

The Military Governor wanted to know something else.

'His Excellency is concerned to be told why the reception is not to be held at the Municipal Centre.'

'Don Luis and I,' said Don Antonio with a quick look at the Captain, 'discussed this at great length and we came to the conclusion that the Caudillo could be more suitably entertained here. The Municipal Centre is somewhat airless and rather — austere. We hoped the Caudillo would care for the best that Torreroja's present-day craftsmen are capable of. However, if Your Excellency is of the opinion — '

'His Excellency doesn't consider it of any importance. He was merely curious. He would like to know who these girls are.'

'Yes, of course; well first of all, they're all local girls — '

'Why are they dressed as they are?' said the aide.

'They're waitresses,' said Don Antonio.

'His Excellency thinks they should wear shawls. They're not modest.'

'Shawls for the girls,' said Don Antonio to Manolo.

The Military Governor was looking through the glass doors which gave on to the unused swimming pool. He whispered to his aide.

'His Excellency is concerned that no one be swimming in the pool when the Caudillo arrives.'

'No one is to swim in the pool,' said Don Antonio to Manolo.

Don Antonio led the way to the back of the café. Virgin lavatory seats were in place, each in its Cellophane until the coming of the Caudillo.

'Now if Your Excellency would come this way — '

They went down the steps and over to the entrance of the Garden of Remembrance. The Military Governor spoke to his aide. The aide spoke to Don Luis, who nodded.

'Is something wrong?'

'A question of security,' said Don Luis.

The triumphal arches were in place. Don Antonio glanced sideways at the Military Governor. What did he think? The sun-glasses gave nothing away. The full effect would not, of course, be seen until the greenery was added. This would have to be done at the last moment; otherwise it would sadden. On the other hand, the mosaic was done; chips of blue, gold, silver and red sparkled like a rigid rainbow. On every side, flowers echoed its brilliance. The Military Governor spoke to his aide

74

and the aide addressed Don Luis.

'What does His Excellency think?'

'A question of security.'

The Military Governor had a new question.

'His Excellency wishes to know why it is necessary for the Caudillo to walk through here at all.'

'The Garden is, I think, the pride of Torreroja. In addition, it is well known that the Head of State is much attached to flowers. Some of the blooms here — And apart from that, after hours in a motor car it's sometimes pleasant to stretch one's legs — '

The Military Governor whispered to his aide.

'What does His Excellency — ?'

'A question of security.'

'Of course,' said Don Antonio as they went to the car, 'these are only the modest arrangements of a poor village — '

'His Excellency is satisfied. You should all be in your places by half-past three at the latest. There is no certainty about the hour of the Caudillo's arrival. You will be informed of any developments which may occur.'

As the Military Governor's car drove off, Don Luis came to the salute.

'He approved,' said Don Antonio.

Don Luis came down from the salute to scratch the lobe of his ear. 'Good. Now — ' It was time for some *seco*.

The day of the Caudillo's coming was exceptionally hot. The women whitening the kerbstones dripped sweat into the clotted buckets. Don Antonio told Pepe to be ready to hose down the triumphal arches so that they might appear fresh and green. Not only was Franco's name displayed on walls and in windows, but Don Antonio had a gang at work inscribing his name, in huge capital letters, in the very roadway along which he was to travel.

'Antonio, is that you?'

'Yes, Mother.' Don Antonio walked into his mother's room. 'Today is the day when Franco comes to Torreroja, Mother.'

'You have told me so.'

'And I shall receive him in the name of the village.'

'I saw him once,' said Doña Elisabeta, 'in nineteen hundred

75

and thirty-four, in the Asturian War. He was like a fighting cock. He saved Spain.'

'Yes, Mother.' He heard the clink of the rosary in Doña Elisabeta's hand.

'He was riding in an open car and later your father sat next to him at dinner in the mess.' The voice weakened; she was telling the beads. 'Jaime, José, María, Sandro . . . '

The knocker clumped on the front door. Don Antonio heard the scuffing of Carmela's slippers. She was holding the neck of her black dress across her throat as she passed Don Antonio.

'Good morning, Carmela.'

Don Antonio said: 'Mr Stern, I was not expecting you to come today.'

'I was not sure,' said Adam Stern.

'Today is a holiday for all the children. My son does not work today. Today is sacred to Spain.'

'I understand.'

'It is a day no foreigner can truly understand. Today we honour God and Spain. And today my son will see the face which saved Spain for God.'

'I understand, Don Antonio.'

'Today carries a lesson, my friend, more important than any he could learn elsewhere, even from a man with three degrees from American universities.'

'Of course.'

'Today my son will come face to face with the destiny of Spain. No one in a thousand hours of school could instruct him in what he will learn in a few minutes this afternoon.'

'Of course.'

'In Spain we care, above all, for the ideal. The Spaniard gives himself for nothing else. Nothing in American life compares with this. Francisco has been out since early morning. He is setting an example for the rest of the children. His mother would have been proud of him. By the way, I would advise you to be in your place early, Mr Stern. Four forty-five exactly, he arrives.'

'Thank you, Don Antonio. Until tomorrow then.'

'Until tomorrow, Mr Stern.'

When Don Antonio left the house, the street was already alive with people in their best clothes. Children were making designs in the dust on a foreigner's car (one was teasing air from the valve on a front tyre), but they scattered, chirruping, when they saw Don Antonio.

'I hope', he said, leaning on his cane, 'that you will all be washing your hands and faces before the Caudillo arrives. My son is already in his place, waiting.'

Even the gypsies, sitting at their café, were dressed in style. Their women were standing around, those breasts jutting, all made up and with flowers in their hair. Of their King, however, Don Ferdinando, there was no sign.

'Good morning, Don Antonio,' they called.

'Good morning, good morning,' said Don Antonio.

The women smiled and looked under their sooty lashes as he went through them. Their brothers, with slicked hair, watched. Don Antonio made a big chest. Everywhere his plans were being carried out to the letter. The village had burst into flower, colour in every corner. Above all, The Cock was supreme. The tower had reached its peak. Strings of coloured lights — the Gala Opening would take place that night — hung across the terrace and hooped the entrance. From the spire of the tower bunting draped to each corner of the café. Even those who had been known to ignore Don Antonio went out of their way to congratulate him. He shook over a hundred hands between the Plaza and The Cock. No man missed the chance of a smile, the touch of his hand. This morning the Mayor was the town. The only faces to pay him no homage were those of some of the special Guardias drafted to Torreroja on security duty; they knew nothing of the village or of its aristocracy. Their boots made a beat of the dusty road.

The Garden of Remembrance was also lined with flags. The silver lettering on the arches glittered in the sun. When Don Antonio passed through on his eleventh or twelfth journey of inspection, he could almost fancy that it was for himself that this dazzling welcome was spelt out.

'Don Antonio, if you could spare me one moment — ' It was the carpenter, López, who was responsible for the temporary building which was to provide shade for Don Antonio and the rest of the reception committee down at the roadside. 'If you could possibly come and approve of what we have done, Don Antonio.'

'Of course.'

Someone rode up on a motor cycle. 'Don Antonio — '

'One moment.' The Mayor shook the frame of the sun shelter. It seemed firm. He nodded and ran his finger along the planing.

'Some sandpaper here.'

'Yes, Don Antonio. At once.' López bowed. López bowed! The morning passed. The sun reached its zenith. All was ready. The Mayor looked up and down the *carretera*, which, in the full heat, lay puddled with mirages. Only the Guardias were to be seen. Don Antonio went slowly up the steps of the terrace. He went through into the washroom and put his face under the tap. He wiped it on his handkerchief. He did not care to touch the clean white towels nor to pass water in the virgin bowls with their Cellophane seats. He went down to Don Ferdinando's field and relieved himself there. The gypsies always used it. Returning, he went into the Garden of Remembrance. The triumphal arches were dull with dust again. The gravel could do with a rake. He called Pepe, who rose from a pad of shade under an orange tree.

Half-past four, the sun hung like a tilted bucket of molten metal in a sky without a rag of cloud. The mountains behind Torreroja were ribbed with shadow, but elsewhere there was no suggestion of evening. Nor was there any indication of the Caudillo's coming. The road carried its common traffic of lorries and cars. Each one that rolled impudently over the lettering which spelt FRANCO on the tarmac received a furious scowl from Don Antonio when it drew level with the café. Luckily, however, the day was so dry that no tiresome blemish was left on the whitewash.

Don Antonio, suit buttoned, shoes glassy, tie tight under his red throat, waited by the roadside. He peered along towards the village. There were not enough people. He sent Manolo to the Head of the Municipal Police: the people must be encouraged to line the route. A quarter to five was almost upon them. He could come at any moment.

A black Seat emerged from behind the castle. Don Antonio's toes contracted against his hot soles. People were crowding to the kerbs. Don Antonio recognised a pair of sun-glasses in the back of the car. The Military Governor was making his last tour. Don Antonio went forward.

'Good afternoon, Your Excellency.'

'His Excellency wishes me to tell you that there has been an unavoidable delay. The Caudillo will not be here for one hour.'

Don Antonio called for lemonade. The heat seemed to be growing. Only the Garden of Remembrance looked lush and cool.

'There ought to be more people,' said Don Antonio. 'Round here, I mean. After all, this is where he's going to stop.'

Actually, he had noticed, the alien Guardias were giving discouraging looks to those citizens who were making their way up to The Cock. They did not seem to appreciate the importance of a packed welcome for the Caudillo. What mattered to them was that there should be no trouble.

To Don Antonio's relief, the gypsies began to come across from their café. Though he despised them for the animals they were, he resented them for their independence and he feared their powers. Now if they were coming, it was because they knew — he didn't ask how — that Franco was on his way.

'Where is Don Ferdinando?' the Mayor asked Manolo.

Manolo shrugged. 'He'll come, when it suits him.'

'He should be made to come.'

Manolo shrugged. 'Yes.'

'Have you seen my son?'

'This morning.'

'I thought he would come here. Well, at least the crowd's getting bigger.'

'Of course.'

The gypsies had gathered in a tight crowd now, their backs to everyone.

'What're they talking about?'

'Who knows?'

'They mustn't turn their backs.'

'They won't, when the time comes.'

A couple of Guardias were standing near the gypsy circle. The slim gypsy boys inspected them. They actually turned round and inspected them.

'Don Ferdinando should keep them in order.'

'He's the biggest rogue of all.'

79

'Don't tell me.'

Don Luis was scratching the lobe of his ear.

'See if you can find Francisco,' said Don Antonio to Manolo.

It was six o'clock. The edges of the sky were deckled with gold. Manolo came back. There was no sign of Francisco. 'No matter,' said Don Antonio. 'Do the girls have their shawls?'

'Taken care of.'

'Find me some more lemonade.'

Suddenly faces were falling forward over the road like blooms lopped by the slash of a cane. A motor cyclist was whipping down the hill from the castle. He braked sharply, scalding dust from the road, and drew up by the Mayor. 'Ten minutes,' he announced and was gone on double exhausts.

The word was passed through the people.

Don Luis was talking to an officer of the Guardia.

Don Antonio took the lemonade from Manolo and drank it quickly, eyes right over the glass along the road. 'That's better. Now, is everything all right?'

'Yes, yes.'

'Make sure. We've got just eight minutes before — '

Half an hour later, a subdued droning could be heard somewhere behind the castle. It rose and rose in power and pitch until it seemed to fill the whole sky. And then, from round the corner of the castle — even the gypsies were staring — came three, six, nine, twelve, fifteen motor-cycle troopers in black leather uniforms with white crash helmets, white crossed shoulder straps and black sten guns. They wore huge goggles. The buzz changed to a drumming roar. Three, six, nine, twelve, fifteen, they were through the village. They were gone. Don Luis pulled the red lobe of his ear. The road was empty. Fully ten minutes passed before people spoke above a whisper.

Now there were Guardias everywhere; they came from the alleyways, down from the castle, machine-guns ready. Don Antonio reviewed them uneasily. Don Luis nodded to the Guardia officer, whose men began to push first the gypsies and then the other people back from the road. Don Antonio watched the gypsies anxiously; if they abandoned the proceedings, he was afraid it would be unlucky. The Guardias continued with their work. They bullied the gypsies back until the last of them all but fell into the beds of the Garden of Remembrance. 'Keep them out of there,' shouted Don Antonio. 'Not in there.'

The droning came again. It rose and rose in power and pitch and then — three, six, nine, twelve, fifteen, eighteen, twenty-one — twenty-one motor cyclists darted into view, bore down on the village and were gone. The attention of the people was fastened on the road. Only the Guardias attended to their business and not to the road. They prodded and peered among the shrubbery of the Garden of Remembrance. Don Antonio worked to control his indignation when, under the instructions of their alien officer, they stepped in among the beds and rooted behind the triumphal arches. They kept jostling the gypsies until one of them suddenly shot out his arm and pointed with his finger, one of those skinny, double-jointed fingers, bent back with its own rigidity.

A single slim figure was ambling along the road. Right down the centre of the *carretera* came Don Ferdinando, his horn-handled cane hung on a leather loop over his wrist, a snappy trilby at an angle on his head, white-and-black shoes on his feet and his dancer's body sheathed in a lightweight grey cotton suit. Round his waist was a red sash and in his buttonhole a red carnation. In his mouth he had a long bamboo cigarette holder with a king-sized cigarette in it. He walked down the centre of the road until he came to the stencilled lettering FRANCO. He stepped with elegant precision into the hollow triangle of the A, paused, made out the name of the Caudillo for himself and with a smile of majesty proceeded towards Don Antonio.

The Guardias looked at their officer and their officer looked at Don Luis. There was much blinking and looking at boots. The gypsies' faces were slashed with white smiles. The people, one or two of them, clapped. Don Ferdinando strolled — how could a man take such long strides and still cover the ground with such slowness? — directly up to Don Antonio and put out his hand.

'Not late, I hope?'

Don Antonio clenched his fists. His teeth ground together. 'Arrest him,' he said to Don Luis, 'arrest him before — before,

before we have — Get him away from here.'

One of the gypsies shouted something. Don Antonio could not understand. They were all traitors, that was certain. They were laughing, the girls were swinging their skirts and pivoting about.

'Get them away from here.'

Don Luis spoke to the alien officer. The officer waved to his men, who waded into the gypsies. Two came for Don Ferdinando. He brought up his cane. 'One moment! One moment!' He twitched his cane. 'One moment! I come to reveal something — an ambush!'

'He's a crazy gypsy. Get him away from here. Get him away.'

'There are people hidden. Concealed.' Don Ferdinando pointed with the tip of his cane at the Garden of Remembrance. 'There!'

'Get him away. He's a madman. He's crazy.'

Don Luis scratched the lobe of his ear. 'Better have a look,' he said to the alien officer. 'Be quick.'

Don Antonio, looking at his watch, said: 'Stay where you are, everyone. Stay where you are.'

But they were all surging towards the place which Don Ferdinando had indicated. The King was among his subjects now, smiling and shaking hands.

'If there's no one there, he should be arrested.'

The Guardias were trampling the whole garden.

'There's nothing there. They'll — '

A sudden thrashing rose in the middle of the green. Like game disturbed by a dog, something was flapping and snapping among the foliage. Don Ferdinando put his eyebrows together and looked at Don Antonio, the King. Don Luis unhitched the flap of his revolver holster. Don Antonio wanted a cigar, a glass of lemonade, a gun. Don Ferdinando spread his arms and the people laughed and cheered.

From a clump of green Guardias, the naked, flat-chested body reared up, like a stripped bird, and for an interminable second, Don Antonio saw a badge of hair and two scraggy legs before the wild, fluttering creature was borne away through the back of the garden towards Don Ferdinando's field. The boy's olive face was sullen, not demonic. His hands were at his front. He went the same way with no suggestion of flight.

A whistle blew. The first car was descending from the castle, which, as the sun dropped, burned scarlet in the evening sky.

'They're coming!'

Another car was behind the first, another behind that. A sequence of wide black limousines streamed out from behind the red castle. The first passed over FRANCO in the road. The second was over it now and the first was almost up to The Cock. Don Antonio stared into the road. The first black car, unwinding a siren like a pennant behind it, rolled past where Don Antonio and Don Luis were waiting. Which car contained the Caudillo? No one had said. The second car went past. The first car was all but through the village. The fourth car was over FRANCO. The eighth car came from behind the castle. The third car was past Don Antonio. The first car was on the road to Malaga. The eleventh car was in sight from behind the castle. The sixth was over FRANCO. In which packed car was the Caudillo? Who knew? The Guardias were rigid at the salute. Don Luis had drawn his stomach into his chest. Don Ferdinando had his hat over his heart. The third car was through the village. The ninth was over FRANCO. Generals, admirals, security men, black car after black car, ribbed with chrome, distinguished with ministerial number plates of the highest priority, all went through. The fifth car had quit the village. The nineteenth was out from behind the castle. The fourteenth was over FRANCO. The dust rasped Don Antonio's eyes. The nineteenth car was over FRANCO. The nineteenth car was through the village. The nineteenth car was on the road to Malaga. One last motor cyclist buzzed out from behind the castle and flitted through Torreroja.

For a minute, the people awaited a miracle. Then the smiles and the giggles began. Among the grinning faces, only the Guardias were stern. The one nearest Don Antonio was whispering to himself: 'With my own eyes, with my own eyes I saw him. In the fifth car. I saw him with my own eyes.'

'I too,' said his colleague. 'In the second car.'

'The Caudillo?' said a third. 'He was leading, of course, in the very first car. I saw him myself, with my own eyes.'

Don Antonio rubbed his thumb along his jaw. He looked round for Manolo. 'Switch on the lights,' he said. He walked

83

along past the gypsies. They bowed. They deferred. They
touched each other aside. The townspeople ignored him. They
fell silent at his passing. He walked the long road to his house
and opened his front door, furtive as a safe-breaker.

'Antonio, is that you?'

'Yes, Mother, yes.'

'It was a triumph, my son. Yes? I heard the cheering.'

'Yes, Mother.'

'And you, my son – you spoke to him?'

Don Antonio stood in the darkness with his mother and
heard the clink of the rosary. 'Yes, Mother,' he said. 'I spoke to
him.'

'And he remembered your father, the Colonel?'

'Yes, Mother.'

'You spoke of their dining together in the mess at Burgos?'

'Of course, Mother. He asked me to bring you his profound
greetings.'

'Your father and he – '

' – were messmates. That was the word he used.'

'They were Christian knights,' said Doña Elisabeta. 'You
went with him through the Garden of Remembrance?'

'I did, Mother.'

'Our dead are not lost. With such a man, our dead are not
lost.'

'No, Mother.'

Don Antonio left the room.

'Jaime, Pia, José, Pepe . . . '

The rocker creaked, the rocker squeaked.

Don Antonio clamped shut the shutters of his office. He sat
down on the rusty *chaise-longue*. He sat there for an hour,
perhaps longer. Then he went into the kitchen. Carmela was
sitting at the table, hands folded in front of her, a shawl over
her head.

'You've heard.'

'I have,' said the woman. 'What do you want me to do? Do
you want me to go?'

'No. If you leave this house, I will kill you.'

'What do you want me to do?'

'Nothing.'

'I understand.'

'Take off your shawl.'

'Yes.'

'She must go from the village.'

'Yes.'

'I will pay whatever is necessary.'

'Good.'

'And the doctor. Whatever is necessary.'

'Thank you.'

'But you stay here.'

'Yes.'

'And no nonsense.'

'I understand.'

Don Antonio said: 'The American will not be coming again. We shall be only ourselves.'

'I understand.'

Don Antonio went back to his office and sat down in his swivel chair. He leaned back. The thick spring at the back creaked as he put his weight against it.

'Fran-cis-co, Fran-cis-co, Fran-cis-co,' the children were chanting in the street.

Don Antonio went to the window and opened the shutter an inch, two inches. The children had gathered under the yellow street lamp. 'Fran-cis-co, Fran-cis-co . . . ' They were in a group by the front door, but Don Antonio could see no sign of his son.

In the hall he could hear their chanting 'Fran-cis-co, Fran-cis-co, Fran-cis-co . . . ' growing louder and more rhythmical. Don Antonio unsheathed his Malacca cane from the umbrella stand.

'Francisco, Francisco, Francisco,' they were calling faster.

Don Antonio threw back the lock and opened the door.

'Francisco Francisco Francisco Francisco Francisco Francisco.' The children were drubbing their fists in their palms. In the centre of them, the spotted dog was busy over the bitch once more. 'Francisco Francisco Francisco. *Olé!*'

Don Antonio scattered them left and right with his fist. He raised his Malacca cane and brought it down with his full force again across the back of the dog. There was a *crack-crack*, like two barrels of a gun. A yelp of agony stabbed out. The dog, laced into the bitch, was rolling, yapping, frothing. The shattered cane in Don Antonio's hand was like a bundle of reeds. Don Antonio's sharp shoes jabbed at the animal's belly and head. The dog slobbered and howled and dragged itself away, broken-backed, still coupled to the bitch. Don Antonio clawed after it on his stripe-trousered knees, hands round its neck, braced from the drooling jaws, and he strangled it. He tore the carcass out of the bitch. She yelped and bit his hand. The teeth were in only an instant before Don Antonio snatched himself clear and kicked the low-reared beast down the road. He took the carcass of the dog, dangling by the neck, past the children and into his house. The door banged. The knocker clumped.

'Can you dispose of this?' said Don Antonio.

'A dog?'

'It had an accident. I had to – finish it. It's not to leave here.'

'I can dig a grave in the patio.'

'Now. Immediately.'

'Very well.'

'If the bitch whelps,' muttered Don Antonio, 'they must all be killed.'

'I'll do it now,' said Carmela.

She took the dog and went into the patio.

On his way back to the office, Don Antonio heard a tap at the front door.

'Antonio – '

'Yes, Mother, yes.'

He opened the door.

It was Manolo.

'I'm sorry to disturb you, Don Antonio. But about the dance – '

'What of it?'

'Does it go on?'

'Of course it goes on. The Caudillo came. The café is finished. Of course it goes on.'

'I thought perhaps – '

'How much did we say for the first drink?' There were faces at the street door. 'Fifty pesetas the first drink?'

'Yes. Fifty.'

'Make it a hundred,' said Don Antonio.

'A hundred pesetas!'

'Yes,' said Don Antonio. 'If the people want to eat the

refreshments prepared for the Caudillo, they must pay for them.'

'A hundred pesetas, they'll never pay it.'

'They'll pay it. You can tell them that I personally will take a hundred pesetas from everyone who comes to the dance tonight. I shall be there in person. To see it with my own eyes. You tell them.'

'Yes, Don Antonio. Don Antonio, about the Caudillo – '

'There was a plot to kill him,' said Don Antonio. 'Some gypsies, I'm told. There've been arrests already.'

'Can I – ?'

'Tell people? Certainly. The danger is past. Tonight we celebrate the Caudillo's escape. I shall expect everyone to be there. It's a question of loyalty.'

'I understand, Don Antonio.'

When Manolo had gone, Don Antonio went into his office and shut the door and sat in his swivel chair. It creaked as he leaned back and allowed himself to close his eyes.

It seemed a long time before he heard the door open and a footfall in the vestibule, the door close and the rap of the ghostly knock. The office was dark as he called out: 'Francisco, is that you? Francisco . . . '

AVE ATQUE VALE

The *Finca Rosario* stood amid pendulous orange groves ('Marmalade on the hoof,' Ben Goldman called them). Its driveway was empurpled with artichokes, pinned 'like flowering hand-grenades against the blazer-blue lapels of a southern sky' (my Durrelling notebook entry). The scallop-eaved farmhouse has long since been flattened under the runway used by big jets taking off from Malaga Internacional Airport. In 1960, however, it was not internacional at all; most of us came by road over the twisty *carretera* from Granada, eight or nine hours' frowning into white sun. Selene and Digby Charlton (the famous director) were exceptions: they had been privileged cargo on Hal Gampel's yacht. He rented the *finca* for them ('The best will have to do, I guess,' the legendary tycoon observed) and then hired Ben Goldman, who just happened to be on the coast, to do the rewrites on *Ave Atque Vale* (provisional title). Producer, director and scribe got out that tooth-comb and settled down to work.

Their toil was undisturbed by noise from the airport. It sported only a tattered squadron of silvery planes which looked as if they had had their nasty day over Guernica and were not likely to fly again, at least until they had been darned. The loudest noise was the coconut clatter of horses' hooves as Julio, the resident groom, exercised the six Arabs which the absentee owner kept in the stables. Julio was a one-armed *campesino* who promised Selene that he could turn her daughter, Rita, into a horsewoman. She was a lonely little girl, which was why we were often asked over to the *Finca Rosario* with our two-year-old son, but Selene was lonely too, especially when valetudinarian Gampel moved his medicine chest to Madrid and began to summon Digby for huddles on the set.

Rome was being built in a day, or two, but there were creative problems that called, frequently, for Digby. At first, Selene did not seem to miss him. She had fallen in love with the simple life and the servants it afforded her. Oh that's not *fair*: she thought Andalusia was just the most beautiful place in the world and all she wanted was to have somewhere of her own down there.

'Do you know what land is?' she said to me one day.

'Isn't it generally to be distinguished from sea?' I said.

'Snotty goddamn limeys!' she said.

'Me and who else?' I said. We were alone with our gin fizzes on the tiled patio, with its two-tone wall-covering of pink and purple bougainvillaea.

'It's five pesetas a square metre is what it is,' Selene said.

'Listen,' I said, 'in that case I'll take two.'

'And Isaiah was telling me how much it costs to build down here — correction: how *little*!'

'Isaiah?' I said. 'Would that be the original one or only little deutero, his kid cousin? Or — hey, wait a minute: it's not *Berlin*, is it?'

'That's Irving, smartass, and it's neither. I'm talking about Isaiah Axelrod. He's the nearest thing to a saint I've yet to come across. He's found this site that's absolutely spectacular and utterly unspoilt.'

'Only one problem,' I said. 'Absolutely spectacular and utterly unspoilt sites can be a long walk from the corner store. What's so saintly about him?'

'He's only revived local craftsmanship virtually single-handed. He's given people hope around here. That's pretty saintly in my book. And by the way, your American accent, I don't know where it comes from, but I have to tell you: it's toadily unconvincing, but *toadily*.'

I didn't altogether like her patchwork Bermuda shorts, but did I say anything? Selene was a bright blonde party with short legs and, looking back, I suspect that I flirted with her less because she was attractive than because she had a very handsome husband: I imagined that there had to be more to her than met the eye, or the ear. She and Digby had been students at Washington State College, Seattle, where she was majoring in Journalism. He had the shyness of the narcissist and she was the first girl to bring him, or haul him, out of himself. If she was short in the leg, she had long enough arms and a precociously prehensile personality. (Her obituary professor deplored alliteration, but a girl couldn't help being what she was, could she?) As soon as she saw Digby, Selene went for what she wanted before what she wanted went. Until she believed in Digby, she told me, Digby never really believed in himself. It sounded like a boast; I hoped that it would not prove to be an epitaph. When it comes to 'for better or for worse', the former can sometimes be the less adhesive option. Up-and-going Digby seemed more and more often to be called to Madrid. My wife's suspicion was that he was beginning to go even more often than he was called.

We were willing, but slightly uneasy guests. Since we were living in a hot concrete box in Torreroja, a few kilometres down the road, it was difficult to resist the cool amenities of the *Finca Rosario*. Hal Gampel (whose collection of Shakespeare and Co. first editions was unrivalled) was picking up the tab, and what high-minded young novelist hesitates for long over sponging on guys like that? Selene accepted her good fortune with generous complacency. Luxury was a joke she was happy to share: drinks and meals were there for the asking, and even for those who didn't ask. Only Julio, the unsmiling groom, showed any reluctance. When Ben Goldman, who had stayed down on the coast to finish revising the purple pages, wanted to go riding in the mountains behind Mijas, Julio's bone-hard expression made it clear that he was not running a dude ranch. Ben had made promises to a bunch of *aficionados* who were in town for the Ordoñez-Dominguin *mano a mano* and Julio was not pleased, which may have been what pleased me. I would never, of course, have agreed to rewrite crap like *Ave Atque Vale*, but Ben's smooth ascendancy over me — his 'impressive' novel was on the *N.Y.T.* bestseller list for the umpteenth straight week, *just* — made me grateful for Julio's stand, and failure to deliver. I took pleasure in parading my rather bookish Spanish in conversation with him and made it pass for intimacy; Ben Goldman was too busy to get his vocabulary from Juan Ramon Jiménez. That gave me my snotty chance, didn't it?

That night, Ben was sore enough to give Digby Charlton long-distance hell on the subject of the new dialogue between

Jesus and the Procurator of Judaea.

'So Pilate has all the lines,' I could hear him shouting, 'so who gets to rise on the third day? I don't need this shit, you know.'

Selene leaned across to me. 'Do you think he should talk to Digby like that?' she said.

'I think he probably should,' I said.

Selene looked lonely at that; I hope I was ashamed. Forgiveness was the nearest she came to accusation, however, and she soon asked us back. It was on that next visit that we met Eli Honneger. My small son having been captivated by the charm of Spanish donkeys, I was cast in the role of Juan Ramon's Platero and was forever being driven on all fours around the patio, while Paul and Rita xylophoned my ribs with their pointed heels. Paul particularly liked me to hee-haw and I was in the middle of a bout of dutiful mimicry when the newcomer sauntered out of the house with Selene. 'That doesn't sound like too much of a *burro* to me,' he said.

Unsolicited criticism always excites warm feelings in me. 'Well,' I said, 'what do you know? Selene's finally found a friend shorter than she is.' It may not have been subtle, but it was quick. 'Listen, pal,' I pursued (I really did), 'if you can do a better *burro* than me, do it. It might just free me for work of more profound cultural significance. Make your pitch, my friend.'

'He has a terrible American accent, doesn't he?' Selene said.

Eli Honneger was not apparently offended. He merely began to swell. He was indeed a short man, with a rain-barrel chest, horn-rimmed eye-glasses and a beige chaplet of ungreying hair. His meat-loaf forearms pumped up and down as he engorged himself in front of us. His face bulged with the pent sound he was about to release. He was a human bellows that suddenly broke forth in an explosion of animal lust so poignant that within seconds its appeal was taken up across the *campo*. The landscape became obstreperous with desire. My small son gazed at the source of the noise with appalled eyes. He began to cry in panicky horror. My wife's imploring face should have been enough to silence Honneger's braying. But Eli was translated; human appeals could not touch him. My son's tears and my wife's horror might as well have been applause; he bowed to them and pumped out loud air with unquenched energy.

Ben Goldman, in his perfectly pressed pants (sorry, prof., but those are the facts as I saw them), ambled on to the patio. He had come from his daily tennis game and was carrying a brace of rackets. Looking at Eli and at my hysterical son and my furious wife, he gave us a star-white smile. Then he went up to the feisty visitor and nudged him with the heel of one of his Slazengers. '*Vaya, burrito*,' he said. 'Beat it!'

Eli Honneger rolled his eyes and exhaled that long and lippy sigh which signals the end of a donkey's mating cry and then, quite as if he had a little bitty tail and a *burro*'s neat rump, he turned and skipped into the orange trees. I saw Goldman look at my wife and I was filled with humiliation. He had a very beautiful wife of his own, and a baby, but they never came to the *Finca Rosario* and he seemed in no hurry for their company.

When Eli had reverted into a man once more, he came back to the patio, grinned at Ben Goldman and scowled at me. Ben might look like an unmitigated Yaley, but his family had connections with the Wobblies (even if Emma was, sorry, no known relation), so he and Eli were soon at a reunion, even though they had never met before. Eli had been a union organiser way back and was in Spain in 1938, with the Abraham Lincoln brigade. He had then gone home and made a fortune in the trucking business during World War Two. Selene's father had been his partner, right? He sold out a marriage or two later and now he was back in Spain with a car full of recording equipment, all set to tape the music of the old *país* before it got buried entirely by that little bastard Francisco Franco. He didn't know too much about *flamenco* and his Spanish was '*buenas tardes, señorita*' and other times of day, but he figured the dollar would do most of his talking for him.

Little Rita looked at the donkey-man and palmed blonde strands from her temples. 'Julio knows lots of songs,' she said. 'He always sings when he's riding.'

'Lead me to him, little lady,' Honneger said. 'Let's go sign him up.'

She made to get on his back. He winked at me and set her on his shoulders. There are times when one can be jealous of absolutely *anything*. Ben Goldman was bringing a drink to my wife and the amused gratitude I read in her eyes was enough to poison mine.

If I had had the wit not to be so self-conscious, I should have returned again and again and so I should have been able to furnish a longer tale than this. Alas, vanity and apprehension, pious disgust at free-loading too freely, combined with the arrival of my parents for a holiday, oh a hundred things (and their shadows) meant that we never again saw Rita or the others at the *Finca Rosario*. I am left with a sequence of images, like cuts from the trailer of a movie never actually witnessed *in extenso*. I know, for instance, that Eli discovered that he and Julio had been soldiers in the same campaign and were soon going for rides together, on those polished Arabs, in the foothills of the *sierra* until one day, when they had become apparently close companions, Eli found that they had never been true *compañeros*, because Julio had fought on Franco's side. I expected to hear that there had been a showdown, but it was Ben Goldman who caught hell when he called Julio a lousy Fascist (out of his hearing). 'Hell,' Honneger was said to have said, 'he and I were in a war together, fancy pants, and I don't give a good goddamn which side he was on: he's a *man*.' After that, Julio took Eli up into the hills and introduced him to some people, his cousins, who were still more or less in hiding, which somehow proved how right the old guy's judgment had been. Exactly when Selene began sleeping with Eli I can't say. I saw them together only once in the half-finished house that Isaiah Axelrod was building for them. And then did I dream, or was it fancy, or malice, that said that Selene was Eli's daughter? Had he really cuckolded his partner one cold Seattle winter? It was certainly Ben Goldman who told me that Isaiah's family in South Africa had bankrolled him to start this huge development along the coast – the *Colonia del Sol* – and that their money came from mines where the black helots got paid in 'knuckles and dimes'. Ben eventually left his beautiful wife and went back to the States and quit writing altogether. Last thing I heard, he was a union organiser in San Diego and weighed two hundred and ten. I don't think about him too much, but my wife mentioned his name, funnily enough, only a couple of days ago.

WORK IN PROGRESS

D o you want to see something beautiful?' Matt Hyams
said. 'Do you want to see something unconditionally
worth seeing?'

'If it's your latest painting, man, I don't have eyes for
anybody else's shit right now.' Fred Torrance, elbows wide on
the café table, tattoos blueing his ninepin forearms, lowered
pop eyes towards the froth on his beer. 'I'm not into com-
mercial art.'

'And I don't show my work to amateurs,' Matt said. He
switched a chair in his big fingers and sat into it.

'I don't dig those pissy distinctions,' Torrance said, showing
a lot of white around ginger-lashed eyes. 'Amateur, professional, those are pissy distinctions; I don't dig them.'

'Amateurs never do,' Matt Hyams said. Torrance's livid
face and cardinal's hat of hair came from a crude rouge palette.
'I'm not talking about anything to do with anybody's work.
I'm talking about a woman, O.K.?'

'I'm a married man,' Fred Torrance said. 'Lead me to her.'

'I'm talking about beauty, ass-hole. I'm not about to lead
anybody anywhere.' Matt leaned back towards lame Justo,
handsome to the waist, and pointed to Torrance's beer and
gave it one more vote. Leaning even further back, he stabbed a
soused *boqueron* from the boat of *tapas* on the zinc counter. 'A
thing of beauty is a joy for ever.' He smiled at a class that
wasn't there, especially the pretty girl at the back who was
slow to pack up her stuff. 'Discuss.'

'A thing of beauty is a joy for about twenty-five minutes,'
Torrance said. 'If you're lucky and it hasn't been too long.'

'Those tattoos of yours are incurable, I assume. I'm sorry for
you. You're really labelled.'

'You're bugging me, Hyams. That's not wise. Bigger men than you have tried bugging me. Here I work all day, I come out for a beer and you start in bugging me.'

'Sailor, huh?'

'That was temporary.'

'And these are permanent. Unless you shorten your arms at the elbow. Maybe you should think about that. So now you're a painter, right? It isn't that easy, sailor. It's easy, but it's not that easy.'

'You professors,' Torrance said. 'You'll never understand. Painting in my book is something has to be invented all over again.'

'When you get to where the rest of the bunch went wrong, I'd appreciate knowing. Only watch out for that Caravaggio, when you get to him. He's fast with a knife. You know Neapolitans.'

'I've been in knife fights, Hyams, unlike you. I have a souvenir.' He pulled up his tartan shirt and showed the blank under his ribs. 'Singapore.'

'I was on Bataan, sailor, and I don't have a scratch on me. Who's the smarter fighter? Justo! *Otra cerveza, por favor.* You want another?'

'Why not? I knew this hooker. Tits that knocked your eye out. Solid. And what a body on her! Two months' money I spent getting her hot little box to open. I'd 'a given more, 'f it'd taken more. I gave her more than she asked, even so. Just to find out what else was on the menu. An ass on her could crack nuts. Tight? I tell you, pal.'

'Yeah, and I kinda wish you wouldn't, sailor.'

'And then what do I do? I go and get married to Eileen Pickles is what I do. Can you figure it? Have you seen her? You've seen her.'

'Don't talk about your wife, will you, please, like that?'

'Did you always talk nice about yours, professor? Because what's she doing right now? Don't bother: I heard all about it. Walls have tongues around here, you know. Torreroja is a goddamn colander; there's nothing doesn't leak out.'

All of a sudden, Matt Hyams had his hand on the red top of the other man's head. Teeth clicked against the rim of Torrance's beer glass. He was hard against the glass and his mouth grew a veteran's moustache from the froth. They were still, the pair of them, working at something that took all their concentration. Matt Hyams crowned Fred Torrance under the heavy hood of his hand. The tattoos bulged: fat anchor, flexed serpent, MOTHER! Torrance braced his head up from a mouthful of glass. If he ducked sideways, the glass would go too and he would eat splinters. The two men sat like acrobats, working without making a move.

'What's this?' Adam Stern said. 'What's happening?' On his shining head, he wore his usual knitted skull cap (faded purple Star of David, dirty white ground); *alpargatas* on his sockless feet. He had a rubber-banded couple of spiral notebooks under his arm; two Venus pencils tightened the tourniquet. The collarless work-shirt was new, from the Widow Serrano, less than a buck and a half they worked out at. 'Is this serious?'

'Serious?' Hyams took his hand from Torrance's head. Swollen redness seemed to rise like a party balloon. Up it came, until Matt punctured the spell by touching one tartan shoulder. On the sly, Torrance measured his mouth between thumb and forefinger. 'The idea!'

'You take some risks, Hyams,' Torrance said.

'We're just a coupla painters horsing around here,' Matt said, 'aren't we, old pal?'

'Have you seen her?' Stern said. 'This chick? Have you seen her out there on the *carretera*?'

'She was on the early news,' Torrance said and sprang an invisible knife and had it up to the fist in Matt Hyams' side. 'Be careful with me, professor, I'm warning you. Because I don't know who you people think you are today.'

'Never explain the precise meaning of that to me,' Matt Hyams said. 'You people. Never explain that, if you're smart. Because one word of wrong explanation and I could just twist your head so you can have a new and close acquaintance with your own backbone. Do I make myself unmistakable?'

'Come on, you guys,' Adam Stern said. 'It's nearly Christmas. Day after tomorrow is Christmas.'

'What're you? A talking calendar? What's Christmas to you? Because it's nothing to me.'

'Christmas is Christmas,' Adam Stern said. 'You've got kids – '

'Who needs reminders? I also have work in progress. I have work in progress and Christmas isn't something I aim to have stand in the way of it.'

'Michelangelo wasn't a family man,' Matt Hyams said, 'but even he took time out to wrap a package or two. You'd always find him on Piazza Navona, Christmas Eve. Are they still changing that tyre out there?'

'She's not changing it that I saw,' Adam Stern said. 'She's just standing there looking like the Botticelli Venus's pretty sister.'

'Botticelli?' Torrance said. 'Shit to Botticelli. Shit to Caravaggio. They're still breaking our balls, those Renaissance bastards. I don't want to hear about Botticelli; I don't want to hear about Caravaggio. I'm looking to get out from under all that shit.'

'There's the door,' Matt Hyams said, 'right there. Go join the Foreign Legion.'

'They *are* the fuckin' foreign legion,' Torrance said. 'Europe! I don't dig it.'

'Ends right down the street,' Hyams said. 'Straight on down; make a left; you're home free. Shake the dust, my friend, why don't you?'

'Living all by yourself,' Torrance said, 'what do you do when you want to get laid?'

'I don't do interviews,' Matt Hyams said. 'You want a beer here, Stern?'

'Forty-something years old, am I right? What happened: it drop off already?'

'Come on Fred, willya?' Adam Stern said. '*Una caña cerveza*, why not?'

'Either of you guys ever make twelve and a half thousand bucks in eight months, a little less?'

'I'd have to go count,' Matt Hyams said.

'Twelve and a half thousand grand in eight months,' Fred Torrance said. 'Mutual Funds. All because I wanted to buy the cunt. Santiago de Chile, São Paulo; you ever see São Paulo? I wanted to marry her is why. A hooker and I wanted to marry her. I wanted to have her. And finally, I realised, there's only one way you have people definitely, that's you kill them. I loved her to death, that woman. *Puta*, she'd done everything and I knew she had and still I wanted her. O.K., so maybe that's why. I'm hip to that. It wasn't sex; it was love. Total. *Asunción*, in Paraguay? I was there too. Up the lousy Paraná. Love. Something you'd never understand. I'd 'a used her snot for caviare, I woulda put it on my toast. Better than Beluga; and I've had Beluga. I wanted that woman body and soul; snot, shit, totally. And then I got frightened it was her soul I wanted more than her body. I was a soul-collector suddenly, I realised, and I knew if I didn't make a break, I'd wind up killing her. Not jealousy, possession.'

'Fred, are you coming to tell these kids a story, or aren't you?' Eileen Torrance had the little girl on her canted hip, Darren against her flat breast, his head damp with commas of dark hair. 'I can't do it all by myself.'

She fired her shots into the room and then she was as good as a gypsy, swinging out of the bar with a flash of bare heels plimsolled in black.

'He doesn't want to do things, he shouldn't say he wants to do them.' She was talking to the sunset as it set its torch to the West. Matt Hyams looked at Fred and then again at the door of the Casino and the beauty from the *carretera* was standing there. She caught Fred Torrance's rage as he yelled a look after his narrow wife.

'I wonder if anybody would help me?' she said.

'Is there anybody wouldn't?' Matt Hyams said.

'I'm a painter, not a goddamn *service*,' Fred Torrance said. 'Stories!' He went, 'Excuse me,' past the girl's glorious smile.

Matt Hyams' hand was twitching like a dreaming pup as he sketched her on a blank slip of air. The sun-struck hair had a black slide in it. Matt's hand took routine inventory of mouth, eyes, neck, breasts (under candy-flossed white angora), hips, legs (in black velvet pants) and two feet in flat black slippers. Oh and beauty, brighter than the sunset roasting in the doorway behind her.

'What can we do for youze?' Adam Stern's voice announced Brooklyn, in case she cared to know.

'We need a place to stay,' she said. 'My name is Lola, by the way: Lola Goldman.'

'She sure doesn't look it, does she?' Matt Hyams said. 'Will you have something to drink?'

'Oh no really. We looked in at the Hotel Concha, but it was kinda minimal minus. I wondered — this is such a pretty little place — could we possibly find somewhere to rent?'

'How long were you thinking of staying?'

'A while maybe. My husband's a writer. He has a movie script to write, which is why we really didn't think a hotel — '

'He's a writer? We have a few of those. We even have a poet.' Matt indicated Adam, and his notebooks.

'A poet? That's terrific. Only it's getting a little late and we have our little boy asleep in the back of the Volkswagen. My husband's having a terrible time.'

'That I don't find easy to believe,' Matt Hyams said.

'Changing this tyre. The manufacturers did the nuts up so tight! Finally this truckdriver stopped and helped out or . . . What kind of poems do you write then?'

'I guess you could say Uncle Ez and I were like cousins under the skin.'

'Your uncle's a poet too? That's nice!'

Justo decided to light the hanging gas lamp. The stump of his wooden leg wore a small-size black rubber sock. The lamp hissed blue and then grew to white.

'How old's your little boy?' Matt said.

'Alexander is twenty months.'

'I'll tell you what you can do,' Matt said, 'and that's spend the night in my house. I have the biggest house in the *pueblo* and I'm all I've got to fill it. Stupid. I have two rooms the other side of my patio you can use tonight, and in the morning we can hunt a place for you to stay.'

'I'd hate to feel — '

'The rooms are there,' Matt Hyams said. 'What's to feel?'

Adam Stern sat when they had gone and took the bands off his notebooks and freed the Venus pencils. They twisted in the rubber before he caught them. Then he pressed open a notebook and wrote 'Letter to Uncle Ez'.

> They don't seem to know you, *zio mio*,
> Botticellis don't dig poets; rhymes
> Diminish them; *a las* sink-oh Della Tardy
> Marries houses, reads poems, dreams and darns;
> But beauty buys no cantos, no cant-oh, no!

Maria Caetano, Matt Hyams' new cook since Paquita quit, swished down to the market with her basket, his pesetas, shaking her head at the poor prospects at this late hour. She had made up the new bed, singing a song full of *corazón*. The little boy, running round and round the patio in his night feet, made her bend at the waist and clap her hands in the doorway: '*Niño, niño!*'

Matt sat by the fire in the big room beneath his studio, reading the *Trib* and sipping *vino tinto* from a thick glass. A slob-bellied bottle in a wicker corset stood by the donkey basket. The fire snapped and bubbled. A passing rascal sold the wood by weight, wet. The smell of paint came down the stairs from the studio, teased out by the heat, like a cat.

Matt smiled at an unamusing article in the paper when he first heard Ben Goldman say something sharp. He read it for a joke until he heard her answer. Ben wanted the kid in bed, Lola; Lola said he had slept all day. Ben wanted to know, whose fault was that? Lola said, 'Why fault?' The kid's feet kept running. Matt Hyams tasted the blood of the wine and wished them happy, the family.

Shod steps slapped the patio and Ben Goldman was in the doorway. He wore white pants, with a black belt, white *espadrilles* and a yellow polo-necked sweater. Matt, in baggy jeans, sailor-sweater, eye-glasses for the *Trib*'s international print, looked at the smooth face and the lustrous eyes and the patent-leather hair and thought Ben Goldman quite a dandy. 'Come on in and have a glass of wine. Or there's some *aguardiente* if you prefer it.'

'You don't have some orange juice, do you?'

'Oranges we have.' Matt indicated a scoop of olive wood heaped with oranges. 'Juice you can make.' The squeezer was on the side. 'Maria went to the market.'

'This is very nice of you,' Ben Goldman said. 'I appreciate it.'

'You're a pretty successful writer, I gather?'

'I don't know about successful. I sold a book to the movies, now I'm taking a shot at the screenplay. I'm off and running, I guess. Have I heard of you, sir?'

'I've had a show or two,' Matt said. 'I'm off and lumbering.'

'Matt Hyams, Matt Hyams . . .'

'You're going to write this screenplay here in Torreroja?'

'Could happen.' Ben Goldman was leaning on the oranges, then tipping juice into a glass. 'Most people don't have our luck, do they? Being able to work pretty well where we choose.'

'It's a nice club,' Matt said. 'Does your wife like to travel?'

'Lola? She wanted to see Europe. She was in drama school, but she jumped at Europe. Are houses like this very high?'

'Just the two storeys,' Matt said. 'No, they're pretty cheap this time of year. A man works in the motion picture industry could afford a couple of them, easy.'

'Matthew Hyams,' Ben Goldman said. 'Didn't you have some problems with H.U.A.C. one time?'

'They had problems with me,' Matt said. 'I wouldn't toss them my friends.'

'I'd like to see your work, if you have any you'd care to show. You still prefer not to talk about it, I guess?'

'You're very perceptive,' Matt Hyams said.

Maria had made *croquetes* with tuna fish; after that came calves' liver, *flambé* in Fundador, with onions. Alexander ran in and out of the room, arms outstretched, banking and soaring. The Goldmans watched him, and each other. Finally, as Alexander began to run low on fuel, and the parents did not move, Matt himself took off, with a sudden roar of engines, swooped on the boy and zoomed him across the patio.

He changed the kid, put him in the portable crib and sat on the floor, big-booted, and told him one of the stories he had fed his own children, in the days before the junior senator from Wisconsin made his move, and his wife seconded it. He heard the voices of the parents admiring the house, laughing together at something murmured more quietly, talking of a third person who really ought to be along.

Alexander cooed for a while and then he was asleep, one hand on the side bar of his cage, the other a soft shackle on Matt's hairy little finger. Ben and Lola could be seen across the dark ditch of the patio, sitting in the golden light of the lamp, mottled by the flame from the olive wood. Matt stood in the darkness, unwilling to bring time again to the table: they seemed immortal as long as he left them alone.

But soon he was leading them up the tiled stairs to the studio they just had to see. How often do you get to visit a painter?

Lola clapped her hands. 'Oh my God, Ben, will you look at those goats? Those are the most lifelike goats I ever saw. Is this charcoal, may I ask?'

'That's charcoal,' Matt Hyams said, 'but pay it no mind.' He took the noisy paper from her hand and crumpled it and threw it towards the shallow basket in the corner of the studio. 'I fouled up on that one.'

'Oh, no,' she said, 'it was beautiful. I don't know how you could do that. That *hurt*. Aren't these drawings just magnificent, Benjamin? You're never going to junk them, are you?'

'You don't do portraits?' Ben Goldman said.

'Goats are people too,' Matt said. 'I do them.'

'They have so much *character*,' Lola said, 'haven't they, Ben?'

Ben Goldman walked to the far end of the studio, as if he had an appointment. A large canvas was hanging there, in shadow. It showed the mountains, with a hard shelf of white houses above the purple shoulders of the hills. 'That's the place I'd like to live,' he said.

'I like the sea,' Lola said.

Matt crumpled another unsuccessful goat. Lola's wince was a little sound. There were more sketches on the floor and on the horizontal door, between trestles, he used for a work-table. She pushed some of the drawings together into a sort of corral, where her arms could protect them. Matt's hand twitched again to capture her, the rhetoric of that body. He wanted to find the line to describe her tenderness, and the tincture of greed that compromised beauty with desire. She pleaded with him to lower his standards, for her sake.

'If you don't have any use for these,' she said, 'I know I have no right to ask, but Alexander would just love them in a year or two. Could I possibly?'

The street door had a sharp knocker on it. It snapped now like the bolt of a rifle on a dud cartridge. Adam Stern was standing in the Calle Queipo de Llana. 'How goes it? I called by because there are big plans all of a sudden for a Christmas lunch at the Roses, those English people in the Calle Tostón?' Adam's sentences often ended on an inquisitive note; he seemed afraid of becoming unintelligible. His sister was in a home. 'And they wanted to know, do you want to come along? They'd like it. Everybody.'

Matt and Adam had not been standing at the door for many seconds when anger flared behind them. Matt heard the scorn in Ben Goldman's voice: 'You don't *do* that, an artist's studio isn't the place you go . . . *scrabbling* in.' Lola's reply was less fierce than Matt hoped; the voice of a thin tourist came down the stairs. Matt found money and gave it to Adam Stern; four turkey dinners.

'Calle Tostón, *diez y seis*,' Adam said, 'two o'clock, Christmas Day.'

'Sailor Fred and his bride among the company?'

'I'm on my way there.' Adam said.

Matt Hyams met Lola and Ben coming down the stairs. Ben was behind her; it looked like courtesy, but he was hard on her heels. There was force in it, he was so close. She gave Matt a golden smile, like something detached from a deck, one of *her* pictures.

Goldman brushed at his trousers, a charcoal shadow. His handsome face darkened in reflection. Lola turned at the bottom of the stairs and bent to share his concern. He frowned and kept it for himself. The 'Why?' in her face was pure appeal to Matt; she could not see how Ben could have her and not want her. Could *he*? She slipped out of her vanity like a veil and stood naked, not nude, in front of the big painter. 'He doesn't want me, does he?' she said, without speaking a word.

Matt went out the next morning to buy presents for Alexander and for the Torrance kids. The booths under the lee of the new church were full of wooden trains, dolls and balls on a string you threw up and caught again in a cup with a handle. When he returned to the Calle Queipo de Llana, Matt heard the rap of Ben Goldman's typewriter. It stopped at the sound of the door.

'Don't mind me,' he said. 'Strike while the keys are hot.'

'She's gone to the beach with the kid,' Goldman said, 'so I figured, make a start. But if I'm taking fuel out of the atmosphere, you say so.'

'The world belongs to everyone,' Matt said.

'Was I out of line last night? Lola thinks so.'

'Nobody forms lines in this house,' Matt said. 'About what?'

'Talking about H.U.A.C. and stuff. It kind of fascinates me, I have to admit it. I was just a kid in High School when it was all happening. Then when you meet a survivor . . . '

'You weren't out of line,' Matt said.

'I'm also sorry about the goats. The way she . . . '

'That requires no apology,' Matt said. 'Least of all from you, because it had nothing to do with you.'

'I get it,' Ben Goldman said. 'We won't be here too much longer. I'm aiming to go find that village of yours in the picture soon as the garage has that flat mended. I like the idea of being high up like that. Where was it exactly, would you mind telling me?'

Matt Hyams tapped his head. 'No vacancy,' he said.

Christmas Day was hot and clear. The Roses, Michael, Sylvia, had put two long tables at right-angles in their patio. Red and purple bougainvillaea dressed the deal. The turkey came in shining foil from the village baker's oven, with a whole flat pan of roast potatoes in train. There were big bowls of salad and fruit. Sylvia had made mince pies. They did not sit down to eat until way past three, but the Torrances had still not showed. Adam told Matt that Michael had paid Fred Torrance's dues, because there had been some nastiness when he called at the house. Fred said again he was aiming to work; Christmas was not a holiday he recognised. He read Michael's generosity for the criticism it surely was and now, it seemed, he was making it difficult for his family to attend.

Ben Goldman and Michael Rose had a common friend in the film business and were soon in professional conversation. Adam Stern went to the Torrances' house and, after a while, came back with Eileen and the kids, all in tears. The turkey was already being carved; chestnut stuffing crumbled on to the table from the bulging back end of the bird. Lola's face shone as she carried plates to the kids. Ben was sitting back from the table, knife-edged white legs crossed, one *espadrille* drooping from an arched foot. Eileen Torrance sat next to him and he drew his chair to be close to her, as if he had been waiting for her.

As the meal went on, Ben Goldman took particular care of

the Torrance kids. He could tell stories too. Matt's wooden train came in useful; he chugged it along the lines in the deal table and tootled over the bougainvillaea to visit one of the Roses' kids on the far side of the Rockies. Lola's beauty pleaded with Matt Hyams down the long table. Her husband gave all he had to the plain kids and their plain mother. Eileen flowered in his presence. Her tears dried; her eyes gleamed. She came alive. Ben Goldman bled the beauty out of his wife and blessed Eileen Torrance with it. No one but Matt seemed to notice. He felt it like a knife in his side. He shook his head at the mince pies and stumbled into the house, across the tiles and out into the Calle Tostón. He was lame with the pain of it as he walked along the *carretera* to the Casino Bar.

Fred Torrance was sitting with a *caña cerveza* in front of him. Matt voted for a beer and squatted down to join the other man, heavy arms along the back of a reversed chair. 'Christmas?' he said. 'I don't even know what day it is.'

A PARTING GUEST

Milstein visited us in Torreroja the same October that I persuaded Matt Hyams to come and play soccer for the first time in the big field next to the Villa Santa Cruz. It was a movable *fiesta*, our football, sometimes Tuesdays, sometimes Thursdays, Spaniards versus *extranjeros*, and Franco take the hindmost. Ramón Caetano and his *amigos* used to spill through the Judas door in the thick green gates of the villa like clowns tumbling into the arena. Behind the blanched perimeter wall, with its machicolation of jagged glass, the turreted house was said to sport a tiled tennis court and swimming pool and an orange grove. It was owned, so the reliable word went in the Casino Bar, by some very nice Nazis.

The South of Spain was *terra incognita* — *¡tierra incógnita, se puede decir!* — for most people in England at the end of the Fifties, but we had been virtually evicted from our Highgate flat, by a trustworthy old lady who had sworn to give us a long lease before we parted with our key money, but not after, and we needed somewhere cheap to live. 'GOT IT!' Milstein said, as soon as I told him our problem. 'GOT IT!' And so he had. He introduced me to a woman of dated elegance — purple gloves and matching Ascot hat — and superior vowel sounds, whose charm would have been consummate had her breath not been capable of stopping Rocky Graziano in his prime, which he then was. I assumed that she neglected to brush her teeth, but she was actually dying, stylishly, of a vile cancer. She owned a beach-front house in Torreroja and she was prepared to let us have it at the only sort of rent I could afford. *¡Arriba!*

We were not sure of the propriety of living in a Fascist country, but it was that or J. Walter Thompson. Scowling at the Falangist insignia, we drove into the sun. Torreroja proved

106

to be a dream, though a dusty one when August made a kiln of the place; I could work unmenaced by old ladies and our baby son was able to play safely on the wide beach. We lived like penurious plutocrats on the few pounds my hot typewriter could earn. Morally, there were telling arguments against being on Franquist soil, but as Milstein himself had said to me, when I was voicing liberal qualms, 'DO YOU HAVE ANOTHER GLOBE BY ANY CHANCE?'

Milstein had not been to university. He was clever enough to go, but he was also, as he had explained to me, CLEVER ENOUGH NOT TO. Frankly, he only ever wanted to be in films and disinterested study did not appeal to him. He had always been eager for the big world and when I met him, soon after coming down from Cambridge, he was already in it, working with one of the eventual founders of Independent Television. I was never sure of the measure of intimacy he enjoyed with the great Bernie, but he appeared to be in on the ground floor, and all set for the express elevator to higher things. He was, he insisted, BLOODY WELL going to help me, WHETHER I LIKED IT OR NOT. I've heard worse threats.

We were of much the same age (in other words, he was slightly younger than I) and we had, as it happened, come to England at much the same time, though from different directions and in different circumstances. In 1938, I came with my parents, from New York, on the M.V. *Britannia*; he came without his from Vienna, via Innsbruck and Trieste. One day he would tell me all about it. My father was British and his, of course, had been Austrian. If we had 'the obvious thing' in common, I was smug enough to reckon that Milstein was a good deal more of an outsider than I was. Nevertheless, he knew his way round London, and Show Business, and I did not. I could say (and I have said) that Milstein latched on to me with prehensile alacrity, but it is also true (though I have said it less often) that I considered I was on to quite a good thing myself. Did not Paul Goodman, the pansexual American, once advise writers never to give needless offence to anyone with access to a printing press? I was no less wary of closing the door in my own face when it came to someone who might one day be able to point a camera at one of my scripts.

Milstein was an enthusiast. He was going places and he

wanted his friends along on the trip. He loved creative people and liked nothing more than the idea of giving them their BIG CHANCE. He thought Bernie a genius, which seemed an over-statement, but when he decided that I was a genius too, it seemed only premature. He longed for us to do things together. He believed in sharing EVERYTHING, especially good luck, with people he CARED about. Didn't I feel the same way? I wasn't sure; what did he have in mind? 'Well,' he said, 'for instance would you LEND ME YOUR CAR?' 'How long for?' I asked. 'THAT'S NOT THE BLOODY *POINT*,' he said, and of course he was quite right. In those days, though, there was something *personal* about one's car, even if it was a Ford Anglia; if there had not been, would Milstein ever have wanted to lay his hands on ours? He maintained, and I believed him, that he would have let me have his, LIKE A FLASH. He would have let me have his underpants in the same spirit and, what's more, he would've expected me to put them on right there and then. His generosity, though it's churlish to say so, was also something of an assault. I was prepared to like Milstein, but he was only prepared to love me, or us.

He had soon asked if he could come to dinner and meet my wife and he told me, at our subsequent Dutch lunch at Schmidt's German restaurant (*Wiener Schnitzel* 3/6d), that he was BLOODY RELIEVED that he liked her. Was it all right if he dropped in from time to time without being specifically in-vited? Real friends were always welcome in each other's houses, didn't we agree? We didn't like to disagree, but when you have a colicky baby, the violent and unexpected ringing of the bell, followed by the impatient knocker, is not always the sound you most crave. After one frosty*ish* reception, he seemed so hurt that I tried to explain, and so did Sylvia, but he couldn't believe our mundane objections. 'WAIT A MINUTE,' he said finally, 'BECAUSE NOW I GET IT!' 'Get what?' 'YOU DON'T HAVE TO WORRY,' he said, and the vigour of his reassurance started the baby crying again. 'I make it an ABSOLUTE RULE,' he went on, 'never to sleep with my friends' wives. NEVER. SO *RELAX*.' My wife was less flattered than he intended by the news that he would not be taking her to bed; she liked to imagine that she might herself have had some say in that particular matter. However, having cleared the air, he was determined to go on breathing it and in due course, touched by his inability to guess that anyone could ever get tired of him, we asked him to dinner again, and he came, again and again.

My forbearance was not wholly disinterested. When he talked, and acted, as if nothing could resist him, unless he himself resisted it, he was singularly convincing. When he said that we were going places, I might wince at the company, but I never doubted that we should reach our ambitious destination. My affection for him grew; it was flawed, but the flaw, like scar-tissue, somehow made the bond more sure. *Oderam et amabam.* I wanted so badly, at times, to wound him that I became quite protective about him. When, having been instrumental in finding us our house in the Calle Tostón, he wrote and asked if he could come stay with us for a week, I promised Sylvia that I would make sure that he behaved and wrote back, with more warmth than I felt, that he should come for as long as he liked. Accordingly, he could hardly be blamed, though he was, when the first thing he told us was that he was planning to stay for a full fortnight. It is not a pretty confession, but I hoped against hope, when he came into the sitting room after unpacking his things, that he would have brought my wife a present, for our small son if not for herself. I hoped it not least because I had a feeling that Milstein had made it charmlessly obvious that he had come to see me, rather than us. However, if his hands were empty, he did bring news of a commission for a T.V. play for which I could not but be grateful, though I continued to wish that he had had the wit to find a small toy train, or a box of duty-free soap, before his announcement that he was staying twice as long as at first proposed. All the same, he was our manifest benefactor and if his presence at our table at every meal every day threatened to strain our patience, and our budget, I shrank from making an issue of it.

On Saturday mornings, we always went into Málaga to the market. Afterwards, the artists of Torreroja had a rendezvous at Antonio's bar, near the harbour gates. The myopic Antonio had wanted to emigrate to Australia, but he arrived at the discriminating Aussie offices in Madrid with a dirty child, having travelled all night, and was refused. They said it was his sight; he knew it was the smell. We drank his *oloroso* and carried home a supply of *seco* and *coñac* in wicker-lagged flagons. We had decided to give a small party for Milstein on the Sunday; he had begun to wonder whether we had any friends apart from him, and we were anxious for him to have some apart from us.

Adam Stern arrived first, in his whitish skull cap with the mauve Star of David on the crown, and I must say Milstein was terrific with him. He told the Brooklyn poet of his plans to get Bernie to sponsor a poetry competition and perhaps to start a little press. He wanted to see more of Adam's verse and he was keen to go with him to some of the peasant *pueblos* near Ronda where the old-time flamenco singers could still be found; they might not have much voice left, but they were still vibrant with *corazón*. (Why shouldn't Adam front a pro-gramme on the Jewish roots of Spanish gypsy music?) Then the Goldmans showed up; the golden Lola ravishing in a black dress, gold earrings and thonged gold sandals, Ben in the Ivy League outfit that promised that he was happy to be around, but was only passing through. (Oh those smart creases in those pristine white pants!) He and Milstein were soon shaping up to each other (Ben was writing one film script from his own novel, the sell-out, and he was ready to do another), while Lola stood by, as if a face like hers had never dreamed of launching a thousand ships. Her exquisite modesty took every eye, but never suffered her to look back. (*Me?*) The smile on that luscious mouth was happy for Ben, because just look at him making rings round this Limey, will you?

Milstein was a big hit with our friends. As he watched us clear the glasses and garner the cigar butts (Havanas were available for pennies), he told us what he planned to do for everyone. No Inspector-General ever issued a more optimistic report. The Pallenbergs were a little down in the mouth after the collapse of hard-edge? He was going to see their paintings in the morning and he was sure Casimir Carlinski would have a wall for their stuff, if it was as good as they said. Matt Hyams already had a gallery, but who wanted to keep a dealer in Miami when he could have one in Wigmore Street? Adam Stern? The next Ginsberg; why not? Milstein finished a dish of *boquerones* — his sole gesture towards tidying up — and said that he hoped we wouldn't mind, but he didn't plan to eat all his meals with us in future. He'd take lunch with a few different people so that he didn't get too bored being alone with us, O.K.? We said that we appreciated his thoughtfulness.

Milstein's salary from Bernie was probably equal to the joint income of everyone who lived in the Calle Tostón, but he had not come on holiday to spend it. He didn't really eat lunch, he told us; he turned up at our friends' houses at *mediodía* only because he could be sure that he wasn't disturbing their work schedule. He never wanted more than a snack and whatever they were having was good enough for him. One night, sitting in our patio while Salvadora produced the first of her many courses, he told us of his active plans to produce Ben Goldman's next movie. And what about the little poetry press and Casimir's asylum for the orphans of hard-edge? One thing at a time! Ginsberg wasn't built in a day. Meanwhile, the hopefuls gave him lodging, and board. However, I am not being sarcastic when I say that, like an inverted Jesus, Milstein sincerely believed that people had only to follow him and they would sell everything they had.

It may sound hypocritical but the last straw, or certainly the penultimate one, came when Milstein, after being an hour and a half late for dinner, said that he hoped we didn't mind, but he was going to stay at the Goldmans' *finca* for a couple of nights. He and Ben had things to talk about, and Lola was the best hostess he'd ever met. We might have been glad to see him go, but we weren't entirely glad to see him go *there*. We felt judged, though no judgment was intended, and rejected, though we were not sorry to have the house to ourselves. Milstein genuinely meant no offence, as he proved by returning a day or two later to ask us a favour: could he borrow our house for his last evening? Did that mean that we would have to leave? Was it for an assignation or what? I was duly chastened when he explained that he only wanted a place to return the hospitality he had received from all our friends during his time on the coast. I could have kissed him when he said that he wanted to borrow our cook as well and give us all a slap-up meal, his treat.

While Salvadora filled the place with the smell of charcoal, Milstein drove our car into Málaga and came back with bottles from a place that was TONS cheaper than Antonio's,

AND BETTER. He was so engrossed in his preparations that he tripped over our tottering infant and left him in unappeased tears. He greeted his guests with Amontillado and a plate full of special salami which had them all chewing the fat in no time. Adam Stern brought his guitar and the black girl he lived with; it was the first time most of us had ever seen her awake. Only Matt Hyams excused himself; he had an old friend in town, from Israel, and he had decided to stay loyal to his Miami dealer. 'Never mind,' Milstein said, 'I'm not sure Casimir cares about FUCKING GOATS!'

The evening went well. It was less of a change for us than for the others, because we were, after all, sitting in our own patio and eating food prepared by our own cook, but we were certainly relieved: our friend had not left without doing *something*. He showed himself an urgent host, heaping our plates, and his own, with the food that HAD TO BE EATEN UP. His pleasure in his own bounty was touching; we watched him take the last leg of stewed chicken ('OH WELL, IF NO ONE ELSE WANTS IT!') like parents relishing a bonny appetite. Mopping bread round his gravy, Milstein delivered the parting guest's last word on his stay. 'Well,' he said, 'that's the first time I've had enough to eat since I BLOODY WELL GOT HERE!'

Did we wave goodbye! Matt Hyams was keeping goal for the *extranjeros* when I told him the story a few days later. He laughed so hard that he took his eye off Ramón Caetano's drive from the edge of the penalty box and it broke his left little finger. It didn't stop him laughing. Personally, I didn't think it was that funny.

THE LAST TIME

'You don't really mean it, do you?'

'It has to be,' she said.

'The kids,' he said, 'right?'

'If you like,' she said.

'The kids and him, right?' he said.

'Right,' she said.

'The faithful wife,' he said. 'You really are, aren't you?'

'That must be why I'm here,' she said.

'Even this is something between you and him. I'm not really in this even now, am I?'

'I don't have any choice,' she said.

'Meaning you've chosen already. Why do you have to be beautiful on top of everything else?'

'I don't think I am,' she said.

'Because you know you are. I love you, and you know what it does for me? It makes me bad-tempered is what it does for me. I could kill you as a matter of fact, you know that? You probably don't have me down for a killer, but I could really and truly kill you right now. That's what love does for me. What does it do for you? I'd like to know.'

'I'm sorry,' she said.

'That doesn't sound like too much. You know the real irony, don't you? If I didn't love you, I could probably get you to stay. I once made love — *they* called it love — to a mother and a daughter in the same night. Believe it or not, I made them both real happy. I was up and gone before breakfast, but they were real happy. I'd left a forwarding address, they'd still be around. I never made you happy like that, did I?'

'Perhaps I should have brought my mother,' she said.

'Because I loved you is why. That gets in the way. Hate and

disgust, that was what did it, but they didn't know, or maybe they did. I felt those now I'd probably be able to get you to follow me anywhere I wanted to go.'

'I doubt it,' she said, 'but I'm sorry you feel that way.'

'I'm sorry I don't,' he said. 'So don't start resisting. Yes you are too. I can sense it in your skin. You're naked and you're already putting your clothes on. Your skin temperature's changed; it's turned against me, like an animal's coat. You're a stickleback suddenly.'

'Please understand,' she said.

'I do understand,' he said. 'All the times we met and you were never really here. You were always thinking about him. We were never alone.'

'No, I wasn't,' she said. 'It isn't true.'

'Then why deny it? What do I care what's true? He's better then me, isn't he?'

'That doesn't come into it,' she said.

'Everything comes into everything. He's better than I am and that's what's decided it, not the kids, not your conscience. *That!*'

'I don't know what you mean,' she said, 'better.'

'I thought this would work out for us,' he said, 'meeting this way – hotel bedrooms, funny hours, secrecy, deception – but somehow it never really did, did it? By better I mean better. I thought I'd be hot stuff, like I was with Marilyn and her mother in that motel in Nebraska, but I really wasn't, was I?'

'You were fine,' she said. 'You were sweet.'

'Only you don't take sugar, do you?'

'I wouldn't have wanted you any different,' she said.

'That's what we shall never know. How I would have grabbed you if I'd *really* grabbed you.'

'I hate to be grabbed,' she said. 'No, it's just all too complicated. I'm not good at complications.'

'You'd be good at just about anything you wanted to be good at, in my judgment. Look at you.'

'I can't,' she said.

'Well, look at me. Seems it's your last chance.'

'It's not as if you're going to be on your own,' she said.

'No,' he said, 'I don't even have that consolation, do I?'

'It's up to you,' she said, 'really, isn't it? You're free.'

'Free! I was, I'd come and haunt you; I'd come and make myself a nuisance.'

'You wouldn't want to do that,' she said.

'So you're really going back to him. But then you never really quit, did you? He always came with you and waited downstairs, the way I felt about it.'

'That's neither nice nor fair,' she said.

'Neither am I. Does that make it any less likely?'

'Oh dear,' she said, 'I really didn't want it to be like this.'

'Oh dear,' he said, 'how exactly did you want it to be?'

'You're right,' she said, 'I really don't know. Nicer?'

'I bet you'll tell him all about it. I bet you already told him most of it. Including that this is the last time. Have you?'

'What is there to tell?' she said.

'How it's better with him.'

'I never told him that.'

'You will, lady.'

'Please don't — '

'Please already! You truly think I'm a nice guy, don't you? You flatter me. I'm not so nice. I'm just a little *too* nice, and that's not the same thing at all. You think you can just pull away from this and no harm done, don't you? No lesions, no sepsis. You go back to him, even-Steven, and everything'll be as good as it was before, maybe better? You think I can be put behind you just like that. An incident.'

'Don't imagine I'm happy about it,' she said. 'I'm not.'

'Dammit,' he said, 'I don't care who's happy. All I know is, you made the decision. I didn't. Which makes you the winner.'

'No one's winning,' she said.

'I can just imagine the pleasure he's going to get out of this. He's getting it already, isn't he? Knowing this is the last time.'

'He thinks I'm having my hair done. He'll have to get his pleasure out of that.'

'What's he going to think of it when he sees it? I just may muss it up a little.'

'You always knew it would have to be like this.'

'Maybe that's what crippled me. The knowledge he'd be crowing in the end.'

'He'd better crow quietly. I don't think he'll crow. I won't let him.'

'This year, next year — you'll let him. Finally, it'll be something to keep warm between you. The one little defused bomb safe in the family locker.'

'Don't,' she said.

'You're going to be good from now on, am I right, Miss Muffet? *Mrs* Muffet. You've had your scary little adventure and from now on . . .'

'I don't know what I'm going to be. I never thought I'd get involved in anything like this. Instead of which, look at me.'

'For the last time, I know. I *am* looking at you. Believe me, you haven't really had the full experience.'

'Full enough,' she said. 'How many times have I come to see you?'

'You never really came at all,' he said, 'did you? You never wanted to. And you think you've seen it all? You think he's the champ? He isn't.'

'I think I'd better be going,' she said.

'I'd like to cut it all off, you know that? Your hair. Leave you bald as an egg and send you home like that, and then watch you live happily ever after, with him, and the kids.'

'I don't know you like this.'

'There's a whole lot you don't know. O.K., the whistle's blown; time's up. The bite you took out of the apple doesn't even show, is that what you think? It can all be made good again? Adam is still the one man in little Evie's life? No, ma'am. There are other men and you know it. You won't be able to stop looking at them, knowing they can all do it for you, every single one of them. You won't ever be back with him all alone in the garden. See one snake, you've seen 'em all? That won't ever be true again, no matter how much you decide you love him after all.'

'Please don't,' she said.

'Because let me tell you something, you missed the big experience; you were never in the final. You never had a black man. Me, I have a conscience; I have a wife; I have all kinds of problems, including loving people. You. That gets in the way. But one day try a black man, because believe me that's something you have to do before you die. And now get your clothes on. Fast.'

'I don't believe in those things,' she said.

'Think about it,' he said. 'Even if it isn't true, think about it. All the time you're being the loyal wife all over again. That's the little splinter I'm going to leave in you and whenever you put your weight down, you'll just feel it, the thorn you can't even see, only it's always there.'

'I never thought you'd be like this, of all the things I thought.'

'Surprise! Your husband'll catch sight of you sometimes and there'll be a look in your eye, a vein that fattens somewhere in your throat, and he'll think you're thinking about me, he'll think that it's the past that's come into your mind, and instead it'll be the future. Something you'll always be sorry until you do it.'

'I really do have to go now.'

'I'll be thinking about you,' he said, 'both of you. You and him. I'll be thinking about the three of you.'

PORTRAIT OF A LADY

I was never quite clear why Roy Powell asked me to come to lunch at the same time as my daughter. Sarah is, after all, a grown-up young woman and his announced purpose was to commission a portrait of his noble wife. Where and why did I come in? Presumably as chauffeur, to judge from the remoteness of Heol Tyn-y-fron (sketch-map enclosed). It is true that Powell sent word that he had always wanted to meet me, but during his twenty years as a publisher he had never had me to one of his corner table lunches at the Étoile or suggested that I compose one of those monographs, for which he had been commissioning editor, about Great Cities of the World. (One of our senior novelists, I recall, wrote quite entrancingly on Manchester.) Understandably, despite his Chancellor's Medal and the Prix de Perpignan, Powell could not live by poetry alone and his career as a publisher had recently ended only because his company's new American proprietors had offered him a generous early retirement to which his muse, recently decked with the Oslo Award, made no objection. He would henceforth devote himself entirely to her rural cultivation. For our first meeting, therefore, I was obliged to drive over a hundred miles into the Welsh hills about which he was so enthusiastically captious in *Daff o'Dales and Other Recensions* (1975). It would, I told myself, be worth it in order to shake a hand which had written 'some of the most mordant post-modernist verse of his dissentient generation' (A.A.), even if I could wish that it had been extended in more accessible circumstances. Sarah and I set out on a numbingly cold day in the post-Christmas rump of December. Despite Powell's minuscule annotations on the photocopied Ordnance Survey sheet, we passed several times through freezing villages with very consonantal names before we managed to take the right turning for Heol Tyn-y-fron.

I must confess that I have always been wary of poets, as of musicians. Are not music and poetry the senior services of the arts? It is true that my first published work was a poem, in the sense that it was a sequence of raggedly printed lines in an undergraduate magazine, but I have never dared to think of myself as a poet, even if much of my youth was spent in the composition of verses, in languages dead enough to feel no pain at my contortion of their syntax. Elegiacs and iambics were my strongest metres, but I could handle Sapphics and Alcaics on a good day. If I learned to avoid false quantities in Latin and Greek, I never fully understood stress and thus I have remained disqualified from versifying in my native tongue. English poetry has rarely meant much to me as a reader. I rate Byron's letters above his Parnassian flights and, when it comes to moderns, I prefer Ritsos or Cavafy to the now surely indispensable Mr X or the ice-bright Ms Y. I cannot understand, though I am ready to admire, the neo-Christian austerities of 'our most plangently penetrating' (A.A.) candidate for the mantle of Mr Eliot. As for the latter, I have only to refresh my memory of his camp acidity to share his distaste for the prospect, now happily remote, of having to meet him.

As we circled and circled (ah, those hosts of Midian, were they using one of Roy Powell's maps?) in search of Heol Tyn-y-fron, my main concern was less to commend myself to 'That mirthful Merlin/ Of the unsmiling grin' (C.J.'s 'Welsh Wails') than to secure the commission for my daughter, thus advancing her career and, if it was not too much to hope, allowing her to pay her own gas bill for the coming quarter. When, at length, we spotted a large grey brick house, which seemed to have sprung up behind a stand, or slouch, of wind-cowed trees since the last time we took that particular bend, it was well after one o'clock and we were both cold and hungry.

A rusty Sunbeam Talbot was parked in the frost-crunchy gravel of the drive, but no prompt welcome opened the heavy front door. Was there anyone at home? Surely our arrival was obvious. Yet we waited. I raised myself to look over the sill of one of the Georgian windows and was unnerved to discover that I was pressing my nose against black paint: the house's glass eye was false. When I pulled the metal bud which, in its sconce of acanthus leaves, served in the office of a bell, it came out a long way on a rusting stalk and produced a jangling so loud that a comedy director might have considered its clangour to be over the top. In the way of things, we could not now long remain undiscovered.

The gauntness of Heol Tyn-y-fron and its general air of being a cadet wing of the House of Usher hardly led us to expect a servant. Hence my eye sought to bless the Shetlanded girl who at last gave us reluctant entrance with the allure of the sophisticated musical lady whom Sarah was destined to portray. The literally thick young person before us proved, in fact, to be the *au pair*. Her thickness was due to the quantity of clothing she was prudent enough to wear. She asked us whether we would like to come in. Guilelessly, we said that we would rather. If it was cold outside, baby, it was colder in. If the hall had been hung with sides of beef they would have been safe against corruption.

A rawly orange fire slumped in the drawing room grate. Our host, wisely enough, was slumped beside it, in a low chair whose tripes were resting on the floor. He was of spectral aspect, grey and black, like a Victorian illustration, hardly the image summoned up by C.J.'s 'Roaring Boy who entertains contradictions'. However, Mr Powell certainly did not appear disposed to entertain anything else very much. He made us no more welcome than a Final Notice. His lack of greeting was so marked that I took out my diary in order to make sure that we had come on the right day. Luckily, my new Christmas watch had a calendar. There was indeed no mistake. We waited for further instructions.

Despite the sombreness of the day and the heavy curtains, hanging from high wooden railings in rugous swathes, the room was without a lamp. There were, however, two discernible pianos and a harp, with falling angel. A very narrow, very high book-case contained a century's supply of compressed magazines. A mahogany table was covered with a selection of antique flintlocks and a crossbow. There were no pictures on any of the walls. Where was that keen interest in the visual arts which might account for summoning a brilliant young portraitist, and her chauffeur sire, from London? On the other hand, there was no shortage of Christmas decorations, though one could hardly call them cheer. Gilded fir cones and sprigs of dusty holly scaled the black book-case and nested on the curtain rails. A profusion of silvered conkers, like E.P.N.S. donkey droppings, was piled on any available concave vessel. The festive impact was muted by the impression that all these decorations had been inherited from Miss Havisham. A heap of her riding costumes and capes appeared to be dumped, in greening pride, on a second large table against the far, damp-pimpled wall. This table was, it seemed, a veteran of foreign wars: lacking a leg, it had been supplied with an upended leather suitcase in lieu.

I decided, after coughing a little, to no noticeable effect, to apologise for our lateness. Our host hoisted a forgiving gesture with a tweedy arm and delivered himself of the disturbing reassurance that there was plenty of time before lunch. Would we like a drink meanwhile? And if so, what? I looked round for some bottles from which I might make a tactful choice. Skeins of unreachable, or at least unreached, cobweb softened the corners of the room and colonised the dado. Layers of ashen dust on more accessible areas suggested the proximity of a grousy volcano. In the circumstances, I thought it malapert to ask for the necessary whisky, as W.H.A. might have put it. I contented myself with saying, 'Personally, I should very much like a glass of wine.'

Our host, who now rose to an impressive height and gestured us towards the fire, proved that he had teeth by giving me a lofty wince. '*Wine*,' he said, as if I had nominated a brew distilled only once a century in a remote Andean hamlet, 'there you have me!'

How does one recover from such a social false quantity, so blatant a mistake in stress? My daughter's commission might well depend upon pitching from the deep bunker on to the green, to choose a prosaic image. What should I have asked for? A Sidecar? A Screwdriver? A Manhattan? A *lager*, old man? I removed my now less blue hands from the fire and played safe: 'Sherry?'

'Medium or dry?'

Choices! 'Oh, dry,' I said.

The glass finally offered from the shadows was doubtless very historical, but it was also chipped and not very full. As I made it last, our host crouched up to the fire again. He neither asked whether we had had a reasonable drive on the black ice nor did he explain his wife's absence. Silence may be golden but gold can be rather ponderous. After remaining off the air for several minutes, I had recourse to interviewing a 'considerable original' (J.S.). What did they do down in Gwent, I wanted to know, or chose to ask, apart from writing seminal verse and practising the harp, which I took to be Lady Germaine Powell's favourite weapon? The Welsh hills seemed not to afford any very lively counterpoint to the cultivation of the muses.

'We go to sales,' Powell said.

'*Sales?* What sort of sales?'

'Auctions,' he said. 'We go to three or four a week.'

'And do you buy a lot?'

'A great deal,' he said. 'We're inveterate purchasers. You see, this place needs a lot of furniture. When we first came here, it was nothing but an empty wreck.'

In view of the fissures across the ceiling and the spearing draughts that pushed past the ill-fitting windows, it was tempting to observe that the place was now a rather full wreck. Instead, I plumbed my glass for the last drop of Amontillado and wondered what my next question should be. Was he of the Martian faction or not? It is so easy to say the wrong thing to prizewinning poets who have recently been praised in Norwegian.

'Ah, here's Germaine,' Roy Powell said, sparing himself further investigation.

I retracted my tongue from the bottom of my glass and stood up as a youngish woman in a Victorian dress came into the room at a peculiar angle. It is not easy to enter in profile and then to advance, without ever looking directly where you are going, between the benefits of frequent attendance in salerooms, but Lady Germaine Powell had clearly practised. She contrived to offer her left profile and then her right, hanging her head forward in the style of someone who seemed to expect to figure on a commemorative stamp, almost certainly of a high denomination.

'I'm sorry to be late,' she said, as if she had come to school without a chitty, 'but I've been feeding Octavia.'

Was this another trap? Had she been throwing antelope to their pet tiger? Or merely some as-seen-on-T.V. crispy-crunchies to the moggy in the back kitchen? Or had she — yes, she had! — been offering one of those lace-covered breasts to the infant Powell? Her wistful expression, neither sullen nor satisfied, made her seem at once younger than a mother and older than a bride. When she sat down, for just long enough to allow mad Blodwyn to deliver what was undoubtedly a re-hearsed announcement, 'Luncheon is served, my lady,' I was surprised by the muscular calves visible beneath the raised pelmet of her skirt. One does not expect anyone so gracious to be equipped to play third-division soccer.

We walked down a flagged corridor which, in Edgar Allan Poe, would have led to something more dire than luncheon. The walls were scabbed with impetigo, while the sagging lintel of the dining room looked as though it needed no Samson to bring it down. There was a huge oak table between the two spinets (one with its lot number still chalked on the side). Under an armorial chimney-piece, another small fire did the hottest stuff it could. I was invited to take the chair by the hearth; Sarah was gestured to take the place opposite me. Since the Arctic Circle passed between us, and she was to be on the north side of it, I took off my jacket and handed it to her. Captain Oakes would surely have done the same, but Roy Powell was surprised. 'A very noble gesture that,' he said. Had I cheated him of the pleasure of seeing Sarah rigidify before his poetic eyes? Hospitality can take some odd forms.

What I assumed to be the first course consisted of turkey and carrot soup. Since it was now well into the afternoon, I had quite an appetite, which almost precipitated me into another error. Until I looked closely, I did not appreciate that the stack of brown bread on a plate adjacent to the north pole was in fact a pile of sandwiches, with slices of grey ham in them. This proved to be our main nourishment. The pudding was pieces of tinned pineapple in what appeared to be diluted toothpaste. By some stroke of culinary ingenuity, this dessert was served tepid.

Now there was, of course, no call for an elaborate meal.

Perhaps only a spoiled Francophile would confess himself disappointed at such a collation. If our hosts had tried to salt it with a little amiable conversation, if they had favoured us with a burst of lyricism in progress or intoned a mantra, well, we should at least have been less aware of the rumblings of our stomachs as they came to what terms they could with the invading provender. But neither of them said an emollient word. Weary of prompting the taciturn, I embarked on a monologue with which I had had some previous small success. It concerned a man who accused me of having libelled him in a T.V. play, in which one of my more delightful characters did indeed carry his unlikely surname, by the purest of coincidences. However, for full denunciatory effect, my correspondent also found it sinister that I had given my character the first name Geoffrey: for him, perhaps understandably, this heaped Ossa on Pelion. But he went a little far, I thought, in advising me that Geoffrey was (his italics) *a rather uncommon name*. My little turn consisted in reporting the text of my reply to him which, in reality, I had been wise enough to leave unsent. In it I dared to doubt whether Geoffrey was *that* unusual and, in substantiation, I cited the views of my lawyer Geoffrey, my accountant Geoffrey, my Uncle Geoffrey and, as it happened, my *Aunt* Geoffrey, not to mention my cook, Geoffrey, and my tortoise (Geoffrey). My house, I made skittishly bold to add, was also called Geoffrey and so was my car. By the time I had concluded my little party piece (it was, I beg you to believe, more amusing when performed than when offered in sober print), both Sarah and her father were convulsed by the accumulated absurdity of it all. Our laughter was forced up the scale towards hysteria by the icy puzzlement with which Roy and Lady Germaine greeted the banalisation of Geoffrey. Little frowns furrowed their foreheads, but only the most vigilantly optimistic auctioneer could have read them for positive reactions. Certain truths must be faced: I was not a hit in Gwent.

When the last of the diluted toothpaste had gone from our plates, we were invited to return to the drawing room for coffee. It turned out to be of a brownish perspicuity, a word which Anthony Burgess was once good enough to remind me carries the implication that one can see through it. One could indeed, right down to the cracks at the bottom of the interesting cups. While we were being grateful for the warmth this drink supplied, mad Blodwyn brought in a basket, as it might be direct from the bullrushes, and offered its infant contents to Lady Germaine. The baby was nut-coloured in a patchy sort of way, rather as if there had not been enough varnish to finish the job properly. Lady Germaine inspected it with grand satisfaction, rather as a *maître cuisinier* might a dish which still had a while to cook but seemed to be going quite well so far. Mad Blodwyn then returned with it to the kitchen, or wherever it was quartered.

Lady Germaine continued to offer her aristocratic profiles, with the effect of someone watching a game of ghostly tennis. I recalled reading that Sicilian women avoid looking directly at men, for fear of losing their virtue, and wondered whether her ladyship perhaps had kin in Partinico. No, her early life had been spent, she told us, partly in Keenya, or Ken-ya as she feared we should now pronounce it. She recalled how her father, the Earl, a resident of Happy Valley, once invited someone to lunch who had stayed for two years. I was uncertain whether this was a stock post-prandial anecdote or whether it was uttered with specifically apotropaic intent. At all events, I was quick to set her mind at rest: she should on no account look out mosquito nets for us. We should be gone well before the spring. Indeed, I said, with italicised force, we should be *leaving very soon*, since we had a good way to drive.

Our host proposed a tour of the house before it was dark, not that it had ever been markedly light. Our circuit established that the Powells must indeed have been to innumerable auctions. Every room offered massive evidence of their acquisitive zeal. Even the bathroom — where the likeliest implement in regular use should have been an ice-pick — was crammed with Victoriana of which its previous owners can surely never have hoped to be delivered, let alone at a price. Black candles swung out on brass arms over the Plimsoll-lined tub, which reposed on rusty claw and ball feet. Dire china objects stood in rush-hour proximity on narrow, pendent shelves curved like long-bows under their hideous burdens. There was an organ in the spare bedroom and a pianola in the morning room. Hymns more ancient than modern were ranged on green brass music-stands. Roy Powell actually switched on a light to enable us to see the vicar's own original emendations to text and setting. The light was as yellow as what it faintly illumined: I had a notion that some auctioneer had sold our hosts one of Edison's original bulbs.

Somewhere in the servants' quarters it occurred to me that Roaring Boy could be spoonerised as Boring Roy; it was hardly a sample of great intellectual resource but it induced a nice warm glow in a house where strong men might have been found huddled around a pilot light. Finally we were back in the drawing room, where the fire had dwindled to terminal pallor. I declared that we really had to be going. Although the issue of the portrait remained unbroached, Roy Powell appeared be-latedly anxious that he had not sufficiently entertained us. If he did not go so far as offering a cup of tea, he did now tell us, with a certain urgency, that he had once been pissed on by a tiger at the Manchester Zoo. This confession had the same convulsive effect on him as the team of Geoffreys had on me: he clung to himself and shuddered ecstatically for several seconds. The hell with it, I thought: if he won't mention the subject, I will. 'I say,' I said, with paternal casualness, 'hadn't you people better talk about this portrait?' There! We had been at Heol Tyn-y-fron for three hours. I could scarcely be accused of importunate salesmanship.

'Ah yes, the portrait,' Roy Powell said, as if he had been asked to recite one of his lesser-known works, only to find that, though he was familiar with the title, he had forgotten the first line. 'The portrait, the portrait . . . ' Lady Germaine appeared strenuously exercised by the mention of the painting. She might have been watching a Centre Court rally which accelerated so pacily that soon she was offering us both her profiles all but simultaneously.

'I think you should be very frank about price,' I said. 'However, I'll leave you to sort out the details. It's not some-thing that directly concerns me. I'll go into the hall and have a look at the library again, shall I?'

I had time to walk six or seven times past the cobwebbed bells on the pantry wall, where the plaster was divided into more counties and boroughs than England had before the great rationalisation, and back as far as the library, whose damp shelves contained the only books I have ever seen which seemed to be *leaking*. Then the drawing room door opened and I heard Roy announce that they would look forward most keenly to seeing Sarah again in order to make a start. In view of her prices, they would have to think about the dimensions, but it was agreed that the portrait should have a Victorian musical motif. Lady Germaine might fondle her harp, or lean on a spinet, or inspect a harmonium, or pedal an organ. *À débattre, n'est-ce pas?*

I made a fulsome speech of gratitude — fiction can be a useful training — and we went out into the sub-zero warmth of the December evening. Although no one could have been spying on us from the hall window, since it was the painted facsimile, we kept our faces wilfully straight until I had edged past the moribund Sunbeam Talbot (was it perhaps some kind of rare musical box?) and we were once again on the road to London. I am not sure exactly what the joke was, but it doubled us up so irresistibly that I had to pull into a lay-by and shed happy tears. 'Never mind,' I said, when at last I was capable of words, 'it was worth it. A commission is a commission.'

'I think I'll paint her full-face,' Sarah said.

When she heard nothing from Gwent for several weeks, she decided to damn well give them a call. The telephone rang for some time. We imagined the compulsively purchasing couple with their hands full of the latest sale-room trophy — several tubas perhaps, or the organ from St David's Cathedral — wondering whether it was worth the trouble of disturbing the dust on the receiver. Finally it was lifted and the Lady Germaine's voice was heard to say 'Yes', in the reluctant tone of a coerced bride at some arranged wedding in nineteenth-century Galway.

'I'm calling about when you want me to come down and start doing some studies for the portrait.'

'Oh the portrait!' It might have been a song, this time, for which the musical lady had forgotten the tune. 'Oh the portrait . . .'

'Yes. We talked about it, you may remember, when we came to see you just after Christmas. It's almost Happy Easter.'

'The thing is,' Germaine said, 'we're moving.'

'Moving?'

'Oh yes. We've found this amazing eighteenth-century rural Gothic folly near Bath. We're selling this and moving there and I'm sure you'll understand that that means all kinds of revisions to our decorative plans. You don't do silhouettes at all, do you?'

'Can you credit it?' Sarah said, when the line had gone dead.

'Leaving Heol Tyn-y-fron!' I said. 'What can have possessed them?'

My daughter considered that one for a moment. 'Perhaps they felt there wasn't anything more they could do to it,' she said.

STANDARDS

How was it that Magnus Molyneux was so promptly established as the star of our Cambridge generation? Did he not arrive by more or less the same train as the rest of us? Was he not given the same indiscriminate welcome that declared itself in myriad invitations to join all kinds of society, from the Caledonians (hoots, toots) to the C.U. Majlis, yes indeed? Did he too not rush to see a tutor having trouble with his pipe who just about remembered him from a scholarship interview, hoped that he would find his way around all right, and send the next one in now, would you be good enough? The memoirist asks himself, and cannot quite catch the answer, when the young Molyneux first dissociated himself from the common herd and felt the bossy thrust of those metaphorical antlers which would mark him as its monarch presumptive. Magnus was neither at a fashionable college nor had he emerged from one of those privileged public schools, freemasonries with lodges at King's and Trinity, which could make smooth the way for their favourite sons. Yet within a few months at the outside, it was clear that Magnus had not merely come up but that he had unmistakably arrived.

Cambridge is not Oxford, nor were the early Fifties like the Twenties. Magnus had none of the showy scintillation of the young Harold Acton. It was inconceivable that he should, oh, take a lobster to a seminar. Unlike Oxonian contemporaries, he did not dream of going camply patrician in purple corduroy or of inviting Orson Welles, *de haut en haut*, to a sherry party (he never gave them) and charging the other guests a quid for the honour. There was something becomingly diffident about Magnus, if not all that much. He was notably unfacetious: even those who accused him, unfairly, of blowing his own trumpet could never say that he cried ha-ha. Did that Irish blood render him suspicious of blarney? Loathing Shaw and frowning at Wilde (the epigram, he announced, was the cliché that dared not speak its name), Magnus embarked on Eng. lit. as upon some unchildish crusade. Disinclined to engage on anything so jejune as 'creative writing', he reassured his scribbling peers by the promise not to compete for the same laurels; his were to be cut from a very high branch. No poet, he was our poets' most reliable, and earliest, friend. They hurried to Selwyn to submit their Eliotesque verses to his precocious pounding. No one knew how, at his age, he knew, but everyone knew that he knew, you know.

Before you could say naif, Magnus controlled all the passes with access to the fancier undergraduate publications. Literature was a vocation and he addressed himself to it, for a while, with monastic severity. No one could call him hairy, but he could be shirty: when I wrote the 'book' for an undergraduate musical comedy, Annie France ran to tell me that it had disqualified me for ever, according to Magnus, from the tally of significant members of our generation. The oracle had spoken, but would not, she made it clear, be speaking again, at least to me. If I sobbed myself to sleep, that was not Molyneux's concern; standards were.

Who can judge, until all the evidence is sifted, just how shaping his spirit was? For thirty years now he has enjoyed that covert, enviable reputation which Proust attached to those professorial medical men whose services are craved only when all other treatment has failed. Thom would rush to him, in a lather and in leather, with muscular strophes hymning the head-on, heart-off collision of tomahto and tomayto. John, who promised so very much and even now writes arguably the best detective story reviews in the world, might never have come through his block but for the timely suggestion that he roast fiction for *Critique*. Magnus became its editor during his Ph.D. studies and his mordant conciseness soon proved how brief a man could be without being witty: a single tick in the margin of a manuscript made its author's day, and could last well into the night. Magnus conferred on a chosen few a measure of the greatness which his own parents had wished upon him at the font, where he had been freely awarded what

Pompey himself had had to earn.

We were not friends. We were scarcely acquaintances. When I was on the point of being printed, by a 'guest editor', in a Young Writers' magazine, Magnus returned to his duties in time to 'pull' my sorry story. A one-line note swore that I should thank him for the decision one day. (It has yet to dawn.) That curt scribble is the only contribution I have been able to make to the Molyneux archive at the University of Texas at Austin: a Xerox awaits the footnote his eulogist may give it. When my first novel was published, I was simple – some might say servile – enough to send him a copy. One reviewer had actually preferred it to *Ten North Frederick*, which came out in the same week. Magnus liked my novel only as much as he liked O'Hara's; and he hated O'Hara's. If he loved literature, he did not bestow many kisses on its contemporary instances. Did I mention that he believed in standards? It is worth repeating; and he repeated it.

Annie France did tell me the exact title of Magnus' thesis and I do remember saying that it was almost a thesis in itself, but since it was never completed, I had no chance to share its swingeing insights into the Romantic delusion whose origins he had traced to a particular moment and place, in Scotland, I think. He had been shrewdly guided by Neil Laidlaw, who knew to a nicety which academic fields could be most profitably ploughed with a view to future preferment. Laidlaw's own record of publications was not impressive, save by its exiguousness, but his return to Cambridge had coincided with a demand for the kind of administrative intelligence he had displayed in A.M.G.O.T. His stint in Germany, where he had married a well-born refugee whose papa had fled to Brazil via Basle, gave the handsome, euphonious Laidlaw all the credentials he needed. He and his dark-eyed lady, whose unfrozen funds irrigated their comfortable life, used to entertain *le tout* Cambridge at their Georgian place on the Madingley road. I went once, thanks to a general invitation to a squad of Footlights, to a Sunday tea where there was informed whispering about The Situation and several people had just come back, if you didn't mind them saying so, from destinations where one should have been in order to understand the reason why 'war criminal' wasn't a *helpful* expression. A member of

C.U.M.S. sang Schubert *lieder* to Kirsten Laidlaw's accompaniment on a Conrad Graf cabinet piano which was said to be a marvel, though I questioned her use of the bassoon stop. Magnus read a book throughout the recital, but it was one of Neil's; indeed, it was the only one. The shortest word in the title was 'Prolegomena'.

Magnus' researches took him, on Guggenheim cash, to Cambridge, Mass. Annie France went with him, on a project of her own; no limpet ever had more independence than Annie. They were married in Provincetown, with a Nobel witness, in a snowstorm. She was pregnant before they returned to London. Magnus had 'got a lot out of the U.S.', including a stock of shirts with button-down collars and a certain impatience to be at the centre of things. With Neil Laidlaw working the points, as it were, Magnus switched from romanticism and steamed smoothly into the Foreign Office. In no time he was doing position papers for people very close indeed to Anthony and Selwyn. Timothy Barrett did a piece for his sordid evening paper about 'The Newest Broom At The F.O.' I took it to be an example of egregious toadying, but it was not received as a tribute by its subject. I should perhaps mention that Timothy was not only the 'guest editor' who had been lax enough to like my juvenile short story, he had also been a suitor for Annie's slim-fingered hand. But that, I imagined, was all in the past. And so it was, as well as in the future.

Suez came as a cruel test for Magnus. Need I remind you that Eden's War sundered families and shattered social monoliths? Despite his master's many favours, Molyneux felt that he could not live Selwyn's lie. Laidlaw advised his conscience-stricken protégé on no account to make government policy the reason for his resignation. If he had to leave, let it rather be because a humbler but necessary task demanded his attention. A hand on the right shoulder at the Athenaeum secured Magnus secondment to edit *Atlantic Studies*, a diplomatic quarterly to which he contributed the milestone 'Greeks and Romans; the new Anglo-American cant', his longest published work. Its mournful tone deserved the black box in which he elected to print it.

Timothy Barrett also moved to editorial duties, but his

mission at *Style* was less high-minded, and much more highly paid. I do not believe that Annie was drawn to him by the money, whatever her friends say. Magnus had never been easy to live with; recent events had made him impossible. She thought first of the children (Peter-Paul and, of course, Emma) and then of herself. When she left, Magnus wore his bruise like a rosette. He distributed so few ticks in his contributors' margins that his reputation for rigour reached its apogee just as his personal fortunes were at their nadir. He might have sneered at such schematic ironies, had they not hurt so much.

Style published several of my stories in the mid-Sixties. It also gave parties at which *Time* magazine's local representatives found spicy evidence that London was swinging, though I never observed any flagrant oscillations. Annie took to asking me about Magnus as if I were somehow his keeper. Had I seen or talked to him at all? Was he really involved with some Boston academic? Had he perhaps known her when they were at Harvard? Annie had the gift of making her own treachery into something which deserved sympathy and understanding.

'Magnus has a lot of respect for you, you know,' she said.

'I hardly think so, darling,' I said, 'though I wish it were true, I suppose. How keen we are that prigs should think well of us! And how priggish it makes us!'

'He admires your . . . *industriousness*,' she said, and was off to embrace a publisher in a ruffled shirt.

During the period when modish militants exchanged purple corduroy for workers' denim and allowed no privet to stand between them and the American Embassy, we were living in a small house off the Fulham Road. Magnus and his new wife (she did come from Boston) took a flat not far away and we began to nod to one another, he and I, when our paths crossed on the way to and from the local primary school where both our first-born sons were going. Magnus had taken on additional duties as anchor-man for an in-depth news programme on the wireless which was listened to by every single member of the cabinet. Harold Wilson's London was clamorous with calls for one's political allegiance. My mornings were shrill with appeals for solidarity; the engineers of round-robins would take almost any sparrow's feather for their caps. One grew weary and wary of so many good causes, but what was good enough for Doris and Karel and Clancy and Ken was good enough for most of us, apart from Kingsley and Bernard and Simon. One day I was telling Tim Barrett about my small experience of Morocco during the troubles, when he said, 'Why don't you go out to Saigon and tell them what it's really like?'

'I've got this script I'm writing,' I said, 'for Curly Bonaventura. About Byron.'

'He'd've gone,' Tim said.

In the end, Timothy went himself. The piece he wrote was, let us make no bones about it, superb. Annie told me that it made Harold Wilson weep. As for Magnus, whose *Atlantic Studies* made sitting on the fence look like a decisive move, he limited his acknowledgment to a tick in the margin of an unparagraphed article alluding scornfully to 'the rhetoric of the day-tripper'.

One afternoon that summer, I walked up to the Boltons to collect my son from school and saw that there was some kind of commotion in the playground. It turned out that Peter-Paul Molyneux had been knocked out by a fall from the climbing frame. There was a strange shyness in his father's attitude to the accident: his emotion embarrassed him just as it moved me. After making sure that all was well, I went home and told Sylvia what had happened and of Magnus' anguish. She had bought a couple of ducks for a small dinner party we were giving that night. Too much for four, would they prove too little for six? I was touched that she was touched by Magnus' misfortune and I telephoned to ask them over. His wife said that she expected it would be all right, but Magnus was at the library. She would check with him as soon as he returned. I have heard more effusive responses to spontaneous kindness and I said that I would await Magnus's reaction with comely humility. 'Huh?' she said.

They came. Our other guests were Miles and Felicity Grantham. He was the headmaster of a suburban grammar school; she worked in the B.B.C. African Service, at Bush House. Magnus put them at their ease by doubting the morality of educational streaming and questioning whether the Corporation had any sort of coherent notion of what it was doing in broadcasting to ex-colonial territories. Pre-dinner drinks were lively. As for Magnus' new wife, Sabina, she did not seem to know or care if her step-son would be back at school in the morning. She was writing a study of valetudinarianism in the nineteenth-century novel.

'Are you ever going to write another novel,' Magnus asked me, 'or has Hollywood completely commandeered your services?'

'Nice of you to put it that way,' I said. 'Actually, I have a book at the printer's at this very moment. I'd send you a copy, except I know what you'd think of it.'

'I doubt that very much indeed,' he said. 'I regard you as a white hope.'

'Let's go and have some dinner, shall we?'

Carving ducks and keeping the conversational stream flowing is not a mammoth task, but nor is it always easy. I swear, and would do so in front of the inquisition, that I raised the issue of whether or not I should sign the latest Open Letter On Vietnam only in order to give the ball another bounce, as it were. Had Magnus been approached, I wondered, by 'The Friends of the U.S.'?

'No,' he replied, making it sound polysyllabic.

'It's not a crowd I'm too sure about and I thought − ' Now came the fatal words. 'I gave Tim a buzz about it actually.'

'Tim? Tim who?'

'Barrett,' I said, splashing fat on to my new twill trousers. Dammit, we were living in the permissive age: we had to be frank and outspoken. I had only been honouring the prevailing ethos. 'After all, he's been there. Saigon. He . . . '

'Are you going to Greece again this year?' Felicity Grantham was good enough to inquire.

'We're talking about something,' Magnus said, 'if that doesn't inconvenience you too much. He what?'

'Oh come on, Magnus,' I said, 'or should it be Magne? He knows more about Vietnam than I do, or even you do. He may not know *everything*, but then the last man to know everything − present company excluded − died at the end of the eighteenth century, didn't he?'

'If you need Timothy Barrett's advice on whether to take a stand, how much do you seriously suppose your signature is likely to be worth?'

'I wasn't thinking of asking anything for it,' I said. 'I just wanted to know what kind of a *galère* I was getting myself into.'

'You remember,' Magnus said to Sabina, 'we were talking about that English tendency to introduce foreign words into a conversation when the topic begins to prove awkward?'

'Do you remember, darling,' I said, 'how we were saying that intellectuals have that habit of talking about you in your own presence as if you weren't there?'

'How any self-respecting person can go whoring off to Tom, Dick or Harry in order to find out what his conscience ought to tell him for himself, I cannot imagine.'

'Oh balls,' I said. 'Have some duck and let's condemn wild-fowling, shall we? Vietnam is a dog's dinner and people who know exactly what they think about it can't have much idea what thought is.'

'I don't think', Magnus said, 'that you have any right to speak like that.'

'This is my house,' I said, 'and — *en bon bourgeois* (note the foreign in there, Sabina) — I shall say what I bloody well please in it.'

I cannot remember how we got through the rest of the evening. We did not own a Conrad Graf, nor even a Broad-wood bi-chord; no one sang Schubert *lieder*. I did my best and Sylvia, I am sure, did better, but we were never invited back by either couple, despite the excellence of the Athol Brose. Some perverse vanity led me to send my novel, when it came out, to Magnus and Sabina, but if I hoped for some conciliatory effusiveness I was disappointed. A brief typed note, signed in his absence, acknowledged receipt. I was sufficiently irked to imitate my great-uncle Jessel's ploy and write a few apprecia-tive sentiments about 'the pleasure your work always gives me' at the bottom of the *Atlantic Studies* paper, before sending it back to him. When would I ever need Magnus Molyneux, after all?

His remarks about Hollywood stung, not least because the place was raw already. In the intervening years, however unwillingly, I have often determined to ram them down his smooth throat. The critic provokes new work not only by his demanding standards but also through his damnable vanity.

Unworthy as it may be, while writing my latest book I some-times fantasised about winning the Booker Prize. It is not everything, of course, but it is certainly something. Magnus would be obliged, would he not, to add my name to that list of significant contemporaries? A novel is no brief labour. My first for a few years was delivered to my publisher a few days ago. The greatest pleasure in writing is being printed, but recognition never hurt anyone's feelings. Might this year be my year? I thought so for a short time, but this morning I read that the chairman of the Booker Prize committee has just been chosen. *Maxima donabis praemia, Magne, mihi?* Scansion does not allow the addition of *num* to the question but I still expect the answer to be no.

TO BE A PILGRIM

When a film producer reminds you that you and he are 'very old friends', you may depend upon it that he is about to break some unpleasant news. And if he adds that he has decided to 'restructure his life', you would be wise to abandon any large hopes of receiving whatever sums of money may still be due to you. At the time, in the early Seventies, when Quentin Pilgrim made these declarations to me, the British film industry was suffering from the chronic palsy which often follows an attack of hiccups in the American economy. Since I had noticed that his office telephones had fallen more silent than routine tact demanded and that his debby secretary, Debbie, had left the *Evening Standard* deeply creased at the Situations Vacant column, surprise was not one of the effects his confession procured. To pile omen on omen, Columbia Pictures had just turned down our joint project, albeit 'with love', as they rather effusively put it. Films with European locations and characters who sometimes spoke in disyllables were not finding favour with the diving dollar.

'I should like to think', Quentin said, 'that this was the big chance for someone in this country to take an informed risk, but you know what the City is like.'

'The City', I said, 'is a four-letter word, somebody once told me. It seems he counted right.'

'What?' Quentin was not bitter, but he was impervious to facile jests. 'They say they want to do things with you, but when you give them the chance, they'd sooner keep their money-bags in the office safe.' During his short, juvenile acting career, Quentin had served several times in the S.S. It was not his Anglo-Saxon style to flash glances of rage and resentment, but he was clearly enraged and resentful. He had started

Albion Productions with idealistic encouragement from financiers who were now not returning his calls, but who did not fail to call loudly for returns. 'This country . . . ' he said again. 'I always believed something could be done here, but now I'm not so sure. The fact is, they don't want you to succeed.' He looked at me with that air of moral reproach which often afflicts those who are about to default on a debt. 'I'm not thinking simply about money,' he said.

Some ten years earlier, Quentin had sworn (quietly) that we could change the face of the British cinema, or at least heighten its brow an inch or two. It was no use waiting for other people to do things, he warned me, at a party in a famous flat where a whole wall was black-and-white Bosch. If you wanted to avoid the rut, you had to be prepared to get out and push. I gave him more marks for the vigour of the sentiment than for the originality of its expression. It was typical of the reforming zeal of those who realise, too late, that they had no business enjoying their public schools as much as they did. Privilege (he had proceeded to Oxford) primed him, like so many, with egalitarian condescension. Had he been a Roman patrician, Quentin would have lived for the Saturnalia, when he would have his annual chance to carry second helpings of vegetables to the slaves upon whose services he called so reluctantly, and so frequently, during the rest of the year.

As he jinked and feinted his way through show business during the next decade, Quentin combined the excitement of worthy causes (who will ever forget People's Cinema or the Film-makers' Workshop?) with the drudgery of careerism. Had not Nye himself said something about the necessity of scaling the commanding heights? Those with no head for them were destined to be petty men for ever. Quentin reached the point where he could tie up a package deal involving, say, Sophia and Greg and, on the same day, be a co-signatory on a round-robin about Apartheid with Doris and Lindsay as fellow-feelers. Head *and* heart, that was Quentin in those hearty, heady days.

Wisely, he never played the hippy: his hair was of regulation length, he was rarely in jeans and grass was not his scene. For all his urgent sense of social justice, he drove a hard bargain and a six-litre Bristol. However much he might deplore the class system, he could never quite lose the appearance of being on secondment from rather better company than he chose to keep. He was a wine-drinker who quaffed ale to put others at their ease. In short, he lived at the busy intersection of his contradictions.

If his own voice retained its unmodified and gentlemanly vowel sounds, he acquired a taste for women from more exotic backgrounds. His first wife was Peruvian, so we were promised, though her name was Gladys and her mother lived in Hounslow. To a snobbish eye, and nose, she was a stranger not only to London but also to soap and water. Quentin himself was always a severely depilated tribute to talcum powder, but his ladies (Gladys did not find long favour) were made of stronger, and hairier, stuff. The latest was a T.V. personality who not only belted songs but looked quite capable of belting her guests on 'The Bobby Baines Show'.

Her given name, so the gossips maintained, was Felicity, but she had once played a copper in a panto and had been Bobby ever since. Her aggressive glottal stoppages often embarrassed the celebrities in the fluorescent red 'hot seat' which her inquisitions had made notorious. It was less often the savage candour of her questions which fazed the famous than their difficulty in understanding them. *Ci-devant* Felicity was a feminist so *engagée* that the mere use of the female pronoun, or of the male, could provoke charges of sexism. The Phillimore Gardens dinner table, to which we were occasionally summoned, to eat food prepared – or at least purchased – by Quentin, was a nervous venue for Bobby's guests. All conversational commerce save hers tended to be contraband.

The 'Pilgrims' were not, in fact, joined together in matrimony. However, they did have a child, Jerome, who excited in me such violent feelings of aversion that I felt obliged to hold long expiatory talks with him in his loud bedroom. He was only seven, I think, when Quentin decided that England was too tight a little island to contain him, but Jerome had all the stereo equipment and discs his mother's contacts could provide. He kept the volume at a force which could reach Eastern Europe. I would yell polite inquiries about school, and the football results, while the Stones rained so brutal a lapidation

on my ears that not even a middle-class liberal could believe
that he wholly deserved it.

'I feel,' Quentin went on to tell me, on that afternoon when
he suddenly elected to tell me everything, 'that I'm living on
top of Jerome. His therapist agrees with me. So does Bobby.
She and I jointly are too much for him. He needs to breathe. So
I've decided that the logical move, for all our sakes, is California. If you want to be anywhere in this business, you have to
be at the centre.'

'Even when the centre's rather to the side,' I said.

'What?'

'How will Bobby feel about leaving the show?'

'Bobby's not leaving anything,' Quentin said. 'I'm going;
they're staying. She couldn't function out there. I'm different;
I've got a lot of contacts. I can't tell you how many people have
asked me to work in L.A. Of course,' he added, 'Bobby and I're
going to get married before we part.'

'Of course,' I said. 'Why?'

'It's still a bourgeois world,' he said. 'There's Jerome to
consider. He's a very sensitive child, you know that.'

I must say they carried the thing off with style. The cere-
mony took place at Marylebone Register Office on the Saturday afternoon and two hours later Quentin was on the Jumbo
to L.A.X. That evening, Bobby went to one of those more or
less weekly ceremonies at which people in the business surprise
and delight each other by giving and receiving beautiful
awards. She pretended to thump her male flatterer with the
tortured metal he had given her as 'Light Entertainment
Personality of the Year', because, after looking at her, he had
said, 'Well, light*er* anyway.' She accepted the congratulations
on her wedding with the old toothy grin and belted out 'My
Way' as if she had no idea Sinatra had a lien on it. The
columnists went to town on her next morning, after she had
danced till dawn with men who were not her husband, but she
wasn't bothered: 'I couldn't dance with 'im, could I, when 'e
was in mid-air and I wasn't? So sod them!'

Out on the Coast, open doors proved stickier than Quentin
had hoped; old friends had new friends and, in Beverly Hills,
new friends are best friends. He had got out fast, before shit
met fan, but the taint of failure clung to him, no matter how

often he showered. When I went to L.A. some weeks later, for huddles over a new script, I saw Quentin driving down Rodeo Drive in a small green Ford. He stopped to tell me that he might be producing an educational T.V. special before Christmas. When that is the best news a man has, he has none that is good. He even spoke of having another try with Columbia on *Rough Shoot*.

'After all, they did say "with love", didn't they?'

'Isn't that Chinese for "without money"?'

'What?' There was more weariness than impatience in his brevity. He still had the straightness of the young officer, but the old sweat was showing through his khaki shirt. The green Ford even had a stick shift. How down could a man be before he was out? I took him to dinner and we talked about a dozen ideas. Every writer has a project he likes to talk about; mine is a T.V. series about Alexander the Great. I told him how the Macedonians cut a dog in half before marching out to battle, their entire force passing between the severed portions. 'Strong stuff,' he said.

'But educational,' I said.

'I don't know what I'm going to do,' he said over the *demi-tasse*. 'I simply don't.'

'Something'll turn up,' I said. 'What about "Underwater Cohen"? Did I ever tell you about that one? My series about a Jewish deep-sea diver?'

The man who finally saved Quentin's bacon was, of all people, Wesley Garrett Jr. Wesley was the son of a star that had set with the Western. He was not a live wire. Indeed, had he not inherited his father's stock, and name, he would never have survived to become an executive, let alone the head of the studio. He was of a taciturnity so impenetrable that not even Bobby Baines could have found occasion to interrupt him. He bored accountants; he sent hypnotists into a coma. But he did give Quentin Pilgrim a job. No one else, it may be, would have cared, at that particular juncture, to be known to be on Wesley's payroll: he had sponsored and released one turkey after another since his assumption of office, and it looked unlikely that he could survive till Thanksgiving. Since the rule was that when a man was fired his appointees went off with him, Quentin's tenure on the 'Creative Vice-Presidency' was likely to be brief, but what drowning man tests the durability of a straw, however short?

Meanwhile, he had an office and a new car and a personalised parking space right outside the executive block. One heavy day, he and Wesley came out into the smog, on their way to democratic pastrami in the Commissary, to see the whitewashed outline of a stiff traced on the sidewalk around their side-by-side names. The main board was due to meet in New York at the end of the week and the word was that Wesley Garrett Jr's head would roll as soon as they had straightened their legal pads. But in those few days, something remarkable happened. Wesley's youngest turkey was released and, surprise surprise, it turned out to be a swan. What's more, it laid golden eggs. The studio's stock doubled overnight. When the board met, its agenda was a mere agendum. To those on the point of ignominious departure, it sent a lease-renewing telegram: 'CONGRATULATIONS STOP STOP STOP'.

Quentin himself had no share in his patron's smash-hit, but those whom Midas touches know the rewards of gilt by association. The sour smell of failure was purged by showers of golden rain. Quentin's own little projects began to achieve lift-off before the end of the runway. He found new friends among his old friends. ('How long have you been here?' they said, and were really sore with secretaries who didn't pass on messages. *Shit!*) He was cosseted with stock options and with a bigger car, which was actually smaller but fancier. (Have you seen that new Porsche with the red upholstery?) As for Wesley, deckled change of address cards were soon in the mail. His side-kicks, who had recently been shaking in their shoes, decided to order bigger boots. Quentin took up with a scenic designer called Randy who had been shacked up with a seven-foot basketball player. She came from Iowa and had never seen a black man till she was twenty years old, and ready for it. Taking her from this black dude was a real emancipation for Quentin. When you do that to somebody, you're treating him as a genuine equal finally, aren't you?

Quentin was put in charge of Worldwide Production, but it was understood that he would be offered something with more scope as soon as things shook down a little. He had Sherryl and

Charmaine, the nose-bobbed secretaries appropriate to his refitted office, and a deep-pile lobby large enough for two-handed handshakes with Dustin and Sidney. He had been at the studio for some weeks, but he had now arrived. At the end of the year, the erstwhile pariahs received six-figure bonuses. When Quentin skid in to London, it was on Concorde, of course, and of course he stayed at the Connaught. I read in the press that one of the great ambitions of his life was to revive American faith in British talent. I waited in all day, but I must have missed his calls. Finally, I decided that it was excessively snobbish not to get in touch with an old friend merely because he was now a big-shot. As I might have guessed, he had no idea I was in town; he would have loved to see me, he said hurriedly on the telephone, but his schedule was so tight. He was off to Cannes next morning and that evening was sacred to Jerome, for reasons I'd surely understand.

'I was just wondering one thing,' I said, 'and that is, what about *Rough Shoot* now you're . . . ?'

'*Rough Shoot?*'

'You remember. Our . . .'

'Oh, *Rough SHOOT!*' He corrected my pronunciation. 'You know what I honestly feel about that little number? Its moment has passed. I hate to say it, but its moment has passed.'

'Then don't say it again,' I said. 'But while we're on that subject . . .'

'Freddie,' Quentin said, 'forgive me, forgive me, but I've got Wes from Tokyo on the other line. Let's meet soon. When are you next in L.A.?'

What Albion Productions still owed me was perhaps 1 per cent of Quentin's next annual bonus, but the debt was evidently not included in the parameters of his present thinking. Money is indeed not everything, but there is nothing to beat it for paying bills. I did not allow myself to become obsessed, but I carried a petty and persistent grievance.

Some months later, I was crossing the States by Whisperjet and sat next to a lady who was going to Beverly Hills for dinner. By that process of divination which goes with the right kind of blue rinse, she guessed who I was and asked if I'd heard the news about Quentin. He had been knocked down while crossing Little Santa Monica and had had both his legs broken by a driver who didn't even bother to stop. 'What kind of person could do such a thing?' my neighbour wanted to know.

I thought about it. 'Maybe a very old friend?'

UNION JACK DEVELOPMENT

Not long after the birth of our first child, when we were living in a small flat in Highgate, Milstein came and baby-sat while we went to a concert. (I remember Victor Gollancz thumping his unvarnished stick on the floor of the Festival Hall and shouting '*Davies!*', in a voice that brooked no modesty.) Milstein arrived in time to see me clearing away my spiral notebooks – always bought at the Librairie Joseph Gibert, in the Boul' Mich – and locking them into a desk drawer. 'Why the HELL are you doing that?' he demanded.

'Look here,' I said, 'there are some things in them that I wouldn't particularly want anyone else to see.'

'WHAT'S THE MATTER WITH YOU?' he said. 'DON'T YOU TRUST ME?'

'It's not a question of trust exactly,' I said.

'CHRIST, I wouldn't go reading your notebooks without permission. What do you think I AM?'

He promises me that I looked somewhat hurt by this reassurance. 'Why?' I am supposed to have replied. 'Aren't you even interested?'

I hope I am not a gross snooper, rifling secrets from my friends' archives or prospecting greedily for skeletons in their cupboards, but I confess that I rarely deny myself a glance at the correspondence on vacant desks, nor can I resist a close reading of the entrails of any strange house in which I happen to be left alone. The writer is a kind of spiritual burglar who leaves with swag that cannot be marked on any routine inventory.

We enjoyed a period in the late Sixties when travel was cheap and screen-writing more than usually well paid. I was easily convinced by the Maughamian gospel that the world should be one's oyster, and that there might as well be an 'r' in every month: why not go somewhere warm and locally colourful and sit on a tropical terrace while itemising the iniquities of the class system or the hypocrisies of colonialism?

An emigré novelist, whose work I had saluted in a review, wrote to me advertising the charms of South America, especially of Uruguay, then celebrated as 'the Switzerland' of its continent, a welfare state where early retirement took place at thirty-five. I inquired nervously about the frequency of revolutions. My correspondent promised that, provided one did not impede the take-over of the main Post Office or the radio station by khaki persons in a hurry, there was nothing to fear. These things caused less trouble than the strikes which were making Britain a by-word for social disintegration. Soon the *tupamaros* were to spill a lot of blood on his amiable version of life in Uruguay, but we were naive enough to set off, innocent of the meaning even of jet-lag which sent us reeling round the *sandwicherias* of Buenos Aires like drunken men.

By the time we arrived in Punta del Este, Gordon was dead. He had painted a seductive picture of the sophistication of '*Esteños*', those summer visitors from B.A. who hopped across the estuary to bring glamour to the resort from which, a generation earlier, they could hear the guns of H.M.S. *Exeter* and her escorts as they engaged *Graf Spee*. Our timing, however, was bad: it was out of season. There were few signs of sophistication, or indeed of life. We found temporary accommodation in a brick block of holiday flatlets whose caretaker was German. He may have been of an entirely harmless provenance, but his domain was divided into numbered '*bloques*' and he assigned us to our quarters with a firmness I could not relish. From our high window we could see Punta del Este's two remarkable beaches, back to back on the point which fingered the Atlantic: one was caressed by a lapping sea, the other − facing in an angrier direction − was thrashed by breakers. A small oil tanker with a back problem had been rolled on to the rocks below our *bloque* and the hard sea was drumming a bass tune on its hull. Soon the rain began to fall.

The helpful German introduced us to a local estate agent.

She was a woman of languorous sighs, and size, who drove us from villa to locked villa in a small Renault, its gear shift under her flowery skirt. Confidence and melancholy were co-tenants of her soft frame: she doubted whether she had anything on her books which we, or she, would like. Punta del Este took on the unexciting aspect of an extremely remote and deserted Le Touquet. Having looked at the umpteenth unromantic holiday home, I asked her where in the world, if she had the choice, she would elect to go. She looked at me with Niobic sadness and exhaled, with unforgettably passionate longing, the single word '*Europe!*'

After a cultural detour to Cuzco and Macchu-Picchu, we alighted finally in Jamaica. The British had abandoned their colonial burden, but not their privileges or hegemony. It was no great credit to my political consciousness, but I rejoiced at the evidence of English-speaking comforts. We might not be rich enough to rent the magnificent spread of an absentee magnate, but we could certainly manage the asking price for a pretty little place with a mere two or three servants. The writer's convenient alibi served to calm my *engagés* misgivings: how could I render that sardonic account of the expatriate life if I had not lived it for a while?

The second son of a Scottish earl made a jollier companion to our house-hunting than the lugubrious *señora*. Gaudy hibiscus trumpeted the splendours of the island. Were those grapefruit trees? Could that possibly be frangipani? Oh Willie Maugham, were these not your footsteps? Lord Gary McGarry arranged for us to move into the little house we had finally chosen, from a delectable selection, with the briefest of delays. Union Jack Development was a few miles from Ocho Rios and its newness was announced by the roughness of the road through its unspoiled pines and by the heaps of yellow rubble visible between us and the aquamarine Caribbean. Our white walls were swagged with purple bougainvillaea and orange bignonia and the screen doors of the living room opened directly on to a little swimming pool where my daughter and I were soon exchanging underwater handshakes. We had, I could be forgiven for believing, at last arrived.

The cook's name was Delilah. On our first evening, she produced a palatable meal of grilled liver and fried plantain, followed by a tropical fruit salad. The next day, she promised, she would take my wife to the market and then she would really show us something. The lotus, it seemed, was to become our staple diet. I defended myself against a charge of parasitism by a routine of industry. There was a quiet terrace off the cool bedroom where we slept in the owner's large bed and there I set up my typewriter and settled down to being no mere tourist.

Union Jack Development would one day sport a shopping mall and an entertainments centre with clubroom, so a brochure proclaimed. Meanwhile, there was not a great deal to do, especially since we did not like the idea of leaving Sarah and Stephen with the black servants whom we had not yet come to love and respect. It was a treat to have them, but it was also a treat when finally they left in the evening, cycling or walking (Miss Ivy) to whatever they called home. The house had no radio or T.V.; if we were not bored, neither were we entertained. Inevitably, we speculated on the character of those who had lived in the place before us. The furniture lacked personality: it had been bought, we concluded, in order to be scorched by strangers' cigarettes and stained by their stirred, never shaken, Martinis. (Ian Fleming's *Goldeneye* was not far away.) Only a large wooden desk, under the angle of the stairs, seemed to have been chosen rather than merely provided. It was in its drawers that I found the drafts of Antonia's letters, and the scraps of her diary.

I was not looking for them, of course, but of course I could not refrain from reading them. A breeze had rattled the paper in my typewriter and I took myself indoors to write my film about mercantile imperialists and saintly revolutionaries (set in an Africa I had never visited). It was while clearing space for my equipment that I had reason to go through the desk so thoroughly. At the back of the deep, dusty bottom drawer I found an album of photographs, or rather an album with some photographs in it. The first pages were crusty with tightly arranged, rather indistinct snaps, after which came a mournful succession of empty black cartridge-paper sheets to which nothing had been, or was ever likely to be, affixed.

The snaps were ill-focused and were mostly family groups. Several of the wincing males wore kilts and appeared to be ranged along a baronial wall, overlooking uncut grass. A very large dog (Irish wolfhound?) had managed to open just one eye and its whiskered master seemed to resent having to do more. I fancied that the poor quality of the definition was due to the shaking hand of the photographer who, of course, did not feature in the perfunctory parade. She was, we guessed, on a trip to meet her new in-laws who had not, it was obvious, come anything like halfway to meet her.

I cannot honestly say whether we began to feel that the house, nice as it looked, was somehow disappointing before, or after, we became aware of Antonia and of what had happened to her. Perhaps we were punished for our catty curiosity; perhaps she had somehow stained the air and blighted the apparent geniality of the place. The drafts of her letters were written in a large, lurching hand, with little noughts instead of dots on the 'i's. At times she seemed scarcely capable of writing a word without crossing it out. Never have I seen anyone seem to stammer on paper with quite such manifest apprehension. Had she married her husband in the face of Daddy's opposition, or did Daddy oppose everything? Even the weather could not be mentioned without the revision of whatever banal adjectives she had first selected. ('Wonderful' was deleted; 'blissful' substituted.) As to the main issue, Stewart was an *artist*, she explained, rather as if her father might not be familiar with so rare a breed, and he could *not* be expected to work like other people, to a *routine*. That was why they had come out to Jamaica, because there were lots of plootocrats who would want to have their portraits painted. These things, however, were bound to *take time*, which was why she was writing this letter. It took no large wit to divine that most of its underlined phrases had been taken from Stewart's angry arguments, and possibly dictated by him. His photographs gave the impression of a rather cold, resentful young man; there was nothing bold or Bohemian in his style as he lounged against that baronial balustrade. His socks were pulled right up.

Antonia seemed sufficiently anxious about her father's response to be reduced to several versions of the same text, but she was more relaxed when it came to her mother, though even with her a draft was evidently necessary before a letter could be sent. It occurs to me now that possibly Stewart insisted on checking whatever she wrote; her nervousness may have owed something to her dread of what her husband would say, or do, if she didn't come up to, or with, scratch. Had he been to one of those rigorous private schools where outdoor skills are inculcated and all outgoing correspondence is checked? Spartans must learn not to be garrulous and never to complain.

Antonia may have liked the climate, or felt that she should, but she soon abandoned the pretence of affection for Jamaica or its inhabitants. The servants began by being 'alright', but soon she was doubting their honesty. Miss Ivy was an idle old grouch (we could not wholly disagree) and Delilah, she suspected, made off with a lot of food. The refrigerator always went wrong soon after it had been filled, with the result that Ivy had to throw out anything that might have gone off. Before a week had passed, the same thing was happening to us. I called Lord Gary McGarry, who said that there had been trouble with that fridge before.

Antonia's bedroom was not conspicuous for what the young were already calling 'good vibes'. The jaggedness of her conjugal life somehow snagged on those who used its furniture. The bed was somewhere to sleep, and we slept in it, but the spell of the West Indian nights failed to work its magic in other respects. The house, we might have reported to Daddy, was O.K., but 'heavenly' would have to be excised, if we were to be honest. The little pool, a dead worm whitening in its alabaster basin, continued to be a pleasure, but once back in the house, I could not shrug off a certain malaise. Even the desk was a sorry accomplice to my work: it bit my knees. Our clothes greened in the closets and had to be hung out, like tripes, until they were dry enough to be brushed back to their original colours. And then dryness itself became an affliction: owing to the energetic activities of the workers down the road, the main water pipe was fractured. It would take several days to ship the right replacement from Kingston town. Miss Ivy carried slow buckets from a stand-pipe near the highway. I tried to type, rigid with guilt and irritation, as her slippers slurred on the hot pathway.

At first, Antonia had been at pains to give the impression that her marriage was a success. She enumerated the drinks parties to which they had been bidden and ticked off the useful contacts they had made. Stewart was flown in private planes to millionaires' hideouts, while she was left in Union Jack Development, waiting for big returns. Was she too mousy to deserve invitation? Did Stewart fancy his chances with rich wives in her tactful absence? Or was he merely drinking in all-male company, weary of her reproachful presence? She told Mummy that she was not a bit bored. Her own company could be preferable to Stewart's: when he came back, he was either fatuous with empty hopes – which led to bouts of boozy extravagance – or else he was depressed and abusive. Antonia was the witness he could have done without. His skill – to judge from a couple of oil-sketches under the stairs – was not negligible, but he was not the kind of artist who could create anything on his own. Without commissions, he sulked. When he could not justify Antonia's faith in him, he lost faith in her. Had it not been for the responsibility of a wife, he could at least have had a good time. Her beauty had been fine in stock-brokers' Surrey, where he had found her, but how irreplace-able was it in Jamaica? Daddy was supposed to be well-heeled; it wouldn't hurt him to stake them for a while, and it certainly wouldn't hurt her to ask. It had reached the stage where they could not even afford the rent. The landlord was a dentist in Montego Bay, who was being adequately patient, but it couldn't last for ever. Fearful that the dentist would come and make an ugly scene, Stewart stayed away more and more. Antonia tried to read; she even tried to paint. The stiff, unfinished sketch of an old dog that came to the house with Miss Ivy announced her untalented resignation.

Antonia's only visitor was the landlord. One day, in despair, she wrote to Daddy telling him of her humiliation at having to go literally on her *knees* to a *nigger*, at having to beg for a few more days, a week. Imagine, Daddy, a woolly-wigged nignog! Previously, I seemed to catch the tones of Stewart, sneering and sniping until she put pleading pen to airmail paper; now I could hear the golf club prejudices of the father played back in order to persuade him to bail out his degraded daughter. Either Daddy had a very hard heart or he wanted her to confess her mistake and come home. The landlord was sorry, but something would have to be done, you know. He was as embarrassed as he was insistent, it seems, because he began to bring her books and records, to alleviate the tedium, and sweeten the pill. She came to look forward to what she also dreaded, the sound of his Chevvy, and its ruptured muffler, on the gravel. There was only one form of payment she could offer. If her father would not help her, what better way to pay him back than by opening her long white legs to a darkie dentist?

For all I knew, the legs were short: I pictured her as a rather vacuous blonde, probably no more than twenty-two or three, with blanched toes in thonged sandals and silvered eyelids. Probably she had been lonely enough to crave the dentist's attentions, in a way. Having done everything she could, she had most likely returned to England, where she might one day tell Mummy of what she had had to do. ('Oh darling,' Mummy would say.) The day had clearly come when she walked out of Union Jack Development, without even stopping to clear the desk. The aura of her disillusionment hung about the house until we left, which was no more than a fortnight after our arrival. The drought continued unrepaired and Lord Gary, warned that we were at the end of our tether, offered us a superb house, with the right terrace and a different class of servant, not far from the Hilton, where I played tennis with an American who had recently taken a line in a Davis Cup tie. And so, one day, seeing us loading our stuff into the hired Ford, Miss Ivy observed: 'Tings are looking strange today.' We had not liked to advertise our defection, even though we were eager to go. Miss Ivy kissed the baby whose first steps she had witnessed in the hot living room and we quit Union Jack Development for good.

If our new cook appropriated ever increasing proportions of the excellent produce for which she went to market, the meals she provided were beyond Delilah's scope. The new pool was so large that elaborately articulated insects could practise formation-skating on its surface. The terrace was bigger than two cricket pitches and perfect for a working writer. Lord Gary was pleased that we were pleased and one day he invited us to his estate for drinks. (It turned out that he loathed Jamaica and was hoping to sell me the whole shooting match.) As we drove through downtown Ocho Rios, a black man in an

open car waved easily to his lordship. A white woman, in a
crisp linen dress, with a skin like lightly bronzed apricot, sat in
the Mustang beside him. She was about thirty and she looked
supremely at home. 'My dentist,' Lord Gary said. I looked
back. How could I reconcile the cool gaze that Antonia
returned, that languid hand so cockily resting on the dentist's
thigh, with the frantic drafts of the letters she had left in the
desk drawer? Would Daddy come out one day and visit them?

BAD BOOKS

Y ou must have been up at Cambridge with Gaines and
Ashman,' Bruce Bentley said to me the other day, when
he had got his tape recorder working. He had already
said it before, of course, when he telephoned to see if he could
come and ask a few questions about the literary scene in the
Fifties, a period now as remote, and apparently as fascinating,
as the Twenties once were to us, though for quite different
reasons. My generation looked back greenly on a time of
sexual licence and financial ease, at least for those with whom
undergraduates were likely to identify, while Bentley regards
the Fifties as a decade of provocative inhibitions and stimulat-
ing scarcity. He turned out to be a curly-headed Ph.D., with
glaucous eyes and a smile as natural as the tails you pin on
donkeys at children's parties. He had been given my number
by his professor, the editor of a grant-aided magazine who
makes sure that my books receive sour notices in his columns,
if indeed they are noticed there at all. One owes such people all
the help one can give them, does one not? I have little doubt
that when Bruce Bentley's 'informative and illuminating
analysis', with its 'revealing anecdotes of the *après-guerre*', is
widely reviewed by those who will remark in it 'the makings of
a new iconoclasm, the more valuable because it is both rigorous and broad-minded', I shall be relegated to a footnote,
while Gaines and Ashman stand as emblems of their period, as
indeed is their due, if justice must be done. I shall frown in their
shadow, like the substitute in a team photograph.

I first shook those already rather famous hands in a crowded
music room in St John's during my second year, after I had had
a poem printed in the *Young Writers' Magazine* (price one
shilling). Gaines and Ashman had, of course, long since

disdained publication in so jejune and juvenile a place, but they agreed to dress the party rather as, in the golden age, the gods could be found at table with mere mortals. Their names were whispered to me by a Trinity Classicist (now professing in California) who saw them rather as literary consuls whose dignity he was making clear to a callow provincial. The enviable pair were research fellows of their respective colleges (only false myth had them sharing rooms in their first year and conspiring, with appropriate ambition, to take Cambridge by the throat, and other parts). In fact, Bruce Bentley was good enough to tell me, they first met at the Blue Boar in their second term, their eyes clashing, as it were, on the same bint. Ashman was reading Geography, but his creative fires were already alight; he had poems to show Gaines, who encouraged the signs of a new voice about to crack. Gaines had already been in Penguin print with a story about army life in a transit camp in the canal zone. At that point, quite clearly, he was the senior partner. It may be argued that he dropped back, like a good pal, or that Peter Ashman's pace quickened, but there is no question that they were soon a pair as indistinguishable in critical opinion as they were in social circumstances. They went together like, as we used to say, facts and 'that-clauses': very, very closely.

When they walked into the music room, no lictors were required to clear the way for their advent: their own *auctoritas* (I was a Classicist myself in those days) served in the office of *fasces*. Ashman had, of course, abandoned geography (abroad was not to be one of his favourite places during his maturity) and the brilliant duo had been trained under the scrutinising eye of that unique master, The Doctor. It was The Doctor's argument, I had no need to tell Bruce Bentley but it may be worth repeating for those at the back of the class, that the creative phase of Eng. lit. had yielded to the Age of Criticism. Since The Doctor, according to the snipers who impeded his progress to academic high office, could create nothing and was able to criticise everything, it was a happy chance that he had been born on the cusp. If all the great novels had already been written, the task of ranking them was hardly less testing than their composition. Gaines and Ashman were recruited to an open-necked élite whose business was the acquisition, and propagation, of accurate taste. Although there could be no new important English novelists (or poets, sorry), the Doctor still had places in his practice for those with stout hearts and sharp scalpels.

Gaines and Ashman commended themselves not only on account of their scholastic merits. In addition, they had not been to Public Schools; their minds were uncontaminated by pansy preconceptions. The Doctor had reason to feel that he had prime, but unshaped, clay in his hands. For the first years of their novitiate, neither Gaines nor Ashman chose to disillusion him. They were prudently wary of his disapproval; those with divergent tastes from The Doctor's would find outer darkness a well-lit haven compared to the place to which he consigned them. Whatever the questionable status of Milton, the Doctor could fling a fallen angel so that his feet did not touch from dawn till dewy eve. Gaines and Ashman were obliged to a rude apprenticeship. They did not flinch, it seems, from a diet of dead ducks. They chomped dutifully on old bones of contention. They learnt appreciation and, more important, they learnt derision. Like apprentice ferrets, they were put down petty holes and incited to flush out paltry game.

Ashman's first published prose, so Bruce Bentley's bibliography will, I believe, establish beyond cavil, consisted of his devastating paragraphs on 'The Author of Sparkenbroke'. It seems that the title 'A frog he would a-wooing go' was appended subsequently, in Ashman's collected papers 1949–64, but the mordant tone was there in the original, presaging the characteristic snap of the major articles that followed. The culmination of Ashman's debunking activities came, of course, with his reassessment of D.H. Lawrence, under the rubric 'Lorenzo, the Tit-Man'. Who can forget the rebuke, more in anger than in sorrow, with which The Doctor anathematised his erstwhile protégé? Gaines, I am promised, agonised for more than a day before almost aligning himself with his friend's defiant dissidence. Bentley will show that John felt some bitterness at being placed between 'the devil and the light-blue sea', as he wryly put it.

The popularity of Gaines and Ashman as critical hatchet-men now seems difficult to understand. Bruce Bentley asked me to offer my explanation. I was, like Baldwin, appallingly frank: we might fear what they would say about us, if they ever deigned to say anything at all, but the generation of the Fifties was as much relieved as intimidated by their bold proscriptions. Whole breeds of dull dogs were put down at their behest; we were excused hysterical Russians and phoney Frenchmen, voluminous Gerries and dated Eyeties, as well as stacks of native speakers too boring or too pissy to be suffered. It was no longer frivolous, so some of us made bold to infer, to listen to, oh, Charlie Parker, say, while checking out Wallace Stevens, one of the few transatlantic brethren excused from the brutal bombardment triggered off by Ashman's *tour d'horizon* entitled 'Crapping on Parnassus'. Gaines matched him, almost, with his 'Hemming and Whoring: the unimportance of being Ernest'. Lilian Ross had done the pathfinding, perhaps, but once the target was illuminated, John homed in like a good 'un.

In the Fifties, Gaines and Ashman were regularly spoken of in the same breath, but they never, so far as Bruce Bentley can discover, actually collaborated on a single sentence. They commented on each other's work, and spoke well of it, with a meum-tuum sense that suggested heavenly twins, but they never coalesced. Resolutely heterosexual, they provoked envy but never scandal. Critically, they were, for all their erudition, on the side of rude common sense. When it came to it, they tended to flatter the mundane view, while at the same time appearing to indulge in paradoxical daring. If they were quick to throw up the windows in order to clear the fetid atmosphere of the ivory tower, the fresh air they let in was the usual stuff breathed by most people outside. Ashman's huge success with his first novel was evidence less of its originality (so a backbiter might gnash) than of his capacity to attune himself to the public taste, while still appearing an 'intellectual maverick' (*Spectator*).

Gaines never seemed to resent Ashman's great leap forward. He spoke well, and frequently, of his friend's novel and was not to be conscripted into reservations. The nasty word was that Peter had been inspired by John's own manuscript version of a novel which he himself was to publish only four months after Peter's and which, in the cruel way of these things, was said to be derivative from what it had actually preceded. Bruce Bentley smirked, but kept silent, when I quizzed him on this. Gaines' book may have blazed the trail it appeared to follow, but its edge was less sharp than Ashman's; its failure, if painful, was not undeserved. The acclaim for John's next slim volume was a spiritual compensation, but the film rights of poems are rarely sold for the kind of money Ashman received for his novel and, in consequence, a gap began to open between the consuls. Gaines took it well. So far from retiring to gaze at the heavens, he applauded like a loyal oppo. Gaines and Ashman continued to use army slang in the groves of Academe, thus announcing their steadiness under fire, or at least smoke. The notation of the pub crawl and the barrack-room furnished their work with vivid recollections of the squaddies' world. (I am thinking, for instance, of Gaines' tone poem 'Bashing Your Bishop for Winston'.)

Ashman renounced his research, as every researcher now knows, and decamped to London, when his first novel became a best-seller. Though young Bentley spoke of it with impressed piety, he did rather wonder why everyone had thought it so funny. Was it truly *that* hilarious when the hero and his classy girl had to put their rain-soaked clothes in the professor of Anglo-Saxon's gas oven and were found by his wife, stark naked, in the airing cupboard waiting for them to be thoroughly cooked on Regulo number six? I did my best to assure Bruce Bentley that all the wits had indeed been struck on the funny bone. The most memorable set-piece in Gaines' unremembered first novel concerned its lecturer hero's drunken attempts to convince an audience of blue-rinsed ladies (that old target was once new) that W.B. Yeats was the national poet of Scotland. The exact location of Innisfree, near Loch Lomond, was indicated on a blackboard map whose general outlines were singularly congruent with those of the female genitalia.

As they negotiated the rougher waters beyond the Cambridge breakwater, it was only natural for Ashman and Gaines to drift apart. You will recall that Byron and the young Gamba, setting off to liberate Greece in two small boats, began by singing and calling to each other, only to have their craft slowly separate until first shouts and then gun-shots were necessary before contact could be maintained. Having put their names to a robust little school, Gaines and Ashman met less often and were reminded of each other's existence more by the literary artillery which both continued to fire than by any personal contact. There were marriages, and a divorce (Ashman's) which may have annoyed Gaines more than anyone guessed; he had once fancied the woman Ashman had discarded. John showed increasing signs of a sentimental sincerity which appealed less to the public than Ashman's explosive put-downs. Gaines had too much honour to abandon his own wife in order to rally to Connie, after Ashman had walked out, but his peace of mind was blighted, even if he refused to reach for the obvious remedy. His books and his poetry grew sombre, as if he were suffering from the guilt of which Ashman showed no signs. His work was marked by a lifeless resignation that left Ashman to become the virtual dictator of his generation of writers. The consulship had been dissolved: Ashman was Caesar, Gaines was, very nearly, *nihil*. Oh, he held visiting professorships and his books continued to appear, but no colour mag solicited his opinions on girls or claret. Ashman always had something tart and topical to say. And if his fiction never again managed to be as blithe or as spirited as it had been in his first novel, what critic dared to say so? He was a forceful polemicist and reviewers were wary of falling foul of his ceaseless tongue. By cutting others down to size, he continued to tower over his contemporaries. Even the new generation of satirists, avid for targets, rarely took a pot at him. When his political opinions veered to the Right, after he had met Lady Caroline, his hold on the intelligentsia was so tenacious that those who might have called anyone else a turncoat were disposed to ask Peter only who his tailor was. In brief, Ashman was a trend-setter. By contrast, Gaines was worthy, but juiceless. His desiccation was a slow process, but it was no surprise when he quit fiction for biography. His wife suffered from asthma; his devotion to her was as selfless as it was exhausting. It is a sorry iconoclast for whom people begin to feel sorry.

When, after a painful period of silence, Gaines published his study of Lionel Trilling, it was, no doubt, shrewd casting on the part of Our Best Literary Editor to send it for review to

Ashman, but it was hardly generous. Ashman's judgment ('Thrilling he ain't') was fair, but it was not very fair; it was nice, but it was not very nice. My tendency to find excuses for everyone inclines me to think that Ashman may genuinely not have seen how brutally he was treating his old comrade. The habit of sarcasm can be a tic like any other; sycophancy had eroded the good-heartedness that was once Peter's moral strength. He went through the motions of loyalty, but his smile had become the snarl of a caged beast, at once alarming to its victim and amusing to the leering crowd safe outside the bars. Bars attracted Ashman a good deal at this point. What a literary historian like young Bentley might put down to a change in intellectual orientation was as likely due to a surfeit of booze. Gaines did not, to my knowledge, complain. He endured. When, by chance, he met Ashman in a windowless B.B.C. hospitality room, before a book programme on which he was roughly treated, on the green light, by the usual soft-voiced careerist, Gaines was so pleasant that Peter later turned with surprising asperity on the anchor-man, even though he had no quarrel with him. It was a kind of apology for the Trilling review, *par personne interposée*, as the frog-eaters say. Gaines was more embarrassed than placated by what he recognised to be Ashman's patronising pity.

That gesture of reconciliation, an ironist might guess, served more than anything else to widen the breach between the once inseparable pair. Contempt hurts more than hostility. Gaines began, consciously or not, to bide his time. His asthmatic wife died and he married another; Connie Ashman was not, as pretty plotting would wish, available, but the new woman seems to have revived Gaines' energy. What she could not do, however, was to prompt him to malice; he was incapable of it. Our Best Literary Editor sent Ashman's new poems to John for review and was rewarded, and disappointed, by an enthusiastic piece. But then Lady Caroline, whose influence on Ashman accounts partly for his increasing snobbishness, wrote a new 'major' novel. It is unlikely that Gaines solicited the opportunity to review it, but — as chance would have it — the book came his way. It was long and it was pretentious; it was smug and it was over-written; it was larded with French phrases and over-sensitive aristocrats. It was not Gaines' cup of bromidic char, any more than, once upon a time, it would have been Ashman's.

If I say that Gaines finally lost patience and decided to cut loose, I should be doing him an injustice, for that suggests that he was deliberately unfair to Lady Caroline. On the contrary, he was mercilessly fair. He merely stopped making allowances for once. If it is hard not to believe that he was lashing out at Ashman through his glamorous wife, I maintain that every bull's-eye was justified by quotation. Ashman was never, of course, so much as mentioned in the article which demolished his wife, but would Gaines ever have bothered with her novel at all, had he not expected every bullet directed at madam to drill the man who stood behind her? Weary of being referred to with ever deeper sighs, Gaines decided to dish it out for a change.

John had by now aged into a frailty which his new lady might alleviate but could not reverse. He cannot, therefore, have looked forward to a physical encounter with Peter Ashman, whose fictional *alter ego* was never above giving Lefties a poke in the eye. However, if the two legends no longer moved in the same circles, the literary life was certain to conspire to have them meet somewhere, sometime. It was perhaps appropriate that the two Men of Letters who had made 'taking a slash' into a figure of poetic speech should come face to face, or rather side to side, in the jakes at the London Library. Gaines walked in; Ashman was in full flow. John blenched, but he did not retreat. Inhibited only for a moment, he proved his soft virility by coming easily on stream. The two were silent until they took their hands to the basin: Gaines had nothing to add to his review of Lady C. and was determined to make no apology. Ashman, so it appeared, was set on cutting his old comrade dead. And then Gaines felt a friendly hand fall on his shoulder. There was no one else in the room; it had to be Ashman's. 'Bless your heart, old son,' he said, 'bless your accurate old heart!'

Gaines pressed the roller towel to his eyes and, when they were dry, looked cautiously at Ashman, as he groped for his spectacles. 'I'm sorry?'

'Nothing whatever to apologise for, John. Nowt. You hit her where she lives. She yelled for three days. She may never write another damned, thick book. All right, you might say she's never written one so far, but plenty of people thought she was the cat's whiskers. You put the boot in, bless your shoemaker's metal toe-caps. The Doctor would be proud of you.'

'Look, Peter, there was nothing personal — '

'You knew, John; you must've known.'

'I knew I didn't awfully like the novel — '

'You're such a gentleman these days, John. When did that start? She was a bloody albatross, my son. I told her to get lost over a year ago, but she thought I was joking. I'm such a humorist, aren't I? But your notice proved it. She wouldn't believe I hadn't put you up to it. You've done me the service of a lifetime. I laughed my head off and she finally packed her bag and buggered off. I'm a free man, and all thanks to you.'

'I should hate you to think — '

'No risk. I'm not changing the habits of a lifetime, John, at this late hour. You know, I've been approached by Matthew to do an anthology of the Fifties? Not too many flowers contended, if you ask me, but he's asked me to pick a bunch and why not? I'll tell you what, we never did anything together, did we, not *together*? Well, why don't we now? Join me as co-editor. Gaines and Ashman ride again, even if they never rode before. What do you say?'

The rest is to be found under Lit. Hist., is it not? *Fan Fare for the Fifties* has not rivalled Sally Gaines' *Food for Thought*, the intellectuals' cookbook, but there were long and encomiastic articles in the *T.L.S.* and in the wide-margined journal dominated by Our Best Literary Editor. I am told that Gaines and Ashman are once again extremely close. John's latest novel has just been reviewed with unmitigated enthusiasm by Peter, who swears that his old mucker is back on his very best form. Sour tongues say that one good turn has deserved another.

THE OLD PRO

It was thanks to Charlie Chapman that I went to work for Sherman Shapiro, if thanks were due. Charlie had been recommended to me by Robin, who had supervised my blooding in show biz and who now felt that his mission had been accomplished. He was moving on to 'larger entertainment perspectives', he told me.

'Very polysyllabic,' I said. 'What does it involve exactly?'

'Don't be hurt, Freddie,' he said. 'Don't take everything personally, must you? Charlie's got a lot of energy and a lot of ambition. He'll look after you so well you won't even notice I've gone. You're not a night-bird, are you? Because I rather am, you know, and that's where it's going to be at − night-clubs and eateries, and that's where I'm heading. Class is collapsing in this country, Freddie, and you're going to see it reflected in the style of nocturnal entertainment.'

'Only if I can keep my eyes open,' I said.

'What makes you this way, I wonder?'

'If you're not going to be an agent any more,' I said, 'you certainly don't get to handle my autobiography.'

'If you don't like the business,' he said, 'why don't you get out of it?'

'When I have the chance to have Charlie Chapman guide me towards an exciting new horizon?'

As Robin's understudy, Charlie had not shown any conspicuous signs of the go-getting skills which would have him opening an office in California before the Sixties had come to their gaudy end. He seemed rather suburban and it would have taken a shrewder eye than mine to read his shyness for the restless drive it concealed. He wore a sports jacket and flannels. There was the arrow of a Parker pen beside the handkerchief in his breast pocket. His hair would have passed muster with his House Tutor. Yet if he had all the allure of a Dickensian clerk in a modern dress production, there was an air of secrecy about him which slightly intrigued me. To be slightly intrigued is scarcely an exhilarating condition, but my very uncertainty about being involved in show biz at all prevented me from taking any positive steps to determine my career in it. I was content to allow chance to reward or punish me. If I did well, I should soon be able to retire from vulgarity; if I failed, I could congratulate myself on the brevity of my shame. Charlie Chapman told me that he would do his very best for me and I told him that he should remember that if we had to choose between a classy project — one that involved working with a blacklisted intellectual in Red flight from the shadow of the late junior senator from Wisconsin — and some crass money-spinner with no social content, he should not hesitate to align me with the quality. I had just finished working on a small British film, mildly satirical and basically unadventurous in tone and story. I liked to think that I was ready to work with someone more demanding. Frank, my director, had been highly professional, but he was not the British Antonioni. Charlie Chapman assured me that he would be looking out for him.

It was not only fugitives from McCarthy who were coming to London in those days. The refugees had perhaps been the first to establish that life did not necessarily begin and end in Beverly Hills, but before long those who came to visit them began to appreciate the charms of London town. (Calling on old friends who had fallen on pseudonymous times was the least that their famous acquaintances could do, and the least, as so often in such cases, was generally what they did.) Pretty soon, independent producers were finding that the costs of filming in Europe were considerably lower than on the Coast. Meanwhile, the New Wave broke frothily on the sands of Malibu. The undertow dragged the talent back to the old continent.

American voices were heard more and more in Kensington and Hampstead (King Alfred's was a preferred school for kids used to a free environment). Birds of passage settled down to roost. There was a Sunday softball game in Hyde Park. You got asked to Thanksgiving Parties. After the snobs and the semi-snobs came the merely fashionable and, as time went by, the executives also had to go where the action was, as the new saying was. My little English comedy would almost certainly have passed unnoticed in America, even if it had secured a modest booking for a week or two in selected cities, but suddenly, it seemed, all the Hollywood eyes were looking at England, and a lot of them were actually in London. Charlie Chapman telephoned me one day soon after my picture had opened, or rather Frank's picture had opened, for we were in the appropriating days of '*auteur*' theory, which meant that any joke invented by the screenwriter had to be credited to the director. Did not the Lord of the Manor always speak of 'his' roses, not the gardener's? Same difference, as cook would have said.

'Freddie, how are you?' Charlie said. He was learning the William Morris trick of always treating a client as though he might have had major surgery since he was last telephoned. If the stitches aren't out yet, they want to be kept posted, don't they?

'Tapping away,' I said.

'You novelists!' he said, deference and reproach perfectly balanced in his voice. The show biz agent was always proud, so he said, to represent someone who had an interest in Literature, but such dedication spoke of a certain duplicity in the author, a lack of singleminded determination which might, under testing circumstances, lead to a touch of the hoitytoities. 'Forgive me for dragging you away from the things that really count, but I've had a call, from Sherry Shapiro.'

'Nice to talk to you, Charles,' I said, looking out on the Essex-Suffolk lawn where our toddling daughter was trying to turn a miniature black poodle into the donkey she craved, 'but who is Sherry Shapiro and why are you telling me all this?'

'Shapiro and Blotky mean anything to you?'

'Never been on my menu to my knowledge,' I said.

'You really aren't a movie man, are you?'

'Very good of you to say so, Charlie. Does this mean that I've failed my test? Am I out as from this moment?'

'He liked your picture,' Charlie said, 'and he wants you to work with him.'

'Shapiro *and* Blotky?'

'I'll explain. They used to work with all the best people in comedy. They worked with Billy Wilder – '

'Not on *Some Like It Hot?*' I said.

'No,' Charlie said, 'something else. They go back to the great days of radio. They worked under Goodman Ace.'

'It can be pretty dark down there, I'm told.' I had had a long lonely day with some lugubrious Jews in a chapter that wouldn't quite come right; facetiousness, like money, can be a great consolation to the high-minded.

'You remember that great line,' Charlie went on, 'about the guy decided to put a clock on the leaning tower of Pisa? He figured if you had the inclination you might as well have the time.'

'They wrote *that*?' I said. 'Hear the crash? I just dropped the Grecian Urn.'

'Goodman Ace wrote it,' he said.

'But they were under him at the time? They *rate*.'

'They just split up is what I'm trying to tell you and Sherry Shapiro is looking for a partner.'

'He just got away from one, so why does he need another?'

'That's the way the top Americans like to work. He's going to move into direction and so is his frankly untalented ex-associate Hymie Blotky. They can't do that together, so naturally – '

'Hymie Blotky didn't like my picture, is that it?'

'Freddie, are you all right?'

'I'm sorry,' I said, 'but don't let's get into metaphysics right now, O.K.?' My American origins (I have never sought to conceal them) tended to assert themselves at the mention of transatlantic cousins. It was as if I were rehearsing an audition with someone who was afraid that I might not be able to hack it with Hollywood characters.

'I told Sherry you were born in the States,' Charlie said, 'because he was afraid that you might be a bit too British for what he has in mind. Of course,' he added, 'if you don't want the job – '

'Look, Charlie, don't start with the "ifs", do you mind? I don't even know what the job is yet. What is the job, yet?'

'It's sixteen weeks at five hundred pounds a week,' he said.

I watched my daughter trying to saddle Sheba. For the price of a couple of hours with Sherry Shapiro, she could have the neddy of her dreams. Did I also see a vision of an Alfa Romeo 2800 Spider, with triple carburettors and a white leather hood? 'Doesn't sound like enough, does it?' I said. 'Remember that Dilys said that I was a screenwriter for the future.'

'I haven't worked the Chapman squeeze on him yet, have I? But I don't want to lash out on the after-shave if you're not interested. I think he'll go to six fifty, maybe even seven.'

'What are we actually going to *do* for sixteen weeks?'

'Freddie, can I speak frankly for a moment?'

'It better not be any longer than that,' I said. 'My tolerance for frankness has its limits. Listen for the pips.'

'You need the discipline.'

'French lessons aren't enough?' I said. 'What the hell do you mean, discipline?'

'If you want to spend the rest of your life writing novels, you only have to say so.'

'If I don't want to eat, I also only have to say so.'

'You like your little luxuries, I know that. And you shall have them — '

'Gee, pop!'

' — but writing arty English films isn't going to put jam on your bread. You need the Hollywood experience and you couldn't do better than Sherry Shapiro. He's been a top-liner for longer than — than — '

'Don't strain after a comparison,' I said, 'I take the point: he's an old hack, right?'

'There you go with your Cambridge conceit,' Charlie said, 'if you don't mind my saying so. Comedy is the toughest thing there is, and the best paid, which is probably why, and Sherry has been up there for twenty years. Forgive me, but I think this is a unique opportunity to learn your trade from one of the masters. O.K., you did a good job on Frank's picture — '

'And he did a good job on mine. Be fair now.'

' — but what's it doing at the box office?'

'Don't talk dirty,' I said.

'That's the name of the game,' Charlie Chapman said, and it was the first time I ever heard the phrase. I wish it had been the last.

I am ashamed to say that, to the best of my recollection, as dishonest witnesses always confess, I never discovered the subject of Sherman Shapiro's movie until after I had been hired to collaborate with him on it. The negotiations took on a life of their own. I incited Charlie to refuse six fifty a week for reasons that were as confused as I was. I dreaded working 'with' someone else, especially if he was to direct the picture, and I was appalled at the prospect of serving a sixteen-week sentence, but the Jews had sorted themselves out in my novel and I was suddenly in the hectic last week when the words poured out and 'The End' was in sight. We wanted to go to Greece that summer and I Could Use The Money.

'Here's the bottom line,' Charlie said, after two or three weeks of Izaak Waltoning with the producer-director-writer whom I was, believe it or not, yet to meet. ('He's working on a novel' had proved a useful line for Charlie: it had intimations of class, with a short 'a'.) 'He's ready to pay seven hundred and fifty a week with a guarantee of seventeen weeks.'

Nausea soured my recent lunch. How could I refuse? I had postponed facing the realities of my peonage, so gilded had it appeared, and so unlikely that Charlie's terms would be accepted. The joke had suddenly grown straight-faced: I was in for it. Discipline was about to be administered. Charlie was blithe, as well he might be, since his work was done. I tried to present the news to my wife as if it were good. So did the messenger tell Clytemnestra that Troy had fallen. To console myself, I arranged for a local taxi to take me to the station in the morning and to collect me in the evening. Riley and I would live the same life for a while.

Sherman Shapiro had hired a big office in South Street. There was a Sam Browned commissionaire in the hall downstairs, to whom I said 'Good morning' with the familiarity which I expected to feel in due course and who directed me to the third floor, 'Lift to your left'. Sherry was wearing a fawn Safari suit and two-tone shoes. I was offered coffee or juice and we sat down to discuss the project. I was, of course, 'welcome aboard'.

The scenario involved the 'mutual entanglements' of two senior American N.A.T.O. officers. We were in the calm period before J.F.K. committed troops to Vietnam and the cachet

of the armed forces had never been higher. Johnny and
Brad were just the sort of characters a wacky comedy needed
in order to delight the U.S. public. Although they were generals, our leading men were young enough to think in terms of
Cary, say, or Bob, or both, and they behaved like much-
decorated, and very sexy, escapees from an Aldwych farce.
Originality was no part of the discipline I was to learn. Sherry
Shapiro was not, however, a harsh master. He sought by every
means to put me at my ease. If we were not old friends by
lunch-time, it would not be his fault.

The first thing we had to lick, after I had scanned the
story-line, was the motivation of the main character, whose
name was Johnny Grunbacher. 'What makes Johnny run?'
was how Sherry put the problem. 'That's what we have to lick,
Frederic.' He had a big typewriter, with a white tongue of
paper sticking out of its wide mouth, all set for the answers. It
was mounted on a steel table with squeaky casters that made
pale furrows in the new carpet as Sherry pulled it towards him.
'He's the motor, is Johnny, and until we know what makes
him run, nothing's going to get started. Tell me, Frederic, are
you married?'

'Isn't everybody?'

'My wife falls down a lot,' he said.

Sherman Shapiro was a rated comedy writer. I wondered
whether this was the beginning of a routine. It was, but not a
comic one. His face lost its smile-lines and I recognised the
schnorrer beneath the skin. Mrs Shapiro was in and out of
hospitals; as soon as she was back on her feet, she was off them
again. Did she drink? I did not like to ask. She was a burden so
grievous that we ceased to consider what made, or might
make, Johnny run. We had seventeen weeks for that. I was
sympathetic, in a wary sort of way, as the morning passed.
After what seemed several hours, I managed to cadge a glance
at my watch. It told me that it was ten minutes past ten. I had
arrived at nine forty. Seventeen weeks minus half an hour had
still to be worked. Laban had it easy.

It may seem funny now, but it was not funny then. From
Mrs Shapiro, we reverted to Johnny Grunbacher. (Did I think
the name was pitched right? I thought it was.) We ran a few
ideas to the top of the flag-pole to see if either of us felt like

saluting them. (You're right: *Twelve Angry Men* that one came from.) We drank some more juice and Sherman asked me if I liked kosher food. 'Does anybody?' I said. He knew this place we could go to. I knew it too: the waiters had all *lived*, and looked it. I had been there with my only orthodox friend. I had felt no vocation to seek others. Know what kosher soup is? It's what ends in your lap.

I have led a happy and pampered life, I suppose, because that day with Sherman Shapiro was one of the longest in it. By the time that we decided to 'convene again upon the morrow', I was, as my Missourian grandmother would have said, 'fit to be tied'. I had heard about Sherman's Golden Rule: never miss a deadline, no matter what, or who. I had learnt that construction is what counts: you have to have your third act. I had eaten of the thigh of a chicken which had seen its great-grandchildren. I had been reminded again that Mrs Shapiro fell down a lot. For a new comedy duo, Sherry and I had had very few laughs.

The hired Jaguar took me home to a meal carefully prepared by a wife who had not fallen down in the least. Normally its savour would have had me hurrying to table, but the *gratin* turned my stomach and the mushrooms completed the up-heaval. I threw my wife's dinner down the drain almost as soon as I had congratulated her on it. She divined that I was not a happy man. 'There's only one thing to do,' she concluded, 'and that's junk the job.'

'How can I?' I said.

'Call Charlie Chapman and tell him to get you out of it.'

'How can I?'

'Dial his number and tell him. Do you want me to?'

I dialled his number and told him. He was not pleased. His reputation was 'building' and this was the kind of thing that would wreck his credibility. He had given his word; I had given mine. Bullets were for biting on. If I wanted to go on being a novelist pure and simple, that was my decision, but otherwise a deal was a deal. I decided, after further consultation with my wife, that I would be a novelist pure and simple. In that case, Charlie said, I could inform Sherry Shapiro of my resolution myself. It was indignity enough to lose 10 per cent of roughly £12,750.

It cannot be claimed that Sherman Shapiro had seemed much of an ogre. I should have been untroubled at the thought of telling him that, though I could not say what made Johnny run, I had every notion of why I should, but I was ashamed of my lack of staying power and certain that a Hollywood Producer (my caps) would take great delight in telling me that I should never work again if he could help it. The commissionaire did not have to tell me that the lift was on the left. I was an old hand already, and a trembling one.

'Sit down, Frederic, and let's get a foot on the ladder.'

'Sherry,' I said, 'I'm very sorry — '

'Something wrong?'

All he needed, that lugubrious face seemed to say, was a *collaborator* who fell down a lot. 'I'm afraid so,' I said. 'You're probably going to be very angry and I don't blame you one bit, but I don't think that I'm going to be able to go through with this. I was sick all night and — '

'Have you seen the doctor?'

'It's Johnny,' I said.

'He's given you the runs?'

I smiled: he *was* a comedy writer. Goodman Ace taught him good maybe. 'You could say that,' I said. 'I'm sure it means that I lack the — the *discipline* to be a — a true professional in this business, but — '

'Bullshit,' he said.

'No — '

'*Bullshit*. You don't want to do it, don't do it. All I can say is, thank God you didn't try to bluff it out for six, seven weeks, waste a lot of my time, and your time, and *then* quit. Life is very short, my friend, and you're too bright to do things you hate to do.'

'Charlie Chapman's furious with me. I shall probably have to get another agent.'

'I can get plenty of agents,' Sherry Shapiro said. 'It's talent I'm short of. You'll get by. Do you know Stanley Donen?'

' "Singing in the Rain" Stanley Donen? No.'

'I saw him at Carl's party last night at Robin's new place and he said he wanted to get in touch with you. He'd give a lot to work with you.'

'He'll have to,' I quipped. 'Stanley *Donen*? Are you serious?'

'No,' Sherman Shapiro said, 'but he seems to be. Go see him. He didn't call you already, did he?'

'I promise you,' I said, 'he did not. He certainly did not.'

'Better run along,' he said.

'Call me Grunbacher,' I said.

'We mighta made a team at that,' he said.

I didn't see Sherry Shapiro again for several years. He 'licked' Johnny and his rival into three acts and directed a perfectly dreadful movie which went down like a lead zepp (there was even a first time for that expression). Hymie Blotky, the no-good, wrote and directed a smash hit at almost the same time. I invited Sherry to the party to celebrate the opening of the picture I wrote for Stanley Donen, but his London office was closed by then. He went back to California. By the time I was making occasional visits to The Coast, he had become involved in television, which my American agents would not allow me even to consider as a source of income. The numbers didn't add up, did they?

I did not feel a persistent obligation to look Sherman up, but guilty gratitude led me to keep asking after him. His wife was still falling down, I gathered, and one of his kids had been dumb enough to get caught in the draft and lost an arm in Nam. He went on turning out the jokes, though, and I was advised not to do any internal bleeding on his account. My Californian agents had explained to me that once you get into video, it's tough to get hired again in the movies, no matter how good your ratings. Sherman Shapiro, they were ready to bet, would never direct another movie and he would probably never get to write one even. He was on that treadmill for ever, baby.

But they were wrong. Sherry was a pro and he was a fighter, though a doleful one. He hung in there (as they were beginning to say) and he devised a treatment catchy enough to interest Warner Brothers. They commissioned a screenplay and allowed the stipulation that Sherry would direct, if they went ahead. He broke surface in places where he had not been seen for years. Stanley and I bumped into him down at Santa Monica, in a fish joint where the M.G.M. crowd used to go when Donen was a hoofer for Gene. He looked worried and said that he was having one hell of a time licking the script, but he'd do it, he'd do it. I didn't have seventeen weeks to spare by any chance, did I? He slapped our shoulders and went back to his typewriter. I wondered if the wheels still squeaked.

The deadline got closer and still the thing wasn't right. There's a saying in the movies: they only read it once. If Warners didn't dig that first draft, it was back to the soaps. Sherry typed and re-typed. He was in hell, but he didn't complain and he didn't resign. He had no latent desire to be a novelist, pure and simple. One day, he came home with a box of fresh carbons and hurried to his workroom. The script was due in the following day. He started to rework some of the material and then he stopped. Something, he knew, was wrong. He went upstairs to his wife's bedroom, where she always rested in the afternoon, and she was lying there, having fallen for the last time. He gazed on her body with horror and undeniable relief. With pity and shame, he saw what he had so often wanted. And as he stood there, suddenly he had a comic writer's dream: his third act came fully grown into his head, like a long-lost kid. He knew that if he reported the death, he would never get that script, or that third act, to Calley and co. He looked at the woman on whom he had spent his substance and he began to laugh. That third act was a *riot*. He went downstairs, shut his door and started to type like a sonofabitch.

The cops wanted to know why he had not gone out of his office for almost twenty-four hours, but he explained that he was an old pro and his wife was used to his ways. A deadline was a deadline and when you gotta go, you gotta go. The screenwriting community backed him up all the way and, in any case, what was to be done? Everyone knew he was devoted to that dull Desdemona of his. Warners okayed the script and Sherry was back in production. I wish I could say that it turned out to be a hit, but life is often weak in the third act, isn't it? One thing they can never take away from him though: Sherman Shapiro had discipline. He never fell down on the job.

THE PEOPLE IN EUCLID

Does he know what he's going to do?' It was a sign of the times that people assumed that if you knew, you would be able to do it. He was the only child of parents who loved but did not need him. They were a couple and he came third. When the boy brought home prizes, his parents admired the crests and the inscriptions. His success was very nice, but it was not essential to them: they were already complete. His happiness was something they desired, but they would still have been happy without it. Responsible and serious parents, in their clothes, they celebrated Christmas, if not Christ, and birthdays with appropriate festivities. His birthdays did not wholly please them, since his age was the calendar of theirs.

He hurried home in the holidays, even from university, but no sooner was he in the flat than he was a prisoner, planning escape, although he had a key. He dreamed of the woman who was waiting for him. When he went to the cinema he disliked all facetiousness, though he relished parody. Happy endings depressed him.

His parents wished no heavier constraints upon him than expecting help with the washing up. Sometimes he imagined that he would enjoy his meals more if he could wash the plates before they were used. There was also the dog. He was expected to walk it in the trim grounds of the flats, which had been built on the site of a noble house. One of his mother's friends lived in a ground-floor flat where, one day, she smelt the glamour of gardenias, although it was not the season. Who would believe that inquiry revealed that her 'entrance' was on the very place where the West Wing once looked on to a peacocked lawn?

His mother knew a number of the wives whose husbands

went to the City on the same train as hers. The women did not have jobs. They had cleaning women called Doreen or Doris or Trixie, whose husband knocked her about. The vacuum cleaner moaned all morning on Mondays, Wednesdays and Fridays. Everything had to be cleaned, even when it was clean. Michael would hear the Hoover bumping against the skirting boards and rattling as it gulped pins. It was as if evidence were being collected, or concealed.

His mother's friends came for coffee, or whisky, after Trixie had been thanked, and told to take care of herself. (Her exact money was on the hall stand.) The free women talked and laughed together, four or five of them. Sometimes one would be missing. There would have been some kind of falling out. Then she would come again. It seemed to Michael (who stayed in his room, studying) that it was a courtesy, undertaken in rough rotation, to be absent and to be talked about by the others. When none of the girls was away, the conversation lacked intensity. It was liveliest when someone had done something 'too silly' or 'beyond belief'.

Sometimes, when Michael was at his desk, his mother would remain alone at the time when her friends usually called or when she normally told him, through the busy door, that she would be back in a few minutes. On those days was she the one who was being too silly or acting beyond belief?

His father began to ask him what he was going to do. Was it an unreasonable question? It was not. Had he any ideas? Between him and his father there seemed to be an interpreter, whose services made it difficult for them to understand each other. To every simple question, and answer, this invisible official appeared to add a disconcerting rider. One day Michael said that he was going to teach. His father nodded, and looked sideways as if he had understood the interpreter, but doubted if he had conveyed the full sense of what had been meant.

Teaching turned out to be a kind of acting. Michael was at school again, but he was a ghost, through whom the children often looked. He squatted down to their height, but they knew him to be transient. Why else would he chide them for their lack of ambition and promise them that the world was rich and wonderful? It was as if he had already been everywhere and seen everything. His colleagues guessed that he would not go on teaching: he gave too much to it.

One day a colleague took him to a party where a man told him, on a windy terrace, that he was mad to be doing what he was doing. He disagreed, but soon he enrolled as a trainee with a television company which was beginning to be rich. Before long, he was directing half-hour programmes. Anna was an actress with a bit of a name but not too successful to refuse taking part in a series about careers. It was called 'So You Want To Be . . . '

Lining up, she told him that she never intended to act. He said that he believed her and she thought him very, very bright. Something cruel had happened to her and he sympathised, by his stance, before he had any idea what it might have been. Beautiful, she was surprised that he was polite to her. Her beauty was asleep and she was grateful for the kiss that revived her. It made him wonder for whom she was taking him, and whether that could possibly be who he was.

Over a last canteen meal they talked of making a proper film together one day. Already something stood between them and what they would really like to do, and be. One night, as they were talking in her Fulham flat, she began to undress. It made him silent. Nakedness seemed to be a disguise. As he made love to her, it excited him to think that she was hiding something.

One evening she took him to see a film in a remote part of London. 'That should have been me,' she said, after the girl had come on. Michael realised who the man in her earlier life had been and in the black and white light of his work, he asked her to marry him.

'Why marry?' she said.

'You prefer to burn?'

'What more can we be to each other than we are now?'

'Unfaithful?' he said.

'Don't,' she said, and agreed.

He resigned from the company which had marked him for early promotion. She sold her flat and they went to live in the country. They found a collapsing cottage on the East Coast, near a small port once prosperous in the wool and wheat trade. He bought a book to learn the grammar of plastering and carpentry. She gardened. They were happy.

He worked as a part-time roundsman for a dairy; she helped in a chemist's shop in a touristy village not far away. Their favourite walk was along a disused branch line from which the rails had been removed. It was ballasted with wild flowers. Sometimes they wore each other's shirts and sweaters; it was as close as they could come to being inside each other's skins. She wore his jeans sometimes, but he could not get into hers.

One Sunday they made love in the open, near the estuary where fleets of swans sailed. He decked her in flowers and she took the quotation for originality. They were in the ghostly, scented siding for hours. As the sun fattened from gold to orange, they went reluctantly back towards the cottage, laced together as if in a three-legged race, past a little cemetery. The branch line served a tall mill, abandoned but still elegant, a high note in a currency no longer valid. They saw a man in a check suit standing on a tower, with a camera. When they came closer, he had vanished. They heard the sound of expensive exhaust.

'I hate that sort of thing,' she said.

'And what sort of thing is that?'

'Don't you?'

He became their mystery man. It was as if he had stolen something from them, if only an image of them as they had been that afternoon when neither of them wanted to see anybody again except the other. Was he the same man whom later that year they saw, in the touristy village, in a motor car Michael happened to know had three carburettors?

'Is that a lot?' Anna said.

'You must ask our friend.'

It must have been the same man who was said to have bought the big house overlooking the estuary. Michael and Anna had trespassed in the grounds with their brambled marbles and knotty espaliers. Oliver was both rich and the son of riches: doubly fortunate, he had made as much in the City as he had inherited. Michael thought of his father and of the regularity with which he had gone to his office, for a salary.

Oliver came by one day when they were clearing and levelling a new part of their garden. He told them that he had bought Adam Place as a final gesture towards his wife and children. If the gesture was vain, it had shooting and fishing rights; one day it would be worth more than somewhat. Workmen were everywhere and gardening contractors were making a Flanders of the grounds, so he rather envied them their solitude. He had never started anything from scratch: even the wife from whom he was estranged had been married before. Probably she would be again.

He invited them to come on up and see the wretched place once the toilers had departed. He rather wished he had a little cottage like theirs, that didn't need the eighth army to put it right. Anna said that they had better go once to the big house, because otherwise they would always be afraid that Oliver would come and invite them again. She said that she had never known anyone like Oliver: wasn't he unbelievable? Michael had been at school and at university with plenty of Olivers. It was strange how quickly one could be at home with everything one feared and rather liked. At the big house they drank wine from the cellar which Oliver had acquired without having the faintest idea it was even there.

Oliver was sometimes there and sometimes not. They never knew for sure. When Oliver was not about, it was a relief; when he was there, it was entertaining. In one wing of the house he reported a library he had not known was there. And then there was this covered tennis court, *tiled* if you please. Did Michael play at all?

Michael talked to Anna about Oliver, about how really awful he was. He was less a friend than a topic. Oliver was everything they were trying to get away from, in a funny sort of way. He was very generous though, wasn't he? He liked to come to the cottage with a bottle or flowers, or both. His place had strawberries and raspberries they were welcome to. God, he thought they were lucky! He admired the two of them more than he could say. He wished that he could have the nerve to start again from absolute zero, owing nothing to anyone. Oh, he was thinking of having some horses. So Michael learnt that Anna once rode.

One autumn evening Oliver asked Michael to come shooting with him on the marshes. There ought to be some duck about. He had a spare Purdy that had been his pa's. Michael had acquitted himself well at tennis and had shot passably in the Corps, though a rifle was not the same as a shot-gun. He had no waders, of course, and of course Oliver did, but would Wellingtons do? They went in silence and in the silence Michael had new feelings about Oliver. With Anna he had pretended not to like the man, and had rather liked him. Now he wondered why he was doing something he did not want to do and who had made him do it. He had never thought it right to shoot for sport, but now he was ashamed at his inexperience. The tide was out and they broached the marsh. Oliver went ahead, loping from dyke to dyke, twisting his heels to disengage from the mud that nipped Michael's feet like cold socks.

They went towards the flat margin of the marsh, among the grey-brown grasses, with their drowned pallor. Michael grew tired and Oliver smiled back at him, as if he had made an inaudible joke. They crouched for a while in the low cover of a sunken punt. A few mallard went by, cuneiform marks creaking along the silken sky, too distant for targets. Oliver grinned at Michael and Michael wondered which of them was the grown-up.

'On we go then.'

Michael became tired, though he was the bigger of the two, or because of it. He kept going, but he grew clumsy. Going over a steep dyke, he tripped, one foot snagged in the mud, the other plunging. His gun barrels snubbed the marsh and came out plugged with mud. They broke the gun and pushed out soft clay cartridges. Then they went on, Michael guessing that they would not get a shot at anything. He completely shucked a boot and the mud nibbled his sock before he holstered it again. Michael was angry at his chosen humiliation; Oliver was in his element.

Suddenly Oliver had a target. They came steeply from the west, black brands on the silvered plate of the evening. Oliver got off both barrels before Michael could fire one. But it was after Michael's shot that one of the ducks faltered into disjointed feathers and drooped towards the far edge of the evening. 'Got to get it, I'm afraid,' Oliver said.

Michael did not imagine that it was a bird. Oliver had wished it on him. Honour required them to walk across the flatness towards the damned creature. They had to go because they might only have wounded it: they were bringing death to it, if it needed it, like help.

They could hear the toothless chuckle of the waves, the limit of the tide, when they saw the ruins of an aeroplane. It had been there for decades, a fighter. Michael was tired but he went to it eagerly, as if someone might still be in it, who needed help. Scandalised by Oliver's indifference, he called out, claiming that there was a body in the mud, just over there, and they ought to do something. Oliver was bothered about the duck. He was sleeved in mist as he quartered the shore. 'There's a body, damn you,' Michael went after him to say, but when he turned again to prove it, he could see no sign of the grave hump he could have sworn was there. There had certainly been the fuselage of a plane, though it seemed no bigger than a hollow log, no sign of wings.

Oliver was angry not to find the duck. They looked for it until the sea was coming up the soft steps of the estuary towards them. The shore was gone for the night. Michael was dependent on Oliver and that made him sullen. He smiled at the mist and shook his head. 'Fool!'

He followed Oliver, private to his officer. Oliver stopped in the stewing mist and said, 'Are we going the right way, do you think?' Michael could hear the tide. He proposed elementary logic; it was behind them, therefore they had only to keep ahead of it and they were home, and dry. 'It may not be so simple,' Oliver said. He seemed pleased to say it. Then they heard water ahead of them and Michael saw Oliver's teeth before he said, 'See what I mean?' Michael was calm, only because he had the feeling that he was being tricked and that Oliver really did know the right way to safety. They veered to the right in the hedgeless maze and new water fattened about their ankles.

Oliver said, 'Jesus, old man.' The mist billowed in soft cataracts. They came to some planks. Was this where they had seen the distant mallard?

Oliver said, 'I mean it, old man.'

Michael had teeth then. He seriously imagined that if the tide came and they were in serious trouble, he would fight with Oliver, to the death, before he went under. He would use the Purdy like a club. Suddenly, but as if it was always coming, as if it had been threading the silence for some minutes, Michael

heard the regular natter of a train on the main line, from which
his and Anna's floral path had once branched to serve the mill.
The train went along the foreshore and its steady sound
stitched a compass on to the hem of the night. They set
themselves and went straight to the hard. The tide swarmed
after them, but they stepped easily out of it.

Oliver had a flask of rum somewhere under his corduroy
and they sat on the bank and swallowed its rough heat. A train
came back from the town at the head of the estuary and they
could see its lights and count its silly passengers. They were
like fairground targets, the faces in the yellow squares, and
they seriously considered potting a pair. Or did they? They
laughed together without declaring the joke and Oliver, as if
this were it, told Michael that his bloody wife was never
damned well coming to live in the big house.

Anna said she was sorry about it. Michael said he was sorry
too, but he was not. He hoped that Oliver would sell Adam
Place which seemed, every day, to be coming closer to the
cottage, and now to be only a step or two away. Michael
thought he had concealed his lack of pity, but Anna sensed the
reserve in him, though she could not read it precisely, like the
optician's bottom line. She feared that it meant more than it
did.

Oliver usually went to London for the week. They could
look forward, in a way, to his coming, and to his going. The
days without him were wonderfully peaceful and their life was
as happy as ever, but it was a life in which Oliver decidedly did
not figure. That was his place in it. At the weekends he had
often been tactful (oh and he did have other friends in the
area), but now that he had confessed that his wife was never
going to come and that he was not sorry, he stayed longer
around at the cottage. He brought them bits and pieces from
the big house which they might find useful. Anna would ask
him to stay for a meal. Afterwards she would say that she
wished that he had not accepted. One such night, Michael
insisted on doing the omelettes and he worked in the kitchen
while Anna entertained Oliver under the medlar tree.

As they were having coffee, Michael disagreed with something Oliver had said, a political matter. Oliver's money had
made him seem clever; he was used to being humoured and he

humoured even himself. Michael rose like an angry tide. Anna
chewed her knuckle as her husband ridiculed their friend.
Oliver tried to answer Michael's sarcasm, but he fell into one
trap after another. When he said goodbye, and thank you,
he hopped from one foot to the other. He looked a bit of an
ass.

Michael said that he had thought it was about time Oliver
realised a few things. He asked Anna to endorse his view that
Oliver was talking total nonsense. 'You don't need me to tell
you that,' she said, and went to do the washing up.

'You think I was wrong?'

'I don't think he necessarily said everything he could have
said,' she said.

Michael said: 'I may have to go up to London.'

Oliver came with flowers and a bottle, to apologise. Michael
had gone to London. He had been writing some lyrics, for
songs, and wanted to see a man with whom he had been at
university, who wrote music. Anna said that Oliver did not
need to explain himself to her. She was making pastry in a
white overall, nothing else.

'I think I upset him,' Oliver said.

'I think he upset you.'

'Anyway, I'm sorry.' He kissed her and, smiling, she held up
white hands in busy surrender.

She was naked in bed when Michael came home, on the late
train, and his bicycle from the station. She was always naked in
bed. They made a pair of soft spoons and went to sleep. Her
nakedness was no longer an invitation. He did not notice it as
Oliver had.

She did not like Michael to be alone with Oliver any more. If
he went up to the big house, she went with him. If there were
going to be games, they had better be for three. 'How many
good games are there for three?' Michael said, but she did not
smile back. Oliver showed them conjuring tricks. He talked
about these horses. Music was written and Michael had to go
to London again, for the matching of words and tunes. He
might not be back that night. He came back and found Oliver
in bed with Anna. They heard the bicycle clicking in the
darkness, and caught sight of its wavering light, but Oliver
pressed her body under his in the bed Michael had built.

Michael had seen the car, of course, in the lane, and the unlit cottage. Oliver said goodnight.

Anna said, 'I'll explain, if you like.'

'I knew after that night,' Michael said, 'when he was wrong and you thought he was right.'

'I didn't,' she said.

'No,' he said.

They were separate again and he desired her with a passion that was stronger than love had been. She was afraid of his desire, saddened and excited by it. He did things to her, and for her, that he had never done before. He reminded her of things she had forgotten. It awakened ambition in her. They were things that her one-time lover had done. She yelped with the pleasure of them and Michael supposed that he was recapturing his wife. He wanted her to be yelping like that when Oliver came to the cottage. But Oliver no longer came to see them both without invitation.

Michael had to go to London again. A singer was interested in 'Romance'. If the song were any kind of a hit, they would be free, wouldn't they? Oliver took Anna to a beamed restaurant for lunch. He told her that his wife and children had not left him; he had left them. He would finish the work on the big house and then he would sell it. There was a boom on the stock market and a syndicate of townees was eager to take it off his hands. He had never been sure that he liked the house. He had come to the country because he wanted to meet her.

'That's silly,' she said.

The contempt that Michael had shown for Oliver during their angry conversation had scalded Anna with a mark that did not heal. She realised how tactful Michael had been in his treatment of her and that she had never been allowed to know the best part of him. He had feared that she would not be equal to it.

Oliver asked Anna whether she had ever been skiing. She said, 'Of course not.' Would she come with him? He would teach her. The pleasure was indescribable and she should have it.

'I work in a sub-post-office,' she said.

'There's no conceivable need for that sort of nonsense,' he said.

How did the cottage catch fire? Was it the unpricked sausages or was it a faulty piece of rubber tubing that allowed gas to escape? The cottage burned. Oliver saw the smoke and came running, but there was nothing to be done. Passengers turned their heads slowly in the windows of the main line train as it went from right to left. The fire engine prevented the spread of the blaze to the woods, but the cottage was black.

Michael stayed for a night at the big house. The three of them talked very sensibly. The moment for violence or denunciation was past, if it had ever occurred. Survivors from an accident, they were stunned into civility. Anna was outnumbered by the other two. It put her at a privileged disadvantage. The woman watched them with wary tolerance, unspeakable solutions on the tip of her tongue. She contented herself with telling Michael that he would be happier with someone who was as clever as he was.

Oliver wanted to give Michael something. There was always money. Michael hoped that the two of them would be happy. He loved them both, he heard himself say. He felt no pain. It was like an amputation. He had once been told, by a doctor with whom he had been at school, of how he had been treating a man with a swollen lower leg and foot, at a clinic on the Persian Gulf. He had supposed that penicillin would cure the condition and told a nurse to clean the infected place. A moment later he heard a scream. The nurse had been obeying his instructions, but when she swabbed the swollen leg, the foot fell off. It was lying on the floor and its owner was contemplating it without evident emotion. He had been bitten by a snake a fortnight earlier and the effect of the poison had been to consume the tissue, including the nerves. The man had walked in on the swollen foot without feeling anything. It fell from the bone like overcooked meat. His relatives arrived with a plastic bag. They took away the foot and its flesh. When the man himself died, all of him would be buried together.

Anna learned to ski. In due time Michael and she were divorced and she married Oliver, with whom she led a smart life. They rode, though he never owned the horses. He wanted her to become an actress again, but she preferred to be with him. One day, when they were buying antiques in a provincial town, Anna told Oliver that she thought she had seen Michael.

She did not think that he had seen them. 'Advantage us then,' Oliver said.

They saw him again, both of them. And again he did not seem to see them. They were less sure that this was to their advantage. They wondered what possible motive he could have for being where they were. He became a topic for them. They were driven to odd excesses ¬ luxurious meals, foreign trips — less for the pleasure they provided than to see how far he might go. They were relieved when he was not to be seen in Paris or Hyères, but they then wondered, at first with a laugh, why they were there.

He made himself present in the background of their lives. As they came to their car, he would be posting a letter. As they entered a bar, he might be leaving it. He was ingenious and they became dependent on his ingenuity. Who was playing whom, and at what? One day they went to a film and he was already in the next seat. Oliver had been a conjurer, but he could not fathom how this trick was done. He became angry. Anna wanted him to be amused, and contemptuous, but he had ceased to be either. He was her husband.

Michael Stein's songs were frequently sung. Sometimes they would be reminded of him only by the pianist in a cocktail lounge or, as time went by, the Muzak in an elevator. It soured Oliver to be so victimised. Like all successful songs, Michael's lyrics were at once general and particular. He asked who was the ghost/ You or me, A or B?/ Who do you blame the most?

Michael was now rich enough to go wherever they went. He went there, but he never attempted to speak to them. His assault was cleverly inoffensive. Oliver hated him. He told Anna that it was possible to hire people to dispose of the damned man. Anna asked how one then disposed of the people one had hired?

They went to a Greek island where pumice stones floated in the sea like ashen dumplings. Michael was untroubled by the solitude to which they sentenced him. Their own speech became laboured. They had to talk to each other. His presence did not silence them, but their words lost their privacy; they were part of a performance. Everything they did became a duty.

Michael moved into their hotel. Soon he had the next room.

Oliver followed him into the heat one day and asked him why he was doing this.

'Doing what?'

'What do you want?'

'Nothing.'

'If you want to see her, go on up and see her.'

'I'm going to the beach,' Michael said.

'Attack me,' Oliver said. 'If that's what you want to do.'

'I don't,' Michael said.

They could not be sure whether he was in his room or whether what they were doing, whatever they were doing, was for their sake or for his. Oliver and Anna retreated into separate ideas of what it all meant and how it might end. All they really had in common now was their essence of Michael. He was their terrible child: he aged them.

When they came down to pay the bill on the last morning, the manager gave them an envelope. In it was a piece of local paper, on which was written: 'Any side of a triangle may be called the base − Euclid.'